Dust to Dust

Poison and Wine
Dust to Dust

DUST TO DUST
(Book Two of the Poison and Wine series)
C.H. Valentino and Eldon Hughes

Thank you for supporting our work.

Visit: www.chvalentino.com and www.ifoundaknife.com
For information about our cover:
www.stephaniethompson.prosite.com

Edited and published by Valentino Books Inc.
Cover art by Stephanie Thompson

To Coye, Charlie and Diann. Heather, my "fine and
uncommon destiny."
And to my Beloved, always. Always for you.
—E. Hughes

To Mom and Dad
—C. Valentino

Authors' Notes

By C.H. Valentino

When I think about it, I can come up with more than a dozen people who deserve my thanks, but none really much more than my parents. As far as people go, they are normal. They like to mow the yard, watch Sherlock, and take their boat out on the Mississippi.

They've been together all my life. They got married in a little park not far from where I live now long before I was around. I guess, that kind of makes them normal, too.

My mom sells copies of my book out of the trunk of her car, cleans my house, and takes me to The Muny to see musicals. My dad mows my yard and fixes just about every damn thing I seem to be able to break. He taught me how to fish and hunt and shoot guns. Mom taught me to cook and laugh and be strong. They both taught me not to be afraid. To create the world I want to live in. To create. To be.

I don't know at what point in life you're supposed to realize that the simple things are the most profound, or that before they were my parents, they were stupid in love and had lives different from what they are now. I'm thirty, so maybe now?

Either way: Kieth and Bunny — you are both extraordinary people. As far as parents go, you're doing great there, too. I love you.

By Eldon Hughes

Every port city in the world holds secrets — small joys that are only hidden to people dedicated to remaining "tourists." New Orleans is no different, in that regard. Sure, the tourist attractions can be fun and entertaining. But out there, away from the Quarter, that's where New Orleans shines. That's where the best food, the best music, and the real magic is.

Please, go visit. Tell 'em I said "Hey."

Prologue

1827 — Baie Chevreuil, Louisiana

Bél fanm se traka.

Beautiful women are trouble. It was his father's favorite saying. His grandfather's and great-grandfather's before that. How many generations of Jaackemel men had echoed those words, Christian couldn't say, but he suspected it had followed them from the Caribbean all the way to the bayous of southern Louisiana, a prophecy to the young and a curse of the old.

Beautiful women *were* trouble, but none as troublesome as the one staring at him now. Body heat curled off her wet hair in vaporous trails. She was lean and long apart from the swell of her belly, which she held like an explanation and an apology in the same breath. Three, maybe four months along. Too far to hide it, that was for sure, which was why they ever came to him at all.

The scent of mossy earth followed her into the cabin. Christian tasted the brine baked into her skin, but there was a softer, more verdant fragrance buried in her blood, cloying like lilacs and sticky as pine. A lifetime in the bayous had taught his nose to be particular about many things: what to eat, where to tread, how to see a gator long before he set foot on its nest. But her scent called to the unique awareness inside him: the real power of the Jaackemel men.

He didn't need her history to know she was a creature of primacy and power. *Royalty.* Not born of the bloodlines of men or passed down through marriage and title, but real nobility. He scrubbed a hand against the bottom of his chin.

This was the most dangerous breed of woman. The kind who knew how to play dead when they were very much alive. A woman who would kiss you, kill you, then walk away with your child in her womb.

If that was the position she was in, Christian didn't ask.

Instead, he plucked open the laces at the base of her throat. The damp cotton nightdress let loose of her shoulders and fell to the floor. Her white skin stippled with gooseflesh as long thin hands moved to cover her more delicate parts.

Christian flicked his gaze toward the copper tub beside the fireplace and snapped. The water swirled in to fill the tub.

"Bathe," he told her in French. "You stink."

Sank up to her neck, she looked softer, less treacherous. Tendrils of red hair floated across the surface of the water, moving in and out from her body. She disappeared once, under and back up, cleansing the last of the mud from her scalp. She pulled her legs to her chest and rested her chin on her knees.

Christian drew a chair to the center of the cabin and sat, studying her, all the while hearing the toothless drawl of his father's voice:

Bél fanm se traka.

There was enough beauty in the swamp, enough mystery to satisfy a man's curiosity, and enough to do the heart didn't get caught up in wishing for something more. Christian wondered bitterly how many Jaackemel men had believed that, too. Scraping, saving, begging. The great-great-greats in his bloodline working until their fingers were too calloused to bend chanting the same, bitter curse: beautiful women are trouble.

But then, where had he come from? Where had any of them come from, if not from a woman? He'd asked once when he was old enough to understand the mechanics of such a thing. The answer he received had been a hard smack from his grandfather's cane; the curiosity quite literally beaten out of him, or at least the notion to ask again.

Now, Christian was alone. His grandfather was gone. His father, too; his body part of the waters he'd worked. The same water he'd taught Christian to manipulate, as *his* father had taught him and so on and so on.

Day in and day out he listened to the distant clamor of the city. Heard the jazz trickling its way down the river, carried on the backs of steamships. They were behemoths of the modern age, glittering with light and steam, people stacked around their rails, not even aware of the noise they produced and even less so of him, until they needed something their civilized world couldn't provide.

Certainly *they* wouldn't miss one woman.

Still, he asked, "Where is your master?"

She stared down at the child in her stomach, as if that was all the answer he needed.

She looked back at him. "Your French is good."

Hers was better, but still clearly not her native tongue. Where she'd come from was probably a much longer tale than either of them had time for.

"Will it hurt?" she asked.

"There are two things that truly hurt in life," Christian said. "Birth and death. Which one are you talking about?"

She slipped back down into the tub, letting the milky-pink water washed up to her lips as she rested her chin just above the surface. Finally, she stood, letting the water drip off the end of her hair before stepping completely free of the tub.

"Could I stay here?" she asked.

Christian shook his head.

"Then I don't have a choice."

There was no sense in adding to her shame. He stood and snapped again. Her cotton nightdress reappeared around her, clean and pressed into lines that made the swell of her stomach that much more profound.

"You always have a choice," he said. "Even if you can't see it. The choice to live and die? You make that every day. You made it coming here. Walking through that door. Sitting in that water as long as you did…"

Even as she realized her error, she was too weak to fight it. When her head slumped back and her knees gave out, Christian caught her easily. Carry enough cypress through knee-deep water, a body is nothing, especially someone so thin and soft.

He lay her on the bed and knelt beside her, letting his hand trace recesses in her face; all her body's efforts confined to one purpose. He combed her hair out until it was a brilliant, fiery wave over her full breasts.

This was not some debutante, another daughter of the admiralty coming to hide her shame. Nor would she ever be. The same world that ignored him, enslaved her. But he could make her a queen, and for that, she would always reward him.

One

Today — New Orleans, Louisiana

Roben LaChance was a rat. Literally a hairless, four-legged lump on a leash outside the Suds N' Scrub on Gravier Street. His skin was the color of ash from the tip of his bald muzzle to the end of his segmented tail, but it was the tattoo gouged into his face that was the most familiar.

The last time Danni had seen him he'd been seven foot tall and towering over her in a banana-yellow Zoot suit. Of course, he'd been a man then. He'd also tried to kill her. So, she wouldn't have given much thought to Roben as a rat, probably wouldn't even have broken stride, except his black eyes were shining with a very *human* hate.

What he'd done to earn such a fate was anyone's guess, but in New Orleans, any guess was good.

Fat raindrops pounded against the tin awning. Fall in Louisiana was like spring and summer: hot and wet. The rain made the air sticky while the heat warmed the oil to the streets' surface. The French Quarter smelled like trash pretty much year round.

Danni shook the water from her hair and stepped onto the dry patch of sidewalk as she waited for the cloudburst to pass.

Roben screeched. The pink nylon leash tied around his throat led back to a homeless woman. She wrapped it around her fist, leaving it just long enough for his back feet to touch the pavement. He scrambled for a minute and then just hung there, swaying ever so slightly in the gusting rain.

"Cute," Danni said.

"Eh. My last one could do somersaults."

Danni unhooked her cell phone from her armband and snapped a photo.

"Where'd you find him?" she asked.

"Curled up in the dry cleaning. Named him Scrim."

The old woman toed the side of her tip jar. Danni peeled a few ones from her running shorts and tossed them inside. "Maybe she'll buy you some good cheese."

Roben lunged forward and snapped at her hand. The old woman jerked the leash a little higher.

"Sorry 'bout that. Last one bit, too," she said. "Had to knock his teeth out."

Roben froze mid-dangle, seeming to understand her words.

By the end of the block the rain began to taper. Danni forgot about Roben and fell back into pace with her music.

She took the same route twice a day: down Conti to Royal then west toward Canal where she could stay in the middle ground until she reached the waterfront. She preferred habits to hobbies but running had become a little of both, a way to pass the time and avoid the quiet chill of her apartment.

The street musicians were already out in their regular spots. They chased her with the shrill squeal of their horns as they shouted call-backs to the commuter crowds.

"There she go! *Go!* Fast as she can! *Can!* Jiji gonna find you! Gonna save you! Gonna stop your shadow man!"

Danni ducked her head and avoided their eyes, desperate to maintain the illusion she couldn't hear them over the music piped into her ears. But she could. Their voices picked at the back of her brain.

Most of the time it was just a static buzz that blended with the traffic and the jazz. At others, it was overwhelming. Prayers of the poor, the sick, and the homeless, a constant choir of need. And there was not a damned thing she could do about it.

She doubled-back up Chartres. The artists at Jackson Square stopped to wave as she passed.

"Give us some good weather, Jiji, yeah?"

The clouds opened. Sunlight lit the gapped cobblestone of Pirate Alley ahead of her. She dodged the larger puddles, ran through the rest, and made it to the cool shadow of the cathedral without breaking pace. She stopped and looked behind her. A dozen hopeful faces stared back through the sun-dappled mist.

Danni ran.

The rain started and stopped three more times before she reached the canal bridge. She kept to the center of the street, avoiding the broken sidewalks as the scenery went from bad to worse in a few upturned lots. Burnt-out houses were as much part of the landscape as the small parks that sprung up in the wake of some celebrity do-gooder. The children in the Ninth Ward had plenty of places to play but fewer to live. And that, too, was her problem now.

To date, Queensland Academy had been a school, a hospital, a museum, and back to a school before being gutted by Hurricane Katrina. The patina ring around the brick still marked the highest point of the flood waters. The second floor had needed all new flooring, doors, plaster… But the roof had been the real expense, taking Danni down to her last hundred bucks and forcing her to do the one thing she swore she never would: *fundraise*.

The hallway was dark beyond the front door. She quietly pressed it back to the latch and scooted down the hall on her tip-toes. Sister Ned was seated at her desk. Steam curled up from the mug in her hands to the white wisps of hair at her temples. She'd forgone her normal nun's habit for a simpler denim dress, which Danni suspected was more about durability than fashion. She was a true Renaissance nun, a Sister of Mt. Carmel.

A single, oak crucifix hung on the far wall, but the rest of the room was bare. Sister Ned liked to keep it simple.

"Good morning," she whispered. She poured a fresh cup of coffee out of the electric pot on the desk. "Breakfast?"

Danni waved away the offer. "I'm good."

"How long you been runnin'?"

"A few hours."

Tension pinched the corner of Sister Ned's eyes. "It's getting worse."

It was more of a statement than a question, but Danni nodded anyway. "My appetite is the least of your worries. Sit down, Sister. Enjoy your coffee before the onslaught."

She waited for Sister Ned to settle again, then sat in the chair on the opposite side of the desk. They shared a quiet moment, reflecting on the inside of their mugs like they did every morning. Sister Ned always spoke first.

"Have you heard from Michael?" she asked.

"He stopped by the apartment while I was out. Dropped off some flowers."

The sister smiled. "He always did have a flare for romance."

Danni wet her lips and considered it. "Is that how I should take them, then?"

"Danni, he loves you."

"Yes, but does he remember what I look like?"

"He hasn't been gone *that* long. And when he's ready, he'll come back."

Danni leaned over her knees, ran both hands through her hair, and came back with a few black, broken strands. It seemed like years had passed when it had only been a matter of months. The Summer of Souls, she jokingly called it, though no one else laughed, least of all Michael. In fact, she couldn't remember the last time she'd heard his laughter or so much as seen him smile. Where he'd once been a constant, shining brilliance in her life, he'd grown increasingly dower, despondent. Distant. And now he was gone.

She tugged the lanyard from the inside of her shirt and thumbed the head of the nail at the end. She'd spent the last several years with it in her chest. At the time, it had marked her debt to The Baron Samedi, the most notorious loa in New Orleans. Now it held a piece of Michael's soul.

The pressure built in the back of her throat. "There was a part of me that thought I was enough for him."

"*You are*," Sister Ned insisted. She stood again and rounded the desk, this time to still Danni's fretting fingers around the nail. "Look at me, Danielle."

Danni steeled herself before looking up, knowing exactly what she'd find. Compassion, resolve, maybe even a little sympathy.

"Michael loves you," the sister said again. "What happened, happened. No use in convincing yourself of things that aren't true or seeing problems that aren't there to see. Besides, we have enough trouble upstairs to pass the time."

How much time? A month? Two months? Danni swallowed hard. *A year*? Exactly how long did he expect her to wait for him? How long did it take for someone to get over being a priest?

"Tell me where he went. Please, Sister. I need to–"

"Run off and see him? Ignore everything you've been told and try to convince him to come back?" She released Danni's hands but didn't move away. "Because he'd do it. For you. Come back as quick as you called, if that's what you really wanted."

"You don't know that."

"Isn't that part of this?" She tapped the nail inside Danni's fist. "You give it a little pull and he comes, willing or not?"

Danni nodded.

"Then do it," Sister Ned said. "Go ahead."

Danni floundered with the idea. She knew what it meant to be on the receiving end of that pull, to be dragged across hell when the choice wasn't hers to make. The Baron had done the same to her for years and probably would have continued had Michael not intervened. Unfortunately, that intervention had left Michael as bound to her as she had once been to Samedi.

The hammer of footfalls broke the silence between them. Kids were like that, asleep one minute, awake the next. Sister Ned patted the tops of Danni's knees and stood.

"Come on," she said. "You can help me get them fed."

Danni gave the nail one last look and tucked it back inside her shirt.

Sister Ned moved ahead of her, flipping on lights as she went. Her make-shift kitchen was impressive, having grown from a single stovetop to a sixteen-burner range, four ovens, and a series of flat griddles that were polished to slick, black glass. She kicked on the flames and motioned Danni toward the refrigerators daisy-chained down the wall.

The floor above them shuddered and water rushed through the latticework of pipes.

Danni nodded toward the ceiling. "We'll need to get

that all covered before tomorrow night."

"Sister Charlotte is bringing a ladder. I figure we can do most of it with white bed sheets. No one will be the wiser, and if they are, maybe they'll kick in for a new ceiling, yeah?"

"Slather on a little Catholic guilt and call it a day," Danni finished.

A spatula shot out from Sister Ned's hand and she cocked a fist against her hip. "Do not underestimate the power of charity. Or shame when that fails."

Danni nodded and tried to swallow the growing lump in her throat.

"Do they have a good life here?" she asked.

"Better than they had on the streets or running errands for Samedi."

That no one could argue with. Still, Danni couldn't recall ever hearing the Sister say the Baron's name so casually before, as if she'd known him her entire life. Something occurred to her.

"You're not afraid of him."

"I know the Devil, Danni. He's got a lot of faces, Samedi might be one from time to time, but I also know this city. Things aren't always as black and white as my rites might suggest."

"That's a hell of an admission to make."

Sister Ned shook her head. "Not an admission, wisdom. The Sisters of Mount Carmel have existed in New Orleans for a long time. Sometimes that means having faith, and sometimes it means blending faiths."

"We're doing a bit more than blending," Danni said.

"They think I'm their patron. I can hear their *prayers*."

Sister Ned shrugged. "Christ had gifts. It was what he used them for that made him different. Hurry up with the fruit."

The first wave of tired faces made their way into the room. They stopped when they spotted Danni standing over a mountain of fresh cantaloupe.

"Well, don't just stand there," she said. "Get over here and help me."

A rush of eager hands quickly made more smashed melon than cubes. Danni hoisted one of the youngest, Jean-Paul, onto an overturned milk crate beside her. He stuffed his cheeks full of fruit and then swallowed with an audible gulp.

"There's a bottomless hole inside that child," Sister Ned said as she passed over two full stacks of pancakes. "Go on, now. You boys say your prayers and eat."

The food was divided quickly but evenly as they all took turns helping each other. One by one, they laced their hands over their plates, formed a quick cross over their hearts, and dove into their breakfasts. Danni scanned the crowd again, counted off the heads, but came up one short.

"Has anyone seen Gabriel?" she asked.

Jean-Paul answered. "Him upstairs."

Sister Ned offered her a bewildered look. It wasn't like Gabriel to miss a meal. The sister tossed her apron on the counter and started for the stairs. Danni stopped her.

"I'll go," she said.

Their collective eyes held a deliberate weight on the back of her neck as Danni moved out of the room. She tried to ignore the words passing between their minds and hers.

Good morning, Jiji. We love you, Jiji. Akeyi yo.

Despite the weight of its meaning, the last one filled her with warmth.

Akeyi yo. We welcome you.

Two

The dormitory was a shotgun room full of beds set perpendicular to the wall. Sister Ned had only recently allowed the older boys to hang sheets between them, in an effort to maintain what little privacy there was to be had in a room shared by twenty-six. From what she could tell, the make-shift walls had been met with mixed reviews, and boasted bold threats like 'STAY OUT OR ELSE' to the rest of the room.

It wouldn't be long before they would need more space than she could reasonably provide.

Danni spotted Gabriel at the back of the room, seated in a pool of sunlight. She stopped to hustle a few pairs of shoes into a neat line, but his attention stayed fixed on something in his lap. She sank down to his bed and blew a cool breath against his ear. His skin stippled, making the charcoal tattoo on the side of his neck look that much darker. All the boys had them, thanks to Samedi.

Gabriel whipped around and clutched his hands to his chest. "No, Jiji, you can't look yet! It's a surprise!"

She tugged playfully at his shoulder. "I hate surprises. Let me see."

"No!"

"Well, I guess you can't see my surprise either."

One shiny eye flashed back over his shoulder. "What is it?"

"Can't show you."

"Please?"

"You know my price, boy."

Gabriel huffed and pushed himself upright. He unrolled a long bed sheet down his body. Danni studied the collection of bottle caps and pieces of shattered safety glass stitched into the fabric.

"Wings," she said with a smile.

"Sister Ned read us a story about Icarus," he said. "I found most of the pieces in the street, and Sister Ned gave me a needle and some thread."

Danni ran her hand over the shoulder of a wing made from a fist full of flattened pennies. It reminded her of Indian beadwork —the Wild Tchoupitoulas or Golden Eagles— tightly stitched together to create a brilliant pattern. The only real difference was the Indians spent months working on their costumes, and Gabriel had been doing this, at best, for a few weeks. Any more than that, and she would have heard about it before now.

"You sewed this all by yourself?" she asked. He nodded. "Gabriel, this is incredible."

The joy slowly slid out of his face. "When Icarus flew too close to the sun his wings melted. Sister Ned said that's what happens when you're too proud."

17

Danni frowned. "Well, what Sister Ned calls pride, I call a design flaw."

She unhooked the cell phone from her armband and angled it around so he could see the photo of Roben as a rat. "Now *this* is what happens to people who are too proud."

Gabriel eyed the fat, lumpy image of a Roben. She had no doubt Gabriel recognized him. Roben had tried to kill him, too. He let out a squeal of laughter, then sobered.

"Did you turn him into a rat, Jiji?" he asked.

"I *can't* turn people into rats."

"Rene says you can," he protested. "He says loa can do whatever they want to whoever they want."

Danni sighed. "There's a little more to it than that. And tell Rene I don't want him talking like that anymore. It upsets Sister Ned."

"Because she believes in Jesus?"

"Among other things, but yeah," Danni said. "And all of you have to take care of her, just like she takes care of you. Speaking of which, it's time for breakfast."

Gabriel nodded and dutifully began to refold his wings.

"Is Father Michael back yet?" he asked.

"Not yet. And he's not technically a Father anymore, remember?"

Gabriel nodded again. Danni ran a quick hand over his head, but when she pushed herself off the bed, his voice called her back.

"Jiji? Do you miss him?"

"Yeah, kid. I do."

He bit the edge of his lip, something mischievous shining in his eyes. "Do you love him?"

Gabriel had lived a harder life than most adults. Even though his face was young, there was a weight in his expression that suggested he understood her hesitation, as well as what it meant. It made him frown.

"He loves you," he said.

"How do you know?"

"He say so."

That simple. Still, Danni frowned.

"Grammar."

"He *said* so," Gabriel corrected.

"Thank you." Danni sighed. "Sometimes grown-up love is really complicated."

Gabriel frowned at her again. "I know where babies come from, Jiji."

"It's not about—" Danni stopped, sat again, and rubbed her eyes. "How are you with secrets?" she asked finally.

"Great! Maurice has a pocket knife he uses to stab frogs in the head and I've never told anyone... *oops.*"

"After breakfast, pocketknife. But first..." She cupped a hand to her mouth. The words came out in a quick rush of air, much easier to say when passed into his ear alone. Gabriel listened, nodding ever so slightly before pulling away, then pinched his thumb against his forefinger and ran it across his lips.

"Can I add your secret to the book?" he asked.

"What book?"

Gabriel jumped over his cot onto a low step stool

19

beside a standing armoire. His fingers barely reached the top. He patted around and returned with a long leather-bound accountant folio. Shreds of paper slipped from inside as he unfolded it across the bed. Some were simple stick-figures drawn in hard-pressed crayon, while others were full pages carefully written across lined paper.

"Every time we get a new brother, they tell us how they met you," he explained.

Gabriel looked shyly towards his feet. "Can I?" he asked again. "Can I add your secret?"

"Yeah. Sure. What the hell."

His small palm shot out. "Quarter!"

"Say what?"

"Sister Ned says anyone who cusses owes anyone who hears it a quarter."

"Hell is not a cuss word."

"Double quarter!"

Danni patted her pocket and pulled out a dollar. "Do you make change?"

Gabriel shook his head.

"Well, hell. And... damn. There." She stuffed the bill into his hand. "That ought to cover me."

Three

"Sorrow is real," the old hoodoo priest said. "Sorrow is honest. There's a lot of power in it."

He cast a sliver of cinnamon into the small fire on the table. The wood sparked and flashed, casting light across the runes drawn into the sand.

Michael let the glow fade before he spoke.

"The sorrow is real, but it's the emptiness that distracts me."

"The emptiness." The old man's voice was deep, gravelly.

His long fingers snapped a piece of cinnamon bark in two. He offered half to Michael and used the other to stir the coffee in front of him. The sweetness filled the tiny cabin. Outside, the night was alive with the sounds of insects and animals, creatures on four legs, two legs, and no legs at all going about the how's of surviving another day.

Michael silently contemplated the why as Zedekiah Brantly watched.

"It's not the emptiness that bothers me," Michael

said eventually. "It's the anger."

"Yes, it is."

"I'm angry at…"

He let the thought fade.

"Everything?" Zed prompted.

"Yes." Michael shook his head. "No. Not everything."

"Now we're getting somewhere. Focus. Separate it out. Name the pain."

"I'm angry at myself. At Reverend Mother for sending me out here. I'm angry at Danni. I'm angry at–"

"Yeah?"

"I'm angry at God." Michael threw the cinnamon stick at the fire. "I knew I wasn't a great priest, but was I *that* bad of a man? He gives her to me and then he takes her away?"

"You walked away, Michael," Zed said. "Can't blame that on God."

"I walked because she made me."

"So, you mad at God or you mad at her?"

"Both."

"And what's that come from."

"Fear." Michael swallowed hard. "It always comes from fear."

"And where does fear get you?"

"At the moment? A shack in the middle of the bayou with an old man who hasn't seen civilization in more than two decades. No offense, Zed."

Zed's boney fingers swept away the runes drawn in the sand. "None taken, just so long as you remember that not being there isn't the same as not seeing. I spent a lot of years in New Orleans, and every time I look, I see it ain't changed that much. More important to see what's right in front of me."

Michael's attention jerked up from the fire. "Oh yeah? And what do you see?"

"A man who's hurting, flailing about for something to hold on to. That's why the old sister sent you to me. Get me to do what she couldn't, and teach you some self control.

"But first we got to give you the tools to communicate, see what you got in you, and make it so you can see for yourself. Latin ain't the only dead language still working will in the bayou."

He selected another cinnamon stick and began to draw in the sand.

"Pay attention. Every rune has more than one meaning. Every series of runes is more than a sentence, more than a message. It's a path your will can walk to achieve a purpose.

"This is *mannaz*…"

Four

Danni ran.

A sob lurched from her throat. Her feet pounded the sidewalk, pistoning in time with her heart, as she clenched her hand around the nail. A warm pulse of blood bubbled in the spaces between her fingers. The grief overtook her in shuddering bursts. God *damn* him! And Sister Ned. And Mother Superior. And anyone else who knew where Michael had gone.

He left her here. Alone, with a house full of orphans and a city screaming her name.

She ran faster. Neon signs turned into vapor trails of light and sound. The buildings lost cohesion. She raced through intersections against the traffic lights, vaulting the benches and fences and people in her path until the fluted jazz of the Quarter was exchanged for the barge horns blasting down the deep center of the river.

The pavement ended at a chain link fence. One hard kick sent her over the top. She drove forward through a thicket of burdock and sun-baked thistle that tore at her skin in stinging slaps. Her toe caught a clump of cement scrub. She pitched forward. Her shoulder struck hard as her body twisted around instinctively to stop her momentum and landed only a few feet from the river.

The seagulls squalled overhead and dove toward the trash-filled eddies only to be chased away by voices farther up the shore. Danni followed the sound to the top of the pier, squinting into the sun to see the men on the dock. Whoever they were, they worked quickly, almost frantically. They shoved raw, wooden crates off one trailer and onto another. A forklift lifted one and carried it to the end of the pier. Two more men hustled to shove the crate off the forks and into the Mississippi. The scrap-wood sides split instantly and disappeared beneath the surface with a loud belch of air.

Danni stood. What exactly were they trying to hide? Another crate splashed into the water, split, and disappeared.

She cut a diagonal path back up the boat ramp and to the dock. Steel shipping crates formed walls on either side of the pier and trapped their voices into a funnel.

"How many more of these things we got?" one asked.

"Don't open them!" another said.

Danni slid around the corner of the pier. A police car sat on the center of the dock, its officer resting against the hood.

"Come on, you pussies! Get them goddamn things underwater!" he yelled as his eyes swept around the dock.

Danni ducked back and waited a long minute.

Finally, satisfied he hadn't seen her, she slid around the edge of the container again.

He was no longer standing at the end of his patrol car.

"Danielle Toussaint."

Danni startled and spun, but he used her own momentum to drive her around, palms first against the shipping container. His thick forearm pressed her cheek against the hot steel.

"Officer Bouchard," she said through gritted teeth.

His free hand started at her hip and traveled across her thigh. He repeated the pat-down on her opposite leg, but stopped when he found the bulge on her hip. It was her *lam te mouri*, literally, a death blade designed to sever souls from their bodies.

Danni winced when he jerked it free from her waistband.

"Well, well. Felon's got herself a pretty little pig sticker."

Bouchard turned it over in her periphery, surveying the bone-handled blade like he was shopping for souvenirs. It flashed in the sunlight and then landed in the river with a *plunk!*

The pressure let off her neck. Bouchard swept both hands around her waist. She stilled herself against all instinct. Breaking his nose would be a shallow victory, and at this angle, he'd have her in a sleeper hold before her elbow finished the swing. Still, she grunted as his hands came dangerously close to her breasts, trying to provoke her.

"Can't say I've ever seen runners come this far off the beaten path, Toussaint."

"I got lost."

"That so?" He twisted her around. His finger traced a fresh scrape on her forehead. "You're all busted up. Boyfriend do that to you?"

"Don't have one."

"Girlfriend, then? I know how you ladies like to mix it up on the cell block."

Danni ground her molar against her tongue and swallowed a wad of spit. Of the few run-ins she'd had with N.O.P.D., Bouchard was the only one who made a point of mentioning her time in prison. Then again, he was the only one who'd taken the time to look it up.

He shifted to see around the side of the container, presumably to where his men worked. She heard another crate smash against the surface before the Mississippi swallowed it whole.

"What's that all about?" she asked.

"Just a little housekeeping." Bouchard's gaze returned but this time it was full of cold indifference. "Nice day for a swim, isn't it?"

He wrenched her hair into his fist, dragging her down, so she was half-bent as he pulled her toward the edge of the pier. "Water looks good, right about here."

The water was warm but no less startling. Danni flailed, sputtering and hissing at Bouchard. He flashed her a quick smile and moved back to his patrol car.

"Come on, boys!" he yelled down the dock. "Let's call it a day."

A semi engine rumbled to life, and then faded a few minutes later. The wake of a passing barge rocked her up against the foot of the pier, pinning her against the pylon as the water and river flotsam washed over her head. She shoved a hunk of drift wood away from her face and began to paddle back to the shore. Her knees found the shoal first, reigniting the pain of the previous fall.

Her feet were almost out of the water when something tugged at her foot. She dug her fingers into the black mud and pulled. It pulled harder. Her hands slipped. Gravel raked against her face as she was pulled back into waist-deep water.

"What the hell?"

Drift wood? A trawler net? This far down river it could have been anything. She scraped her free foot against her ankle, only to be rewarded with another hard yank and a lungful of water as it took her under again.

Five

Sunlight barely penetrated the clouding sediment. Whatever had her foot broke the river bed ahead of her, kicking mud and rotting vegetation in her eyes. The pressure began to build in her chest as she felt herself being yanked into deeper, cooler waters. She tried to focus on a single task. First, she needed to stop moving.

Danni paddled furiously in the opposite direction, choking on the water she'd already swallowed, which only resulted in swallowing more. Her hands sank through the river bed, but it was like trying to grab cold syrup. The deeper she drove her arms into the mud, the colder it got, but there was nothing to hold on to. When she did find something, it wriggled out of her grip.

The panic came back. Whatever was pulling her foot stopped but only to readjust its grip. A hand! It took hold her ankle again and began to pull her deeper. Mouthfuls of mud filled the back of her throat, taking the last of her reserved air. Didn't matter. Whoever it was, they were in for a fight.

Her own scream was muted but fierce. The hand released from her foot, leaving the low current to knock her up and out a few feet. She paddled in the direction she assumed was the surface, but it was hard to tell. She'd lost her bearings to the warm buzz of oxygen deprivation. The water wasn't as cold anymore. In fact, the weightlessness was soft, soothing.

Her mind fought back.

Up! it screamed. *Air!*

A strange thought crept into her mind. She was probably only nine feet from the surface. It seemed so shallow, and yet so deep. But why nine?

"Because that's all the barges need," Michael said.

His face was wrought in a halo of sunlight as they made their way down the promenade, hand in hand. His red hair looked like polished copper under the warm weight of the sun but felt like baby-fine silk when she slid her hand through it.

Her vision began to narrow, filling with white blobs before thinning out. Danni pulled herself into a ball and let the current carry her out to the channel.

"Danni? Danni!"

One voice bled to several dozen, but the sounds of the syllables were tangled in a whirl of rushing wind, too far away to be heard but too close to ignore.

Jiji. *Jiji!*

Danni opened her eyes. She stood on a meadow of long grass. It moved with a gentle, lapping sway. White birch branches crowded the pale purple sky. Children laughed in the distance.

Jiji! Jiji, come play!

She knew this place. It spoke to her, not just in the voices of the children at play, but in every cool kiss of grass and invigorating breath of sweet wind. Bel-koté.

She knew souls were what gave the Baron Samedi his power. She'd stolen her first one from him. The act that had made her a loa. What exactly *that* meant, she also hadn't quite worked out.

The voices of her children, the living and the dead, called to her. They swarmed across the open fields, surfacing and then vanishing in quick forward bursts of light. They reminded her of dolphins skimming over open waters, bounding over each other to be the first to greet her.

Danni laughed freely at the sight of them. It was a melodic sound, even though she hadn't meant for it to be. It triggered her awareness to the other differences in herself. The weight of her body was gone. She noticed the depression in the earth where her foot should have been but wasn't. A perfect silhouette of her body spilled out across the grass. How could she cast a shadow without a figure?

Thought shifted to form. Feet to shins to knees to waist. The rest followed in short order as she coalesced into a solid shape. Whether it was her own imagination or sense of propriety that clothed her in a white, cotton summer dress, she wasn't sure. Regardless, she wiggled her bare toes in the loose earth and stretched toward the sun.

The boys reached her as a group of shimmering, frantic light. They touched her hands, her arms, and her hair before pulling her down to snuggle against her sides. She relaxed, feeling pleasantly warm and at ease. She even

31

thought of Michael knowing he would eventually find her here. He knew the way as surely as she did, assuming he came back at all.

What didn't find her was the grief of his loss, the sorrow she felt for having pushed him away, or the angry truth that she had done nothing of the sort. In Bel-Koté, she was safe from those things. Not even something as sharp and real as the pain of death could reach her here.

Her body was sinking to the bottom of the Mississippi. Even as she watched it happen she wondered how long it would take to die. She hadn't asked or even considered what would happen to her. Could she die? Would she feel it when she did? And if she did, what would it feel like?

The ground against her back gave. Danni fell away from Bel-Koté. She reached for it again but only felt her control ripped away faster. The drop ended abruptly. Sensation returned in the form of a hard smack to her face where it collided with the mossy foot of the pier. Her lungs burned. Her chest felt like it was full of rocks. It only got worse when she took her first breath of air.

She was almost exactly back where Bouchard had thrown her in. The weight of her wet, aching body slowed her progress as she struggled to lift herself out of the water. When she did topple onto the shore, she rolled on her back and spit several mouthfuls of mud onto the bank.

Her sneakers were gone. She opened her hand to the air. Her focus drew down on the knife. She imagined it beneath the surface of the water, and felt it prickle across her senses as she called it to her. It erupted from the water a second later, and she caught it.

Danni lay back against the shore and stared down the length of her body at the nail.

God damn him!

Six

A light breeze blew the sun's warmth across Michael's forearms. His fingers shifted and curled slowly, moving and shaping the dead rabbit beneath them. Sweat beaded across his face, and when he leaned forward, the sweat began to rain.

The rabbit's legs curled up to its belly. A line of sweat slid into the corner of Michael's eye and he blinked, stung by the salt it carried off his skin. Below him the rabbit dropped, dead and still again. Michael sighed and leaned back on his heels.

"This is unholy," he growled.

"Yeah? Tell that to Lazarus," Zed said.

"That was different."

"Because it was God?" The old man chuckled. "You bet it was. God gave Lazarus back his soul. We can't do that. Wouldn't want to if'n we could."

Michael studied him for a minute. "Why not?"

Zed stood, retrieved the rabbit, and tossed it toward the swamp. An alligator's jaws intercepted it just before it hit the water.

"Look, son, we work with the raw materials. If God took that bunny's soul, he must've had a plan for it. Me tryin' to take it back wouldn't just be foolish, it'd be rude. And bein' rude to the Great Conjurer is a sure way to get on His short list."

"But why would I want to bring something back to life if it's not going to have a soul?"

"You wouldn't. But restoring movement, blood flow. That's healing, whether it's a bunny or a man. You bein' able to heal, means you can help. Ain't that what we're doing out here?"

"Yeah."

"Good." Zed reached into a canvas bag and pulled out a dead snake. He dropped it at Michael's feet. Michael jumped as it bounced on the grass in front of him.

"A snake?" he asked.

"Not our business to decide which creature has the right to live or die. Go again."

One day moved into the next. They spent time walking the trails through the bayou. Zed pointed out sweet grass, oleander, and different types of trees, then talked about the when's and why's of their uses. In the evening, they'd return to the cabin. Zed would lead Michael back along the day's walk, but this time Michael would know it through Zed's eyes. He saw what Zed knew about the plants he'd pointed out, carried along by the mysteries he still didn't understand.

One morning, a small leather sack was waiting for him on the table. Michael didn't have to ask.

"Gris-gris bag," he said.

"Will be. Might be," Zed said. "Up to you. Your bag, your beliefs, your power. You've been collecting things during our lessons. Dusts and potions, that white crow's wing. I 'spect they belong in there, but you fill it as you see fit. Bones, stones, dust, rosary beads and the pinky of some old saint… Hell, you can fill it with steel marbles and rubber bands. Truth is, whether it's a bag of junk or the best magic you ever had is up to what *you* believe.

"It's a mojo. It represents what you believe in. Some might say, what you stand for. Magic is just like the Holy Father, son. It all depends on faith."

Michael touched a hand to his heart.

"But be careful what you put in there," Zed added. "Not everything we believe in gets along."

He led Michael out the door into the swamp trails. They weren't much more than tamped down footpaths and reptile tracks with roots big enough to break both ankles if he didn't stay alert. Zed was less cautious and stayed ahead of Michael by more than ten feet the entire way.

"You move pretty quick for an older guy," Michael said.

Zed shot a grin over his shoulder. "And I thought a youngster like you would be a little lighter on his feet."

They stopped at a small, worn crossroads near a line of bushes. Michael could feel the neutrality in the soil like a pillow placed beneath his feet. It wasn't a place to conjure as much as *absorb*.

"Curses," Zed began, "to my mind, are as much about the natural order of things being allowed to be what it is than anything else. Now, I know the church says we're not supposed to wish ill on others, but most times a curse is just getting stuff out of the way so a foolish man can be himself."

He pointed to the pinkish-purple flowers sprouted along the trail. "Take oleander. This beauty can blossom off and on all year around here, unless we get a bad winter. Pretty little thing. But be foolish enough to dress up your driveway, and you'd be lucky if you don't wake up in the emergency room."

Michael could see the plant in his mind as it developed rapidly through various stages of growth. *See* the toxic nature of the flowers even as he smelled their sickly sweet aroma. Zed went on.

" 'Course, some folks might think that if you plant 'em where kids play you deserve whatever misfortune comes your way. Then there's this little guy."

Zed pointed to a low, sprouting plant. "Stinkweed. Gets such a bad rep. Some folks grind 'em up, rub the oil into sand, and spread it where someone else they don't care for will be walking. Says it gives 'em bad luck. That's not a curse. It's just bein' spiteful.

"Not to say there ain't evil out there, or evil intentions. But real evil doesn't do petty. It's more likely to make you feel like the best thing in the world. Butter you up, blow your head up to the size of a Mardi Gras float right before it rips your heart out."

"So you're saying the church is right? There is a Satan?"

"Don't matter what name you give it. There's

darkness out there. What *you* gotta do is learn how to see in the dark."

Seven

John Todd Margolin, better known as Joto, rolled out from behind a tall counter. Mardi Gras beads clattered against the spokes of his wheelchair. It was one of the turn-of-the-century kind with a high, wooden back and cross-thatched seats, which was beyond ridiculous. Joto could afford better. His shop, Chautain Rue, was a mixed bag of dark arts and retail crap, but still one of the most lucrative voodoo stores in the Quarter.

Danni slopped across the threshold, leaving pools of water in the shape of her bare feet behind her.

"Woo, girl! You smell like the warm inside of a chum hold. What'd you fall into this morning?"

She peeled her soaked shirt over her head. It landed at her feet with a wet *fwap*.

"Mississippi."

"We gotta work on your dialect. It's *Missi'sip*."

Joto pulled a clean towel from a pile beside the door and shook it out of a tight roll. He tossed it at her. "You take a wrong turn off the island?"

"Something like that."

He leaned forward in his chair, squinting. "Little bit more than the river did that, I reckon."

Danni touched the blood crusted at the edge of her hairline. "Bouchard."

"He dead now?"

"He's a cop, Joto."

"The question remains."

She scrubbed the towel around her head. "Are you trying to piss me off?"

"Nah, not me. Just seeing how long you're gonna stand there with your shirt off."

Danni let out a frustrated sigh and jerked a fresh t-shirt off the rack. She tugged it over her head, then tossed the muddy towel in his face. His laughter chased her all the way to the back of the shop.

"Don't blame a man for lookin'," he teased. "Blame him for not."

The office was decorated with a few decades of debris; chicken feet, broken beads, loose sets of tarot cards, and boxes of officious-looking papers. A thick, wooden working table sat in the center of it all, bare apart from a crucible smoldering sweet, white smoke.

She scanned the boxes stacked beside the back door, then pulled the knife from her pocket and ran it along the packing tape.

"Any word on my centerpieces for the fundraiser?" she asked.

"Hey! Can you not open my supplies with that thing! Suppose it touches a bit of jou-jou. Next thing you know, I'm missing a few more body parts."

Danni dug through a layer of packing peanuts and frowned.

"What the fuck are these?"

Joto winced. "Saint Jiji dolls?"

The doll was a little bigger than the palm of her hand, dressed in a simple white dress almost the same color of its skin, *her* skin. She slammed it back into the box.

"I've had a dozen people in here looking for icons," Joto explained. "I got the real deal, me, but you can't expect people to keep praying to an empty altar."

"They shouldn't be praying to me at all. And these look nothing like me."

"Well, they do say Made in China."

Joto reached past her and into the box. He tamped the wild tease of synthetic black hair around the doll's misshapen face.

"Like it or not, this is what you are now. These people needed something to believe in and you gave them that. Don't get all hung up on the details now."

"Joto, this is insane."

"More insane than having a nail in your chest? How about stealing souls from The Crossroads?"

"That was different."

"How different? You ain't eating. I know you ain't sleeping. Run as many laps around the quarter as you want to, you ain't gonna fall down. Yous a loa now, darlin'."

He retrieved the first aid kit from a cradle against the wall, unfolded it across the table, then held a wad of fresh gauze up to her mouth.

"Go on," he said. "Give us a little."

Danni dropped into the folding chair beside him and spit into the gauze. He dabbed it against her forehead, the side of her cheek, and the back of her hand. Her skin tingled under each gentle pass he made as the scrapes faded and vanished.

"I didn't ask for any of this," she said quietly.

"Nah. Ya bargained for it, and I'd say as far as voodoo goes, you got a pretty ripe deal. So what if a few mambos want to stick a doll on their altar and pour out a few glugs of gin?"

"They'd do better with a cabernet."

"Yeah? I'll pass that on." Joto tossed the soiled gauze on the desk. "Meantime, I found a houngan in Baie Chevreuil who knew a bit more about Samedi than is good for a man's health. Liked to knock my teeth clear out my skull when he saw me, too."

Danni maneuvered his chin into the light. The cut was barely visible against his dark skin, just above his left incisor. Danni licked her thumb and worked it across his lip.

"I told you to stop trying to meet these people without me," she said.

Something softened in Joto's face. His eyes glazed and drifted before his hand clamped down on her wrist.

"Stop. *Please*. You don't know what that feels like."

She started to ask, but something in his expression said he wouldn't tell her if she did. Danni's hands fell back into her lap.

"What was I sayin?" he asked.

"The houngan."

"Ah. Right. Remember how I told you this wasn't the first time Samedi lost a little more than he bargained for? Last account was a few hundred years ago, on a sugar cane plantation in Santa Lucia called Belle Marseille.

"Back then, they used to boil the cane in big vats. Between the steam and sun and the cooking sugar, the boiling huts would get so hot, the slaves would just fall down dead. So, it was common practice to shut down during the hottest part of the day.

"But, their master, Christopher de'Larousse wasn't that type of man. Didn't care how many of them dropped, he just kept them workin'. So, the slaves called Samedi to blight the crop with cane beetles in hopes it would shut down the show.

"But the Baron double-crossed them. Made his own deal with de'Larousse, and nearly tripled the yield."

"And what was his price for that?" Danni asked.

"The corner stone of Belle Marseille."

"What's so special about a brick?" Danni asked.

"I'm gettin' to it. Hush.

"The slaves decided they had to get rid of Samedi. So, a young slave girl named Emeka stole the cornerstone and called Samedi out to the vats. She told him she would only trade it back for his departure.

"Samedi rushed at her, knocked them both into the boiling cane. Emeka died, but Samedi lost his hold on more than just Belle Marseille. Knocked him back to the Crossroads for a long time. Houngan say, it's the moment he lost his body, and why to this day, he smells like burnt

43

sugar."

"What do you mean, lost his body?"

"Just that," Joto said with a shrug. "Some say the loa have always been, while others say they just men *possessed* by spirits. Time comes and goes, the power changes hands. It takes on a new host, and for a while, the man and the spirit walk together."

"Like me." Danni stared at her open palms and frowned. "I don't *feel* possessed."

"But you don't feel exactly human, either, do you? Can't say I understand it any better than you do. You might try askin' your head of household."

Samedi's brother, The Baron Cemetrie, was the current Ghede family head of household. He'd stolen the position from their other brother, LaCroix. Cemetrie wasn't as vicious as Samedi, but he wasn't what Danni would call kind. She preferred to avoid all of them when possible.

"So, the cornerstone, the slave, what did all this accomplish exactly?" she asked.

Joto snatched a thick leather book from a mountain of thinner bindings. He rustled through the pages and then guided her attention to a bluish drawing in the center of the page. It wasn't much more than a combination of basic geometric shapes: two interlocking circles with a square where they overlapped, three small *x*'s on the outer edge of one arc and three *o*'s on the opposite side. Danni squinted at the text marked in the margin.

"*Débouyé-a*," she read, then shook her head, unfamiliar.

"The Unraveller," Joto said.

"So, what you're saying is I need a brick, some sugar, and one pissed off slave to make me *me* again?"

Joto snapped the book shut. "Voodoo ain't about followin' recipes or reciting rhymes. It's born of raw emotion, good and bad. Love. Hate. Happiness, as well as sadness. That day, Emeka sacrificed herself so her people could live."

"Yeah. On a plantation, as slaves."

Joto frowned. "You're missing the point."

"I think *you* are."

Joto stared at her for a long moment with something softly sad in his eyes. "Guess I let the old man get his licks in for nothin' then, huh?"

"Doesn't seem fair does it?" she asked. "We're running around getting our asses handed to us while Michael's sipping beers in some Caribbean paradise."

Joto barked a sharp laugh. "It ain't no paradise, that's for sure."

Danni ground her teeth together until she thought her molars would crack.

"You've talked to him," she growled.

Joto said nothing, did nothing.

"*Joto.*"

He threw up his hands. "Don't put me in the middle."

"I wouldn't *have* to if someone would tell me where he was!"

Joto shook his head. "Trust me when I say that probably wouldn't go well right now. He needs a clear head and damned if being around you doesn't make everything murky."

Danni started to stand, but Joto held her in place. "Hey. Uh-uh. Sit down and talk to me."

"I don't know how it works in your world, but in mine, you don't complain about your boyfriend to his best friend."

"Your world *is* my world, darlin'. Has been since the moment he walked you in that door." He waved a wide hand around the room. "You think I let just any pretty face come and go through my shop?"

She gave him a weak smile. "If my centerpieces come in—"

"I'll run 'em by the sisters'. Don't you worry about it none."

Danni headed for the back stairs but stopped at the door.

"How'd he get it back?" she asked. "Samedi. You said it knocked him back *for a while*."

Joto sniffed a laugh. "His wife. Maman Bridgette." He snapped to fingers in the space beside his head. "Unscrewed the whole thing."

"Just like that?"

"Just like that. But can you imagine how much groveling it took?"

No. She couldn't. But she had a pretty good idea.

Eight

Saturdays weren't for rest, but they were a break from the scenery of the swamp. Though not much. The only thing not faded about Del's Tackle Shop and Deli was the portable metal road sign in the dirt parking lot that read: COLUMBUS DAY SPECIAL! CRAWFISH-N-COLD BEER BUCKET O' EACH $15

Michael climbed the ramp spanning a series of long pontoons. The store itself was anchored to several concrete-filled oil drums. Del said he did it after he'd been flooded out the first time. Now, rain or shine, he offered good meals and whatever else was on the shelves for a fair price, or at least something close enough to match the need.

Del was a tall, thin man with skin as dark and rough as the cypress trees the store was built around. His high, reedy voice called from the back of the deli. "Hey, now! Where y'at?"

"Hey, Del. Just a supply run."

"Not just. The old man got a box."

Del hefted an oversized box to the counter. Michael

47

recognized the Chautain Rue label and Joto's handwriting.

"You gotta sign here," Del said as he handed off a clipboard. "What'd they do before they give everybody names?"

Michael grinned. "Don't know. Maybe they just trusted each other."

"Ain't it the truth. You need anything besides the usual?"

"Nope."

Del pointed to a table beside the door. "It's pulled and waiting for you in that milk crate over there. Cold stuff's in the blue ice chest in the cooler."

Michael tossed out a few folded bills. "We that predictable?"

"Nothin' wrong with being steady."

"Keep the change."

"Always do."

Michael was still smiling as he set the crate in the back of the pickup. He lifted the box and ice chest in after it and then fished out a beer. The metal newspaper box at the bottom of the ramp still had a paper in it. He found a spot in the shade next to the truck and took a long pull on his beer before unfolding the front page.

The city was promising to rebuild more neighborhoods lost in flooding. Federal Government promising money for levee renovations again. The Pelicans promising a big year. Michael shook his head. More promises that not even the folks making them believed. On the bottom of page three an announcement from the New Orleans Police caught his attention.

"Several reports of strange figures accosting tourists in and around the Quarter," he read aloud. "What makes them unusual, a police source said, is there have been no muggings or assaults stemming from these events. Residents are advised to use caution."

What was unusual was thinking that *not* getting mugged was unusual. He checked the police blotter for familiar names and found none, but there was some new graffiti showing up in the Ninth Ward. The photo was grainy, but from what he could tell it looked like angel's wings surrounding a four-point magnolia.

He flipped to the community section and found a photograph of Mother Superior and several children. Sister Ned stood beside her, holding a large check addressed to Queensland Orphanage. Michael sighed. It was good to see things at home moving forward.

"Excuse me, can you tell me which road will take me to Pintail Bay?"

Michael startled.

"Oh, I'm sorry. I didn't mean to scare you."

Her voice was clear and strong, with just a touch of Irish lilt. Michael eyes started on two impossibly long legs and followed them up to bright red hair and matching lips. Sea-green eyes sparkled behind long lashes. She stood beside a newer Mustang convertible. The bone-white paint looked like it was designed to match her skin. The dark red interior certainly was. He hadn't even heard her pull in.

"Quite alright," Michael said, recovering. He pointed down the road. "Pintail Bay is a mile that way. Look for the rusty sign that says Handy's Marina. It'll be on the left. Road's narrow, but you should have no trouble."

"Rusty sign? That's not promising," she said. Her laughter was low and throaty, and Michael had the sudden image of a happy lioness after an open field kill.

"Beg pardon?" he said.

"Sorry. The rusty sign. I'm supposed to be meeting a man about a boat."

"Ah, well, the sign's rusty. Can't tell you much about the marina."

"Too bad." She cocked a hip against the back end of the Mustang. "How about the area? Can you tell me about that?"

Michael shrugged. "Sports fishermen, small commercial trawlers, duck hunters in season. Most of the large houses are weekend escapes for the well-to-do from N'awlins. You thinking of relocating?"

"Let's see how the boat goes first." She smiled but even that looked predatory.

"Well, it's not the middle of nowhere," he said, "but it's close enough not to make any difference. It's usually quiet, isolated. The locals keep to themselves."

"Sounds like just what I need." She held her hand out. "I'm Catherine."

"Michael." He started to shake her hand, but the beer was in his. He tried to shift it to the other hand, but the newspaper was there. He gave up and went with a smile and a shrug. "Nice to meet you."

"You said 'locals'? Are you not from here?"

"Am for the time being."

"Mysterious," she said.

"Nah, just working on my local custom. Good luck with the boat."

Michael turned out the rest of the beer as he rounded the back of the truck and then slid into the passenger seat. He was half-way down the road when he realized the paper was still in his hand, crushed against the steering wheel.

What about her had unsettled him? Was he just that unaccustomed to being flirted with? He shook off the thought and turned his attention to the road as it dropped off to a dirt track.

Back at the cabin, Michael unloaded supplies.

"You got a box," he told Zed.

"Right on time."

"Something you ordered? You haven't left the place since I got here."

"Why would I have to do that?"

"No power, let alone Internet. You don't even have a phone."

Two thick fingers thumped Michael in the chest. "Stop thinking with your collar, son. Not even about the boring stuff. 'Til you can do that, progress is gonna keep being slow. Got a new challenge for you. You're gonna love it."

Zed used one thick fingernail to split the tape and lift the lid. He pushed some of the contents around and reached deep into the bottom. He lifted out a football sized object covered with a heavy black cloth. Whatever it was looked jagged and misshapen. He dropped it in the center of their work table.

"You ready?" he asked.

"Lay it on me."

Zed whipped off the cloth and stepped back.

"That's a rock," Michael said.

"Indeed it is. Where's it from?"

"Probably a larger rock."

"Fair enough. I'll give you a hint. It ain't from any ground around here. Before the sun goes down, I want you to tell me where it's from, how you know, and why it matters."

"Okay," Michael said. "I'll be back in a bit."

Zed stopped him. "You have everything you need, right here. You can leave the cabin, but no road trips. No books. None of that Internets stuff. Just you. Use your hands, your head, and your heart. The rock'll show you what you need to know."

Michael walked around the table, looking at the rock from all sides. It was a variegated series of greens. Jagged edges shot out on one side while the other was porous like a sponge. He reversed directions and looked again. Light bounced off its faces but didn't cast any color across the table, as if the rock was taking it in, containing it.

He looked back at Zed. "This might take awhile."

"You got 'til sundown." Zed started for the door. "I'm going fishin'. I'll be back with dinner."

Michael sat in front of the stone and wracked his mind for anything he thought he should already know. It wasn't jade, wasn't emerald. It wasn't even a gem, but it looked like it could be. He scooted back and rested his chin on the table, staring at it from eye level. It looked like a piece of Oz.

Without lifting his head, he reached out to pivot the stone. It was cool to the touch, but turning it just gave him more angles. He sat up.

"Okay, rock." He reached out and gingerly pulled it into both hands. "Talk to me."

An hour later he was sweating and his hands were shaking.

"And I'm still just holding a rock," he said to the empty cabin.

He'd tried focusing his attention at one side and then another. He'd tried talking, singing, whistling, and finally shouting. He'd poured water on it, held a match to it, and rubbed it clean with a cloth.

"You're a clean rock."

It was maddening. Hours had passed, he was no closer to an answer, and his body felt stiff and achy.

"Tell you what, rock. Let's go for a walk."

The afternoon sun had slid to the back of the cabin. Sunset was only a couple hours away. Michael let out a slow breath.

"Okay, no pressure."

He circled the cabin several times, shifting the rock between his hands, and then set off down a path that he knew would eventually lead to water. Everything in the bayou eventually led to water. *Everything*, whether it needed to or not.

Seagulls drifted on wind currents. They were joined by larger, darker birds. Buzzards?

Even as he saw them, Michael could tell that they weren't actually there. It was like a picture overlaid on his view of the sky. He looked down and the overlay continued. He saw the desert. Scrub brush, cactus, earthen rocks, and mountains in the distance. He saw animals searching for water. Saw the cactus again and knew there was enough water inside to keep a man alive. He saw plants and knew which would heal sickness and bind wounds.

He looked down at the rock.

"I'm seeing where you came from," he said aloud. "And I know why you're here."

Michael hurried back to the cabin and laid down a thin layer of sand before setting the rock on top of it. He lit some incense and positioned it so that the slow current of air running through the cabin would filter the smoke past him. Then he reached out with his mind.

Nothing came. It was just a rock. He thought about the gulls, watching them float motionless in the sky. His mind wandered. He thought about Danni and the Sisters. He remembered watching Gabriel playing in the orphanage yard. A group of kids in a pick-up soccer game, using a pair of oil drums as a goal. The kids were laughing and trying to keep up with Gabriel as he dashed past them and shot the ball between two cactuses.

Cactus.

He was seeing Arizona again.

Nine

Zed returned just before sundown with a small stringer of fish. Michael had the table cleaned off with the rock set as a centerpiece.

"That was amazing!" Michael said. "What did I do?"

"Dunno, you tell me."

"I was here," he said slowly. "But I was also somewhere in Arizona. I tried and tried and… then it was like it all came to me in a rush."

"Pretty much like my luck fishing today," Zed said. He dropped the fish in Michael's hands. "Couple hours of nothing. Well, they might've been biting. I don't know. I was nappin'. Didn't even bait the hook 'til an hour ago. Let's clean these and cook 'em. You can tell me about it while we eat."

They pan-seared the fish with pine nuts and ate them with some tomatoes from the garden as Michael recounted his findings.

"I know the rock is malachite. I know it's from

55

Arizona. Not exactly where, but Ajo and St. Anthony keeps coming up. I saw an old monk putting it in a box, *that* box."

"Brother Spiro," Zed said. "He was at St. Anthony's before the monastery was. Greek Orthodox. He came to America in the '60's. First to California, then he walked east for awhile. The church wrote him letters, demanding he come home. He'd respond with glowing stories of the beauty and stillness in the desert. Finally, the church decided to come to him.

"They sent men and a crew, built a church and established an order. As is often the case with the Church, they like new, as long as it is familiar. They began remaking his peaceful surroundings into something that looked more like their home. And Brother Spiro took up walking again.

"A good man. A good friend. He makes his home in Ajo now. It's a tiny little place on the way to Mexico."

"And he sends you rocks in the mail," Michael said.

"We send each other items when we see each other's need. For Christmas, I sent him a box of locusts. He had an injured lizard friend that finds them to be a delicacy."

Zed cleared the dishes in the sink and returned to his seat. "So, what else did you get from it?"

"When I stopped trying to force my questions on it, I saw things. A hundred things I can't make sense of. But whatever it shows me I know them. Maybe 'know' is too strong a word, but I *understand* them. I could feel them and how they worked. I wouldn't have thought it possible. It's just a... rock." He looked up at Zed. "Is that normal? How did you know I could read it?"

"I didn't. We got lucky. And you're not reading it. You're tuning to it. You get images, ideas. When you are completely attuned, you'll more than understand things. You'll be able to know them like you'd grown up knowing them. It will speed things up."

"That sounded ominous."

"Good. I don't always get the tone right." He swiped a bit of fish off his chin. "Let's get back to work."

Zed set a bucket in the sink and began filling it with water. He dropped a heavy ceramic cup in after it, then tugged a green ribbon out of his pocket and tied it around the handle.

"What's the ribbon for?" Michael asked.

Zed sat down and grinned. "Give me a minute. I'll show you."

He smoothed the sand on his side of the table and began to draw with a gnarled forefinger.

"I don't recognize that rune," Michael said.

"Not a rune, it's a focal point."

"Looks like a cactus."

"Made you think of where we're going, didn't it? That's rune enough for our purpose."

Michael drew another, just like Zed's, and placed his hands on either side. Moments later, he stood next to the old man, watching the sun on the eastern horizon.

"Wait a minute, that's sunrise. The sun should be setting," Michael said.

"I made a little tweak. We're gonna need the extra time."

Zed pointed to an old straw broom leaning against a boulder. Its handle was ragged and covered in worm tracks.

"Clear off the sand, make a circle big as you can."

When Michael was done, Zed stood on one side of the circle and pointed for Michael to take the place across from him. Zed put his hands together and made a stirring motion. It looked like a gentle wave of air blown in Michael's direction...until it knocked him out of the circle.

"How'd you do that?" Michael said to the sky.

"Pretty well, don't you think?"

Michael sat up. "I'd ask why, but I think I get the idea."

"Good. *Explain it.*"

"Magic has power. Not just influence but direct power."

Zed began the stirring motion with his hands again. "Go on."

"The bruise that's going to come up on my butt is supposed to remind me that magic can hurt as well as heal."

"And?"

"And... a good offense is better than a good defense?"

"Close, but no."

Zed waved his hand. Michael was lifted off his feet again. He flew backward and slammed into the ground.

"You're gonna keep doing this until I figure it out, aren't you?"

"Lasting memories come from two places, Michael. Joy and pain. Choice is yours."

More stirring, more wind, and Michael ended up

looking at the sky again. This time he'd at least managed to keep his breath.

"Mine, my ass," he grumbled. He staggered back to his feet and settled a hand against the gris-gris bag on his belt. "Okay, I have the power to stop this. That's what you're saying."

"Getting warmer," Zed said.

The wind rushed forward, traveling low against the ground and then rising up as it reached him. Michael rolled backwards out of the circle again.

"You don't have the power to stop this," Zed called. "But all you need is well within your grasp."

Michael got up to his knees and reached for his gris-gris bag again.

"What's missing, boy? You don't just put the mojo in the bag. You *are* the mojo. It's in your mind. What got you through growing up? What got you through seminary? What kept you alive all these years?"

Zed's hands were stirring again, his shoulder turning with the forces building up.

"When there were no tools in the bag and before you had the church, you still had you. It's within your grasp. Think, make it so."

Zed's hand waved and the wind roared across the circle. At the last moment, Michael grabbed the old broom and swept it across the ground in front of the rolling wind. Dust and dirt built into a cloud. Michael continued to turn, carrying the broom with him, until he'd made a full circle. The dust cloud tore across the circle. It overwhelmed Zed and he disappeared from view. The cloud dissipated and the roar died, replaced by the sound of Zed hacking and coughing. Michael stood, staring at the old man.

"Not bad. Not bad," Zed choked out. "A little messy. Let me get some water and we'll try again."

He pulled a piece of ribbon from his pocket and wrapped it around his hand. His fingers shifted inside the ribbon, feeling something on the fabric and the wind. The air stirred in front of him and a bucket appeared, the handle already over his upturned palm.

"The ribbon," Michael said. "It was one piece. You cut it into two."

"And?"

"If something was made to be one, and you separate it, the parts are still attracted to each other. They…"

The old man watched him, waiting.

"They can be encouraged to find each other."

Zed nodded. "And sometimes they'll find each other on their own. People can be like that. Elements, too."

He pulled the cup from the bucket and took a long drink. He dipped out a second cup, then turned it over to run back into the bucket.

"Water, for instance, is the most temperamental. It's in a constant state of wanting to be somewhere else. It flows through the rivers, down to the sea, but it's been in the sky and wants to return. So, it heats and evaporates into clouds. It'll hang out there, gathering up with itself, until some part of it gets lonely for the earth.

"We can work with the elements, some better than others, but not like that Army Corps of Engineers does. They build levees or widen the river, force the elements to stay where they want it." Zed paused to shake his head, sadly. "Water's gonna find its way, no matter what man says. But if we work with it, it will carry us, refresh us, feed us, and in turn, we can coax it along and show it direction.

"Same is true of earth, fire, and air. Coaxing is far better than contesting. Nature's gonna win. In the end, it'll blow the earth, bury us deep, and water our graves."

Michael stared at the broom in his hand.

"What are you thinking on?" Zed asked.

"The wind, the earth. Forces that great. Why would they listen to my little broom?" Even as he said it, Michael knew it wasn't right.

"They didn't, did they?"

Michael shook his head. "The broom was just the focus. The feather in my gris-gris bag would do just as well."

"There you go. Now, did it have to be in your hand?"

"I…" Michael stopped and considered it. "I'm not sure."

"Picture the feather," Zed said. "See its length, feel the hardness of the nib, the weight, the down in your hand. Feel it? You sure? Good, now…"

Michael's empty hand moved like the sweep of a pen on paper. Dirt swirled at his feet, pushed into the air and across the circle. Zed clapped his hands together once.

"There you go. No greater force of will than imagination."

"That's just amazing." Michael followed the dust as

it settled to the ground. "And exhausting. I feel like I swept this whole mountain and all I did was move a little dirt."

"It gets easier as your focus improves, which it needs to, *fast*. There's a lot ahead of us, and not all of it is, shall we say, scriptural."

"Yeah, I'm not sure how I feel about that."

Zed shrugged. "There are some things the commandments don't cover. You are going to have to figure out what you're willing to fight for, when, and how. Anything around you may or may not be subject to your will. But everything in your gris-gris bag had better be or else it don't belong there. Let's see what you've gathered, you tell me what it means to you."

They sat on the ground and Michael carefully emptied the pouch onto his leg.

"Now that you know you don't have to pull things out to use them," Zed said, "you need to understand having faith in them is what makes the magic flow your way."

"Faith in them is faith in me," Michael reasoned and then asked, "But because I chose them? Or because they chose me?"

"More like some of both. What you got there?"

Michael held up the white feather. "From the white crow we saw that first morning. It felt like a good sign, hopeful."

"Uh-huh," Zed said. "Now, I know a hoodoo man who can use a feather like that to fly a short distance. You might want to stick to things on the ground. We already saw you don't fly so well."

Michael smiled and exchanged the feather for a

stone the size of his thumbnail. The outside was rough, the color of road gravel, but the inside was a myriad of circles that ranged in color from pink to deep burgundy.

"Fire agate," Michael said. "It was next to that sleeping alligator. Still can't believe he let me have it."

"That old boy don't care about rocks. Just peace and quiet."

"And the marshmallows I offered him."

"He does have himself a sweet tooth. What's it mean?"

"Concentration, defense, truth."

"Not just truth," Zed corrected. "*Honesty*. Not a better lie detector out there. Drop that in a liar's hand, it'll burn 'em like the fire it's named after."

They continued sorting through the items on Michael's leg, discussing them one by one. Zed pointed to a triangular bone shard with brown etching on it.

"What's that you have there?"

Michael held the piece in his palm. He still recalled its complete shape, what had been a box, specifically a portmanteau. He hadn't thought much of it at the time, probably would have dismissed it altogether if he hadn't felt the weight of the five-hundred souls held inside it. Let alone *heard* them like some music box from Hell.

"It's part of the portmanteau that Danni broke," Michael explained. "It reminds me that good can be accomplished just by doing the right things, even when you don't know why."

"That's a pretty happy memory for such a sad face," Zed said.

"I miss her," he said simply. Zed motioned him to continue. "I lied to her, neglected to tell her I was a priest. Had I, she probably wouldn't have kissed me." Michael rubbed a small circle in the center of his chest. "Probably wouldn't have taken a piece of my soul, either."

Zed nodded slowly, seeming to understand the depth of the waters they were treading now.

"High price for one kiss," he said.

Michael shrugged. "It won her her freedom from Samedi ultimately."

"So, it's a debt."

Michael dropped the piece back into the bag. "Yeah, in a way. I guess it is."

"And the cross?"

Zed took the small silver crucifix from Michael's lap and held it up to the light. Michael followed it with his eyes, a familiar warmth stirring the memories to the surface.

"My mother gave me that when I joined the seminary," Michael said. "To shine the light inside me, no matter how dark the outside got."

Still, Zed didn't move to drop it back into his hand, and of everything he'd seen, it seemed to displease him the most.

"Crosses are good mojo, and they're powerful symbols in hoodoo," Michael insisted.

"Not this one," Zed said. "At least, not at the moment. It's another debt, an obligation. I told you, everything in that bag has power, and not all power gets along. Right now, you're carrying two kinds of debt to two *very* different people. That kind of load can drive the magic down, make you weak and vulnerable."

"So, what am I supposed to do? Choose between them?"

"Could," Zed said thoughtfully. "Be better if you put down the debt. Maybe go see your mother and tell her how it is."

Ten

By six o'clock Danni had paced the hallway outside Sister Ned's office nine times. She stopped to check her reflection in the cool, green glass of the door. Mother Superior had suggested her outfit be stylish with an emphasis on *demure*. The best Danni could come up with was a black, chiffon cocktail dress and a cream blazer, but no matter how many times she pressed them, they still looked second-hand.

Sister Ned didn't even look up from polishing the scuff off her shoe.

"It'll be fine," she said.

Danni released a long, shaky breath and ran a hand across her stomach. "I feel like I'm going to puke. Again."

"Pregnant?"

Danni gave her a withering look.

"Come'er." Sister Ned opened a deep drawer and retrieved a jar of peanut butter and a single spoon. She worked a liberal dollop onto the end and then shoved it into Danni's mouth.

"Uhg! hate peanut butter!"

"Eat it anyway," the sister said. "It'll give your stomach something to grab on to while you give your speech."

"*Speech?*"

Sister Ned adjusted the starched, white coif around her ears.

"You didn't think you were going to make me put on this damned thing and beg for money all by myself, did you?"

Danni jerked the spoon from her mouth and swallowed a few times.

"Mother Superior made you wear that, not me. But now that you mention it, you do look kind of…"

"Impoverished?" Sister Ned finished for her. Danni nodded. "That's the point. God willing we'll only have to do this once a year. Turn around."

She did. A thin, glistening set of white pearls encircled her throat. Sister Ned fastened a clasp at the back of her neck.

"My father gave them to me when I turned sixteen," Sister Ned said. "When I took my vows, I couldn't bring myself to get rid of them. They suit you." She motioned for the leather lanyard still hanging around Danni's neck. "Let's leave the voodoo outside tonight, huh?"

Danni's hand dropped from the pearls to the nail. "I'm not sure I feel right about that."

"I've watched over that boy longer than you've been alive. I'll lock it up. Don't worry."

But she did worry. The momentary calm vanished

as Danni lifted the nail from around her throat. As angry as she was, she hadn't been without that piece of him in months. It disappeared inside the drawer. Sister Ned made a show of tugging solidly on the handle, checking the lock, and motioned for Danni to lead the way toward the kitchen.

Sister Ned had been right. The bed sheets did a marvelous job of covering the ceiling while also managing to create a warm atmosphere. The rest was done with simple, red Christmas lights and some well-placed mirrors. Softer, pink light reflected up against the bottoms of the white swells overhead. Sister Marie Claire and a few others were finishing the careful task of lighting tea lights at the heart of each jeweled centerpiece.

"Oh, thank God," Danni breathed.

"Amen," Sister Ned echoed. "Ladies, this looks fantastic."

Sister Charlotte's voice boomed down from atop the ladder, hidden behind the cloud of billowing sheets. "Let's just hope that waterline holds through the night."

A wrench screeched as she put another half-twist on a pipe before climbing down to the floor. Danni felt the tension unwind from between her shoulders. They could do this. They *had* to do this. There was no other option if she wanted to keep them all together.

Danni turned to Sister Ned.

"Where are the boys?"

"Upstairs. I asked them to *quietly* hang their decorations before they got their costumes on."

"It's a brilliant idea, by the way, letting them trick or treat with the donors."

68

Sister Ned shrugged. "Eh. Two birds, one stone, as long as Jean-Paul doesn't bite anyone's hand and Maurice doesn't light them on fire."

"Or stab anyone," Danni added. "Which reminds me, I need to talk to Maurice about something. I'll be right back."

The rumble of voices in the dorms was low but rushed. The older boys tugged the younger ones into tights, barking out orders for grease paint and Scotch tape as needed.

"Where's my hat?"

"On the bed, stupid."

"Which bed?"

"I need a pin. Gabriel!"

"*Shhhh!*"

Softer then, "Gabriel, I need a pin."

Gabriel hopped over a bed to where Rene was struggling to keep a sheet in place around his waist. Gabriel shoved the silver safety pin through the knotted sheet. It slipped and drove into the tip of his finger.

Danni knelt beside Rene. "Here, sweetie. Let me."

She wiggled the pin into place, smoothed the wrinkles from the sheet, and tipped her head.

"Toga?" she asked.

He reached back for a circle of brass wire with two orange maple leaves worked into either side. He set it on his head.

"I'm Hermes," he said.

Danni chuckled. "I'm beginning to see a theme here."

She turned a full circle around the room. Zeus to Apollo to Hercules, all the way back to the injured Icarus at her side where he was nursing his finger between his teeth.

She knelt again and drew the soft end of his finger between her lips. His face stayed placid as the room fell silent around them. She tasted the coppery hint of blood as she worked her tongue over the end of his finger. When she withdrew, the pinprick was gone.

Gabriel's voice came out in a stuttered whisper. "*A-akeyi yo, J-jiji.*"

"No," she said firmly and stood. "Tonight, my name is Danni. That goes for the rest of you, too. I'm not going to lie to you. It takes a lot of money to keep all of you here. So, I need your help, and that means, no talking about Jiji. Do you all understand?"

The downstairs chime rang and the main doors opened. Danni moved to the window. The first group of black-suited men and willowy women moved up the stairs. Danni blew out another long breath and felt Gabriel's fingers curl around hers. When she looked back, they were all there, watching, waiting. Smiling. All at once, they rushed to swarm her legs, which pressed Gabriel tighter against her side.

They pulled her down, wrapping their arms around her neck and pressing their cheeks to hers the same way they did in Bel-Koté. She wondered if it was instinctual or if they experienced the living, breathing memories of their souls being with her on infinite fields of green grass. If she were to ask any of them, it would only be Gabriel. She pulled back from him and held his face between her hands, searching his eyes.

She could feel his soul just beneath his pulse, almost *see* the structure of it at the center of his eye, like a tiny supernova imploding and bursting out with the radiance of a thousand suns. The longer she looked, the clearer she could see his past, present, and ephemeral future.

It wasn't just a maternal connection; it was far greater than that. Gabriel's future, the fate of his soul, rested in her hands. He – *all of them* – were bound to her. Another truth crystallized around the thought: she was just as bound to them. It was like hearing her heartbeat, or seeing inside the softest most vulnerable parts of herself. She cared for them, but they *sustained* her.

Danni pulled back from Gabriel suddenly, breaking the spell of the last several seconds. He reached for her again, but she caught his wrists, almost too hard. She softened her expression as she brought them to her lips, kissed his knuckles, and tucked them back against his chest.

"Finish getting ready," she said. "Sister Marie Claire will come get you for dinner in a bit."

Their tentative acknowledgements followed her out of the room and down the stairs. She stopped on the landing and pressed her forehead against the window and tried to take a full breath. The sensations, the turbulence. *The noise.* It was back, and she could hear the boys most clearly. Staring into a child's soul was one thing, but hearing the innocence of their prayers… it was almost too much.

I hope Jiji likes my costume. I hope I get to stay up

late. I hope I get chocolate tonight.

More voices rose up, fleeting desires of the guests in the floor below her.

I hope this isn't an all-night affair. I hope I can get a good tax write-off. I hope… I hope… I want… I need…

Danni staggered and palmed the wall as she slid down to the floor. Every time she tried to catch one, another would rocket in above it. Pretty soon, it was like trying to dig through sand. The voices piled in faster than she could make sense of their words.

She sunk down into the stairwell and reached for the only soul she knew would shut them all out. Her hand grasped frantically at her throat, but she only felt Sister Ned's pearls. The nail, the piece of Michael's soul. It was gone. She ground her fists against her temples.

"Be quiet."

She heard it before she realized she'd said it aloud. The voices refused, surging to encompass all of Queensland, the block, the street, and then the entire city. New Orleans howled with pain and need, begging her to answer their prayers. She pushed back against them, but just like the Mississippi had stolen her air, the noise stole her ability to focus.

That's where Mother Superior found her, balled up against the wall. The stern warning in the old woman's eyes quickly melted to genuine compassion, albeit slight.

"Anxiety attack," she reasoned. She hefted Danni to her feet. "Best way to handle it is to move."

Danni tried to focus on her face. It was more than an anxiety attack. It was an all out assault. But the minute her hands found Mother Superior's slight but strong shoulders, the noise stopped and the air rushed back into her lungs.

They didn't have the best relationship, especially since Michael had decided to leave the church for her. Nuns didn't believe in voodoo, and for the moment, it was the anchor Danni needed to pull herself back from the storm of voices.

"I have never been so happy to see you," Danni wheezed.

"My God works in mysterious ways," Mother Superior said. "Are you all right?"

Danni nodded. "Better now."

The nun's attention traveled up the stairs toward the dormitory with a serious question in her eyes. "Are the boys—"

"They're fine. We're fine. Thank you."

"I'd ask what for, but I'm not sure I want to know."

At that, Danni shook her head. "No, you probably don't."

"Well, then, if you're ready…"

She motioned Danni down the stairs and into the crowd. They broke apart just past Sister Ned's office, but the heat of Mother Superior's gazed stayed on Danni's neck all the way to the dining room.

Eleven

Tuxedo-shirted caterers moved through the tables with the speed of silverfish, clearing down plates as unobtrusively as possible. A waiter paused when he reached for Danni's untouched plate, but she waved him to take it. If she didn't have an appetite before, she certainly couldn't keep anything down now. Sister Ned gave her a soft look of concern, but Danni waved her away, too.

She let her eyes drift around the room, trying to pick out a single face she recognized but quickly decided it was a lost cause. The guest list had come straight from the vicarage registry, a lot pulled from the Garden District and other richer, *whiter* sections of the city.

A hundred years ago, they would have been sugar barons, cotton kings, and riverboat giants. Now, they were corporate CEOs, doctors, lawyers, and real estate moguls. The table decorations looked like dismal tinsel compared to the fat, studded sparkle of the women beside them. There was at least ten-thousand dollars worth of couture seated less than a table-length away. A sudden sweat broke out inside Danni's thrift shop heels.

Sister Ned patted the top of her hand. If her eyes said anything, it was: *relax*.

Mother Superior stood. The polite chatter faded to the tinkle of glasses and a few hand-smothered coughs as she moved toward the podium.

"Thank you all for coming tonight," she began. "It is with the most humble spirit that we welcome you to the newest incarnation of this historic building: The Queensland Home for Boys."

Danni covered a wince with her napkin. The name needed work.

Mother Superior continued. "The Sisters of Mount Carmel have always endeavored to protect and provide for this community. Today, that protection means feeding and clothing twenty-six boys orphaned by Hurricane Katrina."

Technically, they weren't orphans until Samedi killed their parents while Danni watched. It was her darkest memory of New Orleans, probably of her life, and hearing Mother Superior's watered down version of it only made her feel worse.

Her attention began to drift to where some of the older boys were mixed in with the guests. The younger ones had been assigned to the sisters' tables, as much to reinforce good table manners as manage the herd.

Danni's eyes stopped on a woman seated at the opposite side of the room. Her hair was swooped up off her neck into a loose chignon, a bone-white comb holding a red lily just off the center of the bun. She flashed Danni a quick but ruthless smile. Again, applause erupted around the room. The woman extended her finger toward the podium where Mother Superior was motioning Danni forward.

The hand off was quick. Danni struggled through a brief introduction. Once it was over, she sighed. The sound echoed across the room, carried out on the microphone and signaling more exhaustion than she'd meant to convey.

"I won't waste time telling you something you already know: we need your support," she said. "These boys need your support. More than that, they need what every child needs. Love. But you can't love someone you don't know. So, if you'll allow me: Rene?"

Rene's haloed head popped up from his plate. He stood, proudly displaying his costume for the crowd.

"Rene has joined us tonight as Hermes…"

She called them to stand, one by one, noting their unique talents, their likes and their dislikes. The crowd responded with soft *aww*'s and gentle laughter.

It wasn't until she looked at the ceiling she felt a hard jolt of fear. The bed sheet hung low in the center. A droplet formed on the underside of the sheet, quivering under the weight of the gallons of water behind it, shuddered, and fell. She followed it all the way down to a table where it landed inside the centerpiece, snuffing out the single tea light.

Danni felt something inside her whither. What should she do? What *could* she do? Short of evacuating the entire room, that much water would hit at least half the guests. The only other person who noticed was the woman beneath it. She followed Danni's gaze back up to the center sheet and the dangerous swell, where another droplet had already formed.

A tremor began in Danni's hand, passing up through her arm and into her shoulders. Her teeth clattered, stammering her words.

"G-gabriel, is n-nine." The corner of the sheet began to give. "He enjoys soccer, but is not fond of carrots. Tonight, he's dressed as Icarus…"

Danni watched the knot unravel with slow-panicked horror. The water sloshed and spread out in a big white wave. Her hand shot forward, more instinct than reason, and a single word escaped her lips.

"*Flé.*"

The water seemed to soften, spreading out and out, but never falling, at least not immediately. Instead of water, white petals breezed out over the room, raining down on the heads of the guests, the nuns, the boys.

Gabriel looked startled, then spread his arms wide, welcoming the soft, perfumed embrace of falling magnolias. The crowd rose to their feet with roaring amusement.

The only people who didn't stand were the nuns. Sister Ned and Mother Superior exchanged words beneath their breath, but Danni didn't have to guess to know what they were. If looks could incinerate, she would have flashed into non-existence right then and there.

Twelve

Danni's ear was on fire, pinched between Sister Ned's thumb and index finger as she was dragged into the small office again. Mother Superior wasn't far behind, along with Sister Charlotte.

"I swear, Reverend Mother, I tightened that pipe," she protested.

"I'm not concerned with that, Sister," Mother Superior said.

She closed the door quietly, leaving Sister Charlotte in the hallway, and turned on Danni. "But I would like to know why you felt the need to pull such a stunt."

"What did you expect me to do? It would have ruined everything!"

"You don't know that!" Mother Superior snapped.

"Welcome to our orphanage. Please give us money. *Sorry about the bath?*" Danni shook her head. "Besides, it wasn't something I had a lot of control over. It just happened."

It didn't put Mother Superior at ease. "The only

reason I agreed to any of this was because Sister Ned assured me you had your other…*issues* under control."

Danni crossed her arms and glared at Sister Ned. "Thanks."

Mother Superior continued. "The boys don't need to be exposed to voodoo. They're children, easily romanced by the thrill of magic and easy answers. They need the clarity to make their own choices, whatever those may be."

The anger burned up the back of Danni's neck, and she struggled to keep her voice even. "I'm doing the best that I can."

"And yet what you just did jeopardizes *everything* we're trying to build here!"

"Excuse me?" Danni stepped up to meet Mother Superior, toe to toe. "Are you forgetting who's been funding this goddamned thing since day one? Everything I have is on the line, and I wasn't going to let some stupid, broken pipe ruin all that!"

"At what cost, Danielle? Last time we invited you into our home, you placed the entire sisterhood in danger. Or did you forget about the enormous viper that punched through the floor of my convent?"

"That's cutting the fat on a lot of details there, Sister."

"But not the point. If you can't control yourself, you're a threat to everyone around you."

"Just because Michael–"

"This *isn't* about Michael, but yes. You're a threat to him, too."

The words thudded around in Danni's head like a

brick tossed down a stairwell. Each time she thought it found the bottom, it rolled forward again and dropped more weight into her gut.

Mother Superior smoothed the clean lines of her habit back into place. "Now, the boys are waiting. Let's get this done as quickly and *quietly* as we can."

She didn't wait for agreement before jerking open the door and disappearing down the hall. Danni stood alone with Sister Ned.

"And you? Do you agree with her?" Danni asked.

No answer was an answer in and of itself. Sister Ned hesitated before she said, "He loves you, I know that."

"*But?*"

"But, I'm not always sure he knows why."

Danni was only half-aware that Sister Ned had moved out of the room and been gone for several minutes before she took a full breath. When she did, it rattled with the growing sob threatening to explode from her throat.

"They're not very grateful for a group of nuns, are they?"

Danni spun to find the green-eyed woman in the door. Her dress was almost as painfully white as her skin. If it hadn't been for the red shawl drawn around her shoulders, she could have been a bride set for the altar.

"They mean well," Danni said.

"Oh, cut the shit. I'm going to give you money." She extended her hand. "Catherine Daye," she said.

"Danni–"

"–Toussaint. Yes. I know. Impressive trick, water into flower petals. Not kid stuff, then again, you're not a kid, are you?"

Catherine laughed at the surprise on Danni's face. The rich, thick chords penetrated every corner of the room. "My mother was from Central City. Grand'ma, too. Both mambos. I know real voodoo when I see it."

Danni gestured in the direction the sisters had gone. "Then I guess you know what flew up their ass as a result."

"Oh, better than you know. But I'm curious. Nuns? Orphans? Seems a little low-brow for your kind of skill."

"It's complicated."

"Why don't we get a drink and you can tell me about it?"

Uneasiness stirred Danni's gut. Catherine seemed to read it as hesitation, when in truth Danni was only struggling to place the familiarity of her voice. The soft, lilting melody tied on the ends of her words. Where had she heard it before?

Catherine opened a slim, silver clutch and tugged out a check. She held it out to Danni. "Go on. Take it."

Something else stirred in Danni's gut when she read it. "A hundred thousand dollars?"

Were those words even right?

"This is a fundraiser, isn't it?" Catherine asked. "How about that drink now?"

Danni's eyes went from the check in her hands, to Catherine, and back to the check several times.

Finally, she said, "I can't. I promised I'd take them trick or treating."

Danni held the check out to Catherine again, but she made no reach to take it back. After what seemed like an appropriate length of time, Danni laid it in the center of Sister Ned's desk.

"Thank you," Danni said.

Catherine's nod was slow and measured, her smile barely a half inch of movement, there and gone.

Danni started out the door, but stopped when she spotted Sister Charlotte in quiet conversation with Sister Marie Clair. Their eyes dove back to the floor, but she didn't miss the fear in their faces when they saw her. It had been a long time since any of them had looked at her that way.

She stepped back into the office, closed her eyes, and let out a long sigh. When she opened them again, Catherine's hand was open between them. Her long, slender fingers looked as elegant as carved ivory, tipped with glossy red polish.

"Just one drink?" she offered again.

The weight of a thousand different pressures lifted when Danni took her hand.

Thirteen

New Orleans was alive. Jazz bounced down the damp streets of the French Quarter, rocking out of doorways to mix with the voices on the packed sidewalks. Costumed party-goers whooped and raised their go-cups at the passing cars. Especially Catherine's.

She pulled the comb from her hair. The wind shook her loose curls to long, fiery ribbons, which gave her a far more predatory look. So did the occasional flex of her hand around the steering wheel.

"What do you do?" Danni asked over the rush of the fast moving air.

"A little bit of everything, but mostly, I own a strip club in Storyville."

Suddenly the ostentatious car, the white-over-red interior, made a lot more sense. Danni wondered briefly if she had one to match every outfit.

"Isn't that all just the housing projects?"

Catherine nodded. "Skin and section eight goes hand in hand. You up for it?"

The anxiety she'd felt at the banquet took on a new shape under the suggestion. It was anything-goes in Storyville, and as far as Danni's body was concerned, nothing had *gone* in a long time. Still, she gave Catherine a quick nod.

The engine wound up and they flew toward the darker edge of the city. Near St. Louis Cemetery One, Catherine slowed to allow a walking tour to cross.

"I guess Halloween is prime time for ghost hunting, huh?" Danni asked.

Catherine scoffed. "Most of those people couldn't find a ghost if it was stapled to their forehead. Besides, hasn't been a spook in St. Louis One since Anne Rice put it on the map."

The traffic signal changed, but Catherine kept the car idling in place.

"Give it a listen then. *You* should be able to hear how empty it is."

Danni focused on the interior maze of statues and stone walls. She'd been in cemeteries before, most of the time trying to get out of them. Quickly. She'd never paid much attention to what they *sounded* like. As far as this one was concerned, it was as still and silent as the...

"Nothing, see?" Catherine said. "Just a tourist attraction."

"So, are you..." Danni decided there was no polite way to ask that question and let it die there.

"As powerful as you are?" Catherine shrugged. "I have my moments. But, my mother's mother was a slave, her mother was a slave. And they were taught to believe like slaves. Fear. Reverence. Humility. Once you place those kind of restrictions on a bloodline, it's hard to come back from."

"Pardon me for saying so, but you're awfully white to be so closely related to slaves."

A shadow filled the corner of Catherine's emerald eye as her tone slipped to a raw whisper. "Not every slave in this city was black."

Catherine pulled into the empty lot where the Iberville Projects had once been. Katrina hadn't dealt them much damage, but that hadn't stopped the city from demolishing them, finally stripping out a long-held thorn in their side.

The Mustang rolled over the broken curb and into the grassy low-land beneath an expansive oak tree. The headlights flashed over the trunk, outlining two men hidden in the shadow. Bodyguards. Had to be. Men didn't come naturally with that kind of brawn, and if they did, they didn't dress it down in black-on-black turtlenecks and jeans, and then go skulking in an empty field on a Saturday night. The engine died. Catherine snapped once and tossed her keys at the nearest one.

"*Ici. Conservez-le avec votre vie.*"

He caught them against his chest. "*Oui, madame.*"

The second bodyguard trotted around to Danni's door. He was the smaller of the two, but not by much. He held the door open long enough for her to stand before taking her seat, his knees bunched up to his chest. His friend joined him, backed the car onto the street, and disappeared. Did they just stand there, all night, on the off

85

chance a car might pull up?

Catherine led her out a few feet across the barren field and stopped. One heel shot out and stomped twice against the ground. The sound echoed back, deep and hollow. A burst of light cut a perfect square in the center of the dark yard. Catherine tossed a quick look over her shoulder and then descended the stairs. Danni hesitated but followed.

The smell of sweet cream and candy rose up to meet her, while the deep bass beat hammered home the idea that they were moving deep underground. It thudded against her skin as the cooler air gelled the sweat on her back. The stairway ended in a room made entirely of polished black glass. A few low couches and tables sat in the center while a bank of amber windows overlooked a much larger chamber.

Danni moved to the windows. There were hundreds of people below her, rising and falling to the percussive music, while men and women spun wildly on poles in all four corners of the room. Light bent off their naked bodies, but no one seemed to be watching them. The rest of the crowd was in their own state of undressed debauchery.

Catherine pulled a glass stopper from a bottle in the center of the table and poured out a few fingers of pinkish liquid. She offered Danni two glasses, one full, one empty. Danni took the full one.

"I don't need the other," she said.

A thin eyebrow climbed up Catherine's forehead. "You don't spit for your patron? Brave, girl."

Danni let the question die there and moved closer to

the window.

"Are we at the back of the club?"

Catherine's reflection nodded. "My private suite. The main entrance is a few blocks up, but the view is better from here."

"I thought you said strip club."

Catherine moved up to join her at the glass. She was a full head taller than Danni, but only because of the stiletto tips on her heels. Bare foot, they were probably an even match, in height if nothing else.

"I provide the club, they strip. Come on, I'll show you the rest."

She led Danni down a black hallway lit with blue LEDs. A mirrored ceiling gave the floor a warped effect. Danni brushed her hand against the wall to keep her balance until they reached a massive star field. Catherine stepped down into it, but it took Danni's eyes a second to adjust and see more than just the starry oblivion below her.

The walls were the same solid black as Catherine's private suite, but here the LEDs alternated frequencies, appearing to twinkle and giving off enough light to see a hundred or more cable-held, glass stairs. The entire thing jumped and swayed under Danni's feet. Catherine reached back and caught her hand.

"I won't let you fall *just* yet," she said.

She waited for Danni to find her footing again, but it was difficult. The stairway didn't appear to end in either direction, so there was no stationary point to focus on, and Danni had to keep a balancing grip on Catherine's shoulder the entire way down.

Eventually, Catherine stepped off ahead of her. Danni heard her heels counting off a more solid surface, even though it still looked like the vast blanket of stars. It wasn't until she was level with a floor Danni realized how far down they'd gone, and the underfoot starfield was actually a square infinity mirror. She stared back up the staircase.

"That is incredible. I didn't think they put things this far underground in New Orleans."

Catherine smiled. "You'd be surprised at what a well-placed hydraulic system and a few million dollars will get you."

The room was round but bare, except for the chunky pairs of art deco columns staggered where the room split off into longer hallways. Catherine turned down the closest corridor. Danni could still hear the thumping club bass, but now it seemed to be coming from above her. Her eyes rose to the low, black ceiling. The lasers and strobes on the dance floor flashed hard against the crush of bodies above them. Catherine tapped a fingernail against the ceiling.

"Two-way mirror. The whole floor is made out of it."

Her gaze followed the line of her arm beneath the skirt of one of the few women still wearing clothing. "Provides an *evocative* vantage point."

Danni was more interested in Catherine's face than the ceiling. "Are you…"

There was no polite way to ask that question, either. Catherine's green eyes snapped back, full and round, but her expression was more diablerie than surprise.

"Gay?" Catherine asked.

Her laughter echoed off deeper in the building despite the plush carpet corridor it traveled. It felt sexy and alive, brushing against Danni's skin in melodious waves.

"What a *painfully* Victorian attitude. You need to get away from those nuns. You've subscribed yourself to their values but did you ever ask yourself *why*?"

She started to walk again, talking and guiding Danni's attention as she went. "One man, one woman. That's the party line, isn't it? But it barely scratches the surface of what we are capable of feeling."

They stopped outside a dimly lit room. Inside, a plush couch was positioned against the wall. A man sat as a dancer swept over him in a back-bending arch. Her movements were slow, provocative, an erotic ballet just teetering on the edge of something much darker. Neither she or the man seemed to notice Danni or Catherine, too focused on one another.

"What is sexuality if not the capacity to experience erotic sensation, regardless of gender or a pre-defined philosophy about what is right and what is wrong?" Catherine asked.

The next room was a series of more wrong than right. Same dim lighting, same slow dance, but this time, the space was occupied by a larger audience. The dancer was stripped bare and suspended from the ceiling by a black-leather braid. The backs of her thighs were covered in red welts.

A man stood. He pulled a wide cord through his fist. The dancer whimpered when he leaned into her face.

"Do you submit?" he asked.

Whatever her answer was, it was incorrect. The strap came down hard against her skin and left a fresh ribbon of pink in its wake.

The audience took turns asking the same question before hammering a whip, a riding crop, or, in one case, a wooden spoon against her. Each time, the dancer would rock her head back, her face wrought with bliss.

Danni's eyes traveled down the hallway. An anxious quiver started in the backs of her knees when she realized how many more doorways they were yet to visit. If Catherine was moving toward a point, and she certainly seemed to be, Danni hoped she would make it quickly.

Thankfully, they continued in silence, passing by the rooms that offered new and exciting versions of the same song. Leather, lace, wax, and food. Bodies folded at impossible angles, in varying combinations. Male-female, male-male, female and several males, the inverse of that. After a while, it stopped seeming real. It wasn't love, hell, it wasn't even sex. Just meat meeting in dark places.

Danni kept pace with Catherine, but they never reached a junction in the wall. Still, the rooms kept coming, one after the other, a spiral of depravity. Finally, Danni had to stop.

"It doesn't bother you?" she asked. "To be the mastermind behind all this... stuff?"

Catherine turned and braced her hands against either wall. "Bother? Sweet pea, it *empowers* me. A hundred years ago, do you know what this place was?"

"Bedrock?"

"Storyville was the red-light district for *all* of New Orleans. They bound slaves to their beds, let the rich come and go. Blacks and whites, men and women, treated no better than cattle. Beaten, raped. And they endured it because they had no choice."

Catherine tossed her chin back toward the rooms they'd already passed and went on. "But *these* people endure it because they *do*. Down here, 'no' only ever means 'not yet.' And in that, they are liberated from the world above."

Danni let the thought settle before speaking again. "But even you must have lines you won't cross."

"Me?" Catherine pressed all five fingertips against her breast but appeared genuinely surprised. "There is no line I will not, and do not, willingly traverse."

The hallway finally ended, but the last room was dark. Danni started past it, eager to leave all she'd seen behind her until a muffled cry called her back.

She stopped. Her ears strained against the heavy silence, searching for it again. As sharp and cleanly as she'd heard it, it was gone. She shook her head. Maybe she'd imagined it, wanted to hear it just so she'd have something tangible to object against. She glanced back at Catherine.

"See something you like?" she asked.

It might not have been an invitation, but it was as close as Danni was going to get. She reached into the dark room, patted the wall, and found a light switch. The overheads snapped on. Where the other rooms had been covered in dark fabrics and plush furniture, this one had been painted to present the illusion of being sky-bound. White, supple clouds lay over a backdrop of clear, seamless blue. On a far wall, a mountain of fat, plastic toys overflowed onto the floor. She took a full step forward.

Bunk-beds, cribs, cradles…They lined the walls, mismatched but clearly well-used. It smelled like powder with an undercurrent of spoiled milk. The more sense it made, the less she wanted it to. She turned back toward the door.

An old man bent forward over his lap, seated on the edge of a pine rocking chair. She hadn't even noticed him when she'd entered. His face was so grizzled it made his age impossible to guess. He was just…*old*.

Thick, yellow fingernails chased an itch across the backs of his hands, which seemed like more than enough friction to tear his mottled skin. He studied her, tipping his head side to side, and then said something, in French or Creole.

The blood pounded between her ears.

"What?" she heard herself ask. "I-I don't understand." Or she understood perfectly and didn't want to. "What… what is all this?"

Catherine gripped the doorway on either side but didn't move past the threshold.

"Do you know how many single mothers I employ?" She shrugged. "Daycare."

Danni's eyes narrowed on the old man, still rocking back and forth, murmuring some foreign language. Catherine mumbled something in response, which caused him to stand.

He shuffled toward Danni, using the time between each step to readjust his focus. When he reached her, he pressed his thumbnail against the base of her chin, forcing her head up a half inch. His breathing was heavy and wet. He held it for a full minute before releasing through his mouth.

"*Reine*," he whispered. He whipped around to Catherine and said it again. "Reine!"

"*Es-tu sur?*"

French. They were definitely speaking French, but whatever the old man said after that came out too quickly. The only word Danni caught, he repeated several times. *Reine*.

Eventually, Catherine's gaze shifted back to Danni. "Are you coming?"

The old man was trembling, and his quiet murmurs had become gibberish in any language. Danni stepped past him and started down the hall behind Catherine.

"Wait," she said and set a hand against Catherine's shoulder. "What does that mean? *Reine*?"

Catherine stared at Danni's hand and smiled. "It means *queen*."

Fourteen

Catherine led her up a much less elaborate stairway than the one they'd come down, and they wound up in the private suite again. The dance floor crowd had thinned, and those who were left were making slow, languid circles around the poles. The music and lights were softer, warmer somehow, but the buzzing in Danni's brain only seemed to worsen. She wanted to vomit, if only to expel the horror of the last few—

How long had they been down there? She searched for a clock, but couldn't find one. She slid down into one of the low chairs. Catherine poured out a fresh glass from the crystal decanter and passed it into Danni's hand.

"How easily you assume the worst of me, Danni."

"I'm sorry. You said there was no line you wouldn't cross and then I saw a nursery so close to all that." She sipped the drink. "Is that really the best you could come up with for a babysitter?"

Something changed in Catherine's face, as if she were willing herself to be calm, which looked nothing like calm at all.

"Jaackemel is quite capable. He cared for me, for a time."

It made it better, but only a little.

"But, down there?" Danni asked. "So close to all that?"

"In your mind, where is it that they come from? Heaven? The stork? Certainly someone as attractive as you has at least experienced sex once or twice."

Danni shrugged. "Once or twice."

"Though not lately it would seem. You're so repressed I can practically taste it in the back of *my* mouth."

Finally, *anger*. It rushed over her neck, bringing with it all the chemicals Danni needed to feel clear-headed again.

"Not everything in life is repaired with an orgasm, Catherine."

"Of course not. Sometimes there's pain involved."

"And how exactly did a girl from Central City become the Queen of Carnal?"

Breathless laughter lit the bottoms of Catherine's eyes, but her voice was thick with remembered pain as she settled in the leather chair across from Danni.

"I was young once. Stupid and pregnant. I heard about a houngan in the swamp who helped people like me, for a price. I had nothing to offer him, at least, not money.

"I rode the bus out as far as it would take me and walked the rest of the way. It was probably eight or nine o'clock by the time I reached his door. I was sick with fever, swollen with a child I couldn't care for. He took me in, bathed me. Let me sleep. When I woke up, my child was gone. But he took something else, too."

She slipped the strap of her dress down to reveal a jagged scar where her left breast should have been. It started just below her collarbone and vanished where it curled beneath her arm, easily the width of two fingers. But the cuts had not been clean or even or remotely merciful.

"That's awful," Danni said. "I'm sorry. I... I was going to say, I know the feeling. Missing part of yourself you never expected to lose, but I don't. Not that way."

Catherine considered her for a moment and then tossed back the ends of her drink. "You seem embarrassed," she said.

When Danni nodded, Catherine went on. "Well, I suppose that makes us even. Perhaps it *is* short-sighted to keep children in close quarters with such things. I've never understood them, I know even less about their care. But you, you seem to have it in spades."

"Honestly," Danni said with a sigh, "I have no idea what I'm doing, either."

She stood and walked to the windows overlooking the crowd. It seemed like she had exchanged one troubled orphanage for another, only here the orphans were dignity and moderation. Still, the prayers didn't change. *I hope... I need... I want...*

So much want.

There was a void just beyond their desire, as if nothing could satiate that hunger, but that didn't stop them from tossing everything they had into trying.

"Catherine, look," she began. "Your club is

definitely something. I like you. I *really* like your money, but more because of what it will allow me to do for my boys."

"You really love them, don't you?"

Danni nodded once. "They are my first priority, always."

"Except tonight," Catherine said, chuckling. "No, no. I wasn't insulting you, just pointing out if you don't take care of yourself, you're no good to those you care for. Speaking of which, are you hungry? You hardly ate at the banquet. *Tomas*?"

A door opened farther down the room. The bodyguard was back, this time naked from the waist up and haloed by a rich, red haze. His jeans were fitted but well-worn, and threadbare holes offered glimpses of his muscular thighs, like he'd been chiseled out of a few tons of smooth, pink marble. The bowl of cherries in his hands only seemed to heighten the effect.

Danni wet her lips and took a step backwards. She landed against another equally smooth chest. She hadn't even heard him come in. A dark shadow of stubble lined his square jaw. His skin was darker, almost bronze, and radiated visible warmth. Not just strength, but actual *power* like a gold current rippling beneath her hand. She touched him just above the bicep, letting the sensation roll out against her fingers, studying it and then losing interest in its source as it climbed down her arm and across her chest.

With Michael gone, it had been easy to ignore the want. The *desire*. Anticipation was one thing, exciting, provocative on its own. But it had been weeks, no, *months* since she'd felt the touch of another human being. Most of her days were spent in the company of nuns and children. No time to think about the ever-present tension just below the surface of her skin, but here, it re-doubled on her like a deep water swell. She tried to clear the tension from her throat, but it only seemed to make it worse.

Danni snapped her hand back from his skin.

"I'm sorry," she said quickly.

His dark brown eyes swept over her, unabashedly greedy.

"*Why*?" he asked, but it was a salacious 'why?'

Catherine extended one finger and made a come-hither motion.

"Laurent? *Venir ici*. I do believe you're making our guest uncomfortable."

Laurent slunk away but not out of the room. He positioned himself against the wall and kept his eyes on Danni. Just the weight of them sent a pleasant wave of itches down her spine.

"I don't know what you're doing, but whatever it is, stop it," she hissed.

The wave of power broke instantly, but Laurent's expression was sour.

"Forgive him," Catherine said. "He's not accustomed to being refused."

Danni ran a hard hand against the back of her neck. "And I'm not accustomed to being... whatever that was."

"*Wanted*," Laurent purred. "Most desperately."

It hadn't felt like desperation so much as drowning. Danni shook her head.

"I have a Michael," she said quickly. "A boyfriend. I meant, I have a boyfriend."

Catherine ran a polished fingernail across the top of a cherry before pinching it between her fingers. She rolled it against her lips. "Tell me about him. Your *Michael*."

His name sounded suddenly foreign, as if in a single breath Catherine had stripped him of all familiarity. Danni blinked hard.

"He's my–"

"Boyfriend. You said that." She pushed the cherry past her lips then spoke around it. "Did I miss him tonight?"

"No, he wasn't there. He's… actually, I don't know where he is."

"That doesn't sound very promising." Catherine leaned in over her crossed knees. "I like you, too, Danni. You've got spunk, but you're wound entirely too tight. There's something inside you, begging to be released.

"The nuns, the children? I thought they were your chains, but now I know there is *someone* else holding you back."

Catherine kept her distance. She didn't need to get closer. All her tactics were wrapped up in sharp, piercing words.

"What good is a man who won't come home to you?"

Laurent was back, and so was the heated power coursing off his skin. One, solid hand ran the length of Danni's neck. He hooked his fingers under the collar of her jacket. What made her sit forward and let him slip it off her shoulders, she didn't know. What she *did* know was that she wanted to feel his hand on her bare skin. She didn't have to wait long.

He started at the base of her skull and worked his way down, over her shoulders, across her arms. His breath was hot and wet as he whispered against her ear.

"I want you," he said.

She was vaguely aware that the liquid heat encircling her lips wasn't Michael's. What startled her was *she didn't care.* Laurent tasted like the sweetness in the air. His tongue slid across hers in time with his hands. Firm gliding fingertips passed over her breasts, her stomach, and her hips. She felt them curl to fists as he chased the hem of her skirt. Her knees parted, involuntarily, and she felt a cool rush of air caress her inner thighs.

Danni broke from Laurent's mouth and glanced across the short distance between the chairs. Catherine's green eyes were hooded with lust and darker things.

"Oh, don't stop on my account."

Catherine stood. Without prompting, Tomas unzipped the back of her dress. It slid into a pool at her feet, and she stepped free.

Her skin was the same color as a frosted dawn, except for the long, rugged line carved over her chest, which was still remarkably beautiful. Tomas slid in behind her then sat, pulling her into his lap. Her red hair glowed with a kind of incandescence that ignited the energy between all four of them.

Laurent said something else, but Danni missed it, too caught in the sight of Tomas' hand kneading

Catherine's breast as he ground her against his lap.

"What?" Danni asked Laurent.

His voice was thick around his accent. "I said, tell me what you want me to do to you."

She looked at Catherine again. Her head was thrown back in ecstasy against Tomas' shoulder while his fingers slid down to the red hair at the apex of her thighs.

"That," Danni whispered. "Do *that.*"

Fifteen

The sun was setting over distant mountains and turning the saguaro into long shadows. Michael could see the waves rolling off the desert below him, but he didn't feel the heat. He'd been here all day but never felt hot or cold. Still, he was covered in sweat. Had been for hours.

Zed had him practice focusing on the malachite, trying to recapture the sense of where it had come from. Michael quickly learned it wasn't so much focusing on the rock as the area *around* it, coaxing the things at the edge of his perception into focus.

"It reminds me of being in the confessional," Michael realized suddenly. "Listening to the voice on the other side of the screen stammering through a litany of minor sins."

"Particularly the children," Zed added as he shaped new runes in the dust at his feet.

Michael nodded. "More often than not they weren't there to confess anything other than their fears, have someone to tell their troubles to. I'd stare at my rosary, let the words float down around me, and I could see what they were talking about... *really* see it. Beatings, abuse, some horrible thing they'd witnessed and couldn't understand."

"And then," Zed said. "You'd leave the confessional, having given them what meager words you could, and you'd go do something to fix it."

Michael nodded weakly. "Sometimes I could. Maybe get the kid to a safer place, or–"

"Maybe not," Zed said. "We were bound by the rules of the church. Sanctity, piety, confidentiality. Rules and codes laid down thousands of years ago, only to be twisted and bent by the interests of mortal men."

Michael grinned in the growing darkness. "Mother Superior said that's the kind of thinking that made you decide to retire."

"She's very tactful, that woman is. I've always been a learner, me. A thinker, a scholar of faith. But the more I learned, the more questions I had. Made me see those of us in the habits were special, but not that special.

"You pick any major religion and they all come down to the same things. Be honest, treat others like you want to be treated, remember where you fit in, and don't take yourself too seriously."

"Some of that is the same thing."

"Comes down to it, yeah, it is," Zed agreed. "They all have different words for it. In the Wiccan Rede, it's 'harm none.' Over time, the Christian church turned that into 'thou shalt nots.' Hoodoo now, it's a bit more of an understanding that you risk getting what you give, what the Old Testament referred to as 'an eye for an eye' if'n you get caught."

"But the church tells us that God is always watching," Michael said.

"Oh, yeah? So, if He's always watching, we're always gonna get caught." Zed frowned. "How many times you see someone not get caught?"

"A few," Michael admitted.

"That's why I quit. Current teachings of Christianity still say God is watching, but it's our fault. Other faiths tell us *their* deities might watch if we ask for help and aren't too greedy. But most of the time, we have to watch out for each other and ourselves. Speaking of, you cold?"

Michael shook his head.

"Really? You've been sweating all day. You're still wet. You may not be cold here in your head, but I bet your body back home could use a fire."

Michael came back to himself and instantly felt the cold. The sweat stuck his shirt to his back and sent a chill down his spine. The cabin was still and dark, but the air was much heavier than it had been in the desert.

"And that's today's lesson," Zed said. "While you're off learning and doing, don't forget to give home its due."

Michael moved to get the fire going. His thoughts traveled to the idea of home and all the things it meant. New Orleans, the convent, and Danni.

"We still talking about the cold?"

A knowing smile crept over the old man's face. "I just teach, son. What you take from it is up to you."

Sixteen

Sunlight filtered through the curtains and cut into the soft parts of Danni's brain. She rolled away from the window only to have it thrown open a moment later.

Sister Ned glared, her head wrought in the fierce, white light. "And I was *so* hoping you might be dead."

"Something I can do for you?"

Danni's voice sounded harsh in her own ears, raw and full of glass. She tried to sit up and failed when the room whirled one direction and the bed another.

"You can start with where the hell you went last night."

"Out."

"*Out*," Sister Ned repeated. "It's been awhile but can I assume, given your condition, that still means drinking until dawn while a dozen strangers work themselves against you?"

"Why, Sister Ned, who'd have guessed you had a naughty streak."

A hard slap slung Danni's face sideways against the

pillow. The dull throb in her head turned into a full percussion march. When she opened her eyes again, Sister Ned didn't look a bit remorseful.

"Those boys stayed up half the night waiting for you to come back! Took me and Sister Charlotte two hours to convince them to go to bed."

Danni sat up and massaged the sting in her jaw, but her cheek wasn't the only sore section of her skin. A pleasant tremor ran across her thighs when she stood. *Laurent.*

She tucked the sheet around her bare skin and moved toward the kitchen with Sister Ned at her heels.

"I warned you about building up their hopes on false promises."

Danni swallowed two full glasses of water before responding, but even then it sounded smug.

"They'll get over it, I'm sure."

"Get over–" Sister Ned sucked in a sharp breath and then released it slowly.

Danni cocked a hip against the kitchen island and tried to pull together the details of the previous night. Catherine had brought her home, she remembered that much, but after that... She lifted an empty bottle of rum from the counter, sniffed the top, and felt her stomach roil. Yep. Definitely rum.

Sister Ned was moving around the apartment in a search for answers of her own. There wasn't much to look at. A bed, a couch, a coffee table she'd rescued from the curb. Sister Ned stopped above a shattered vase and a dozen bruised roses scattered across the floor. She stooped down, and when she stood again, there was a rose cradled in the palm of her hand. The anger in her expression was quickly replaced with concern.

"It's because he's gone, isn't it?" she asked.

Danni waved her off and moved toward the bathroom. Sister Ned followed her.

"We all assumed it would be easier for you because you've been alone before, and you know how to deal with it."

She set a gentle hand on Danni's bare shoulder. "He didn't intend on this. None of us did. Come back to the convent with me. We'll tell Mother Superior and she can–"

Danni spun around, angry. "Are you kidding me? Mother Superior isn't going to help me, especially where Michael is concerned. To her, I'm just the Delilah of the Mount Carmel."

"It's not that way."

"Oh, for Christ's sake! Slap me again before you start patronizing me. I'm not confused about exactly where I stand when it comes to the sisters, and you shouldn't be either. I'm not one of you. I'm the exact opposite. I drink, and I cuss, I stay out until dawn, and I do voodoo because, like it or not, I'm a loa, whatever *that* means!

"Now, I left that orphanage in the Sisters' hands because I needed a babysitter. But if you can't handle a few little boys, then I'll find someone *else* who can."

"Danni, you don't mean that."

"I do, and I will."

Danni held open the door and guided Sister Ned into the hallway. "Now get the fuck out of my apartment."

Seventeen

Michael was hot.

He'd already stripped down to his thin white undershirt but even that was sticking to his skin. Six weeks in the swamp didn't even compare to the brittle air inside Chautian Rue. It stung his nose and smelled like burnt pralines.

He struggled to sort out a pile of herbs, checking them against Zed's supply list. Sweat rolled down his forehead and smeared the ink on the page. He mopped it away with the back of his hand.

"Man, you got something against air conditioning? It's hotter than Hell in here."

Joto glanced up from the table and patted the sweat from his upper lip, as if noticing it for the first time. He jerked two glass bottles out of a crate beneath the table and slid one to Michael.

"Good guess," he said.

Michael caught the bottle and tore the cork out with his teeth. The water hit his lips, almost too cold to swallow.

It made his head ache, but he chugged it in three full gulps. It had a cooler, earthy flavor than city water, like he was sipping it off the top of a wet stone. He worked his tongue against the roof of his mouth, trying to place it.

"It's blessed," Joto said before he could ask.

He tucked the other bottle between his knees and rolled across the room with one smooth push to a oak cabinet, then paused long enough to cast a quick warning over his shoulder.

"Hold on to your ass."

The cabinet doors opened and the heat intensified. Joto tugged the cork out of the second bottle and emptied it inside the cabinet. The pop and sizzle was immediate. A cloud of white steam filled the small room.

When it cleared, Joto unfolded his fist for Michael to see, though he wasn't sure *what* he was seeing. It tumbled around in the crease of Joto's hand, the size and shape of a black marble with a hunk missing out of the side. How could something so small produce so much heat?

Michael blinked the sweat out of his eyes. His reflection in the stone blinked a second later. He swallowed a gasp and tried to shape his focus on the space around Joto's hand.

The room faded in and out in stuttered bursts. The smell and the heat hit him again. This time, he knew exactly what it was, but more importantly, *where* it had come from.

"The Crossroads."

"Right in one," Joto said. "Found it stuck in my spoke. Damn near melted my wheel. Been tryin' to keep it cool until I can return it."

Michael stayed motionless as Joto wrapped the pebble inside a clean cloth before tucking it back into the cabinet.

"Why not just get rid of it?"

Joto frowned. "Ever read 'bout the drought of '36?"

He had. "Samedi did that, too, huh?"

"Nah. Houngan named Alcide Lambreaux. Swiped a piece of rock from the Crossroads and tossed it in the Missi'sip. Messed up the whole weather pattern for North America."

"But *why*?"

Joto shrugged. "For kicks, I reckon." He met Michael's glare. "What? Not everyone doin' magic in the Delta's on the side of the angels like you and I is."

Michael resumed sorting the herbs but kept a careful eye on Joto. "Then what are *you* doing at the Crossroads?"

"Not by choice, man. Never by choice. Damn Ghede got me by the heels."

Michael's eyes shifted back to the pile of herbs and stayed there. "I suppose that's something else we have in common."

His hand traveled to his chest where he massaged the damp collar of his shirt against his skin. Did Danni even know he was back in New Orleans? He doubted it. She wasn't the type to sit and wait for him to find her. He'd half-expected her to show up in the swamp. When she didn't, he found himself trapped between relief and longing.

Joto seemed to follow the thought. "Brother, you gotta talk to her sometime."

"And then what?"

"You've seen her, right? You were a priest, not a corpse."

"Don't be a jerk."

"Fine. You *talk*. Tell her how you feel. And then you shut up and listen."

Michael leaned over the table. How did he feel? Not nearly as out of his depth as he had a few months ago, but still awkward. His world was no longer split into two clear paths, right and wrong, good or evil; it was just a matter of degrees.

Even New Orleans felt different. Without his collar, he was just another man on the street, yet he could feel the rhythm in the air, drumming in time with the magic he'd never noticed before. People looked at him almost as if they were sizing him up, or down.

Finally, he dropped the hand from his chest and said, "I'm not ready yet. Still got work to do, you know."

Joto sighed and pushed another bag toward him. "Weird getting used to a new skin, isn't it?"

"That's just what it feels like. New skin."

"The other one was too tight anyway. Whatever you're doing out there, though, it's working. Not a lot of people could'a picked that pebble out for what it was."

Michael thought about it. "Have a question for you. When you concentrate on it, how much of the conjuring community can you feel? I mean, how in touch are you?"

Joto frowned. "That's like asking the local banker

how rich he is, Michael. Any answer is bad for business."

"What I'm trying to figure out is how in touch with each other the community is here. I'm feeling things in the Quarter I never have before, seeing people I've never noticed. And I felt some of them see me, too."

"Okay, that's a problem," Joto said, then called out to the front of the shop. "Guido! Leave us alone. Anybody comes in, I'm out."

"You got a two o'clock session with that lady from New York," Guido hollered back.

"Tell her the spirits contacted me about her, and set her up for the same time tomorrow."

"Cool. We can charge her extra."

Joto rolled back to the cabinet and began pulling down items as he spoke. "I thought you were wide open just 'cause you was with me, but that old man probably hasn't had to think about shields in a coon's age.

"First things first, we got to get you some protection to get you around town. Hell, to get you back to the truck. But don't walk south. Remember Sadie? Wears the lime green fairy costume and the baseball cap?"

Michael nodded. "I used to have lunch with her a couple times a month."

Joto dumped an armload of junk onto the table and went back for more. "Psychic vampire. Not dangerous really, but you walk by her you'll be pissed off for the rest of the day and have no idea why."

He came back with a final armload and went to work shuffling through a series of amber bottles, pouring out their liquids into a bowl. It made a kind of vibrant soup until he used a bundle of sage to mix it into a smooth, gray goop.

"Back then," he said, "the collar was your shield whether you were wearing it or not. Your mind's way of protecting you from the reach of others. Not just attacks but the day to day interactions with people like Sadie. Most of the time she don't even know she's doing it. But you wander across somebody who recognizes what's awake in you? Brother, you're a buffet in sneakers."

Joto tapped the sage against the edge of the bowl. "Okay. Get your clothes off."

"Say what?"

"We're going to do a quick cleansing and then get a little protection around you. Come on, get 'em off."

Michael peeled the damp t-shirt over his head. "I'm not buying one of those crappy souvenir shirts."

"I'm not selling one, either. Besides, you couldn't afford it."

"You got that right. Turns out a vow of poverty does not adequately prepare a guy for a life out in the world. I'm gonna have to find a job."

"I hear the sisters are looking for a handyman."

"They can't afford me."

"My, how quickly the fallen get high and mighty."

"I mean they can't afford anyone," Michael said. "Repairs to the convent had pretty much wiped out the coffers before I left. I'll bet anything they do have they're giving to the orphanage. Boxers, too?" he asked.

"Thanks, no. Save that for Danni." Joto rolled toward him, twisting the sage into a tight bundle. "Don't look at me like that. Now stand still."

Joto produced a lighter and set fire to one end of the sage. He let it burn for a full minute before blowing it out. As the smoke swelled off the smoldering end, he rolled around Michael and chanted under his breath. He made three complete circles before opening his eyes and wheeling back.

"That ought to do." He dropped the sage into a metal work sink. "Now for the protection."

Joto pulled the remaining sprigs of sage off the counter, grabbed the bowl, and rolled back to Michael. "This is a few things."

"I can smell the patchouli," Michael said.

"Yeah, and you can smell the mugwort, too." He dipped the sage into the bowl and stirred the mixture a few times, and then painted a quick line on Michael's stomach.

Michael jumped. "Hey!"

"Stand still, ya' wimp."

Joto painted lines on Michael's forehead, nose, and chin. "It doesn't have a color, and doesn't stain the skin. A half hour from now no one on the street will know you've been warded."

He painted the top of each shoulder and reached toward Michael's chest

Michael's hand shot up to cover his heart. "Wait. Can she... will she still be able to..."

Joto rested his hands in his lap and studied him. "Got something you want to ask?"

Michael hesitated, then sank back against the edge of the table. "She ever ask about me? Does she know we talk?"

Joto nodded. "Don't ask, don't tell, don't cry."

"That's harsh man."

"Yeah, well if you don't ask then I don't have to lie to you, and ain't neither of us gotta cry about it."

"That bad, huh?"

"Been better," he said, then stopped and thought about it. "Well, been better for you, anyway. She came with problems. You let me know when you're ready to step up, but you better do it while it's still yours to step up to."

Michael glared at him. "What's that supposed to mean?"

"Please, bro. That woman's power was born from the wickedest hurricane this city's seen in a century and that ain't even the most interesting thing about her. Not gonna be long 'fore someone else takes notice."

He dipped the end of the brush back in the mixture and held it up, waiting. Michael stepped forward again and Joto drew a quick rune over his heart.

"Done as done can be. Get dressed."

Joto went back to the counter, grabbed a funnel and a small amber bottle, and poured the remainder of the gray goop into it. He plugged the bottle with a stopper and dropped it into Michael's hand.

"That won't wash off, if you're wondering. But it won't last forever, either. Touch it up in a few days, and get Zed to teach you about shielding."

"Not sure when I'll see him again."

"You back in town, then?"

"Yeah. Got a few obligations to take care of."

Michael finished sorting the herbs and packed them into a box. Before he left, he let his hand drift over the charms and trinkets on the shelves. He stopped on a velvet-lined box of silver crosses.

"Are these consecrated?"

Joto nodded. "By Father Frannie himself."

"How is the old guy?"

"He's good. Still sharp. His golf game is suffering. Doesn't get around like he used to. But he's enjoying his retirement in Abita Springs."

"You go all the way out there to get these?"

Joto nodded. "And the holy water. I make a beer run every now and then. The home won't let him have any, so I slip a little in when I can. It's a fair trade."

Michael stared at the crucifix. "You never asked me to do it."

"You aren't a lonely old man who used to play stickball with us in the streets."

Eighteen

"I don't know why this took so long."

Michael's voice followed the light, bouncing down the hallway of the empty mausoleum. Sun poured through the high, glass walls. He sat on a marble bench across from a row of name plates.

The last time he'd been here the wall of low profile slots had been blank. Now, almost every one held a name, a date of birth, and a date of death.

He did the math on a few, coming up with ages that seemed reasonable and natural. Seventy-four, eighty-nine. Ninety-six; a good, long life.

His mother's sat in the middle. Forty-one. He'd long since made peace with the how's and the why's of that number. Less than ten years from the age he was now, more than ten years gone.

His eyes travelled from his mother's nameplate to his brother's. He liked to imagine he could see Joey's wry smile as clearly as it'd always been. But he couldn't. Too many years had made his memory hazy. Michael swallowed the growing weight in his throat and continued.

"Got a few things I need to tell you. Probably ought to start with the cardinal sins, work my way to venial. That day in the car, it was me behind the wheel. Me who crashed, and me who hit those people. Joey took the blame. Watching out for us, again, but I let him. And it was my fault he went to prison. My fault he died there."

By the time he reached the last sentence, he was out of air. He sucked in a deep breath and continued.

"I tried to make up for it, give myself to God, just like you wanted. Turns out God didn't want me, but we gave it a good try. And if he can forgive me, I better forgive myself. I hope you can, too."

He sorted through his gris-gris bag until he found the cross she'd given him. He held it between his hands, concentrating until it glowed. He centered it between the two brass markers before pressing it into the marble. The silver flattened and seeped into the stone as Michael settled back on the bench.

"Just because I gave up the collar, I didn't give up everything it stands for, only what it was keeping my heart from. I love you and Joey, and I miss you both. I wish you could've met Danni. You would've liked her."

"I don't know about that. But she'd have liked that you love her," a familiar voice said behind him.

"Baron Cemetrie," Michael said and stood. "Imagine the surprise."

A slight figure, as dark as mahogany, leaned against the exterior glass and then *through* it. The whites of his eyes burned out of his shadow as he came to stand opposite

Michael. His summer suit was made of white poplin and framed with a burgundy bow tie. A flat-topped straw hat spun slowly in one hand. The other rested over a long, ivory cane.

"Somebody does magic in my house, you think I'm not gonna come see why?"

Michael stepped aside as Cemetrie moved to inspect the wall. The Baron's power flexed hard against his skin, heady and wet, alive but not, yet so familiar. Michael struggled to place it, weighing it against what he knew of Cemetrie and his brothers. The loa weren't gods any more than they were men, stuck somewhere in between. The danger in dealing with them was crossing that line, regardless if you knew where it actually was.

"I meant no disrespect, Baron," Michael said.

Cemetrie's power flared a second time. The air left the room. Even the light stopped moving against the glass. Michael *had* felt this in the swamp! The image of the rabbit and then the snake came back to him. The stillness and the noiselessness, it had been inside both animals even as they began to move.

Michael didn't have time to reason any further before it vanished. The light and air stirred. Cemetrie traced the silver where it had melted into the stone and nodded his approval.

"That's a nice thing you done there, showing respect. I appreciate that. You're a good boy to your mamma. I appreciate that, too. So, you get a pass." He raised the cane in warning. "Just this time, though. You hear?"

"I do," Michael said. "And thank you for watching over my family."

Cemetrie motioned him forward, and they walked back toward the mouth of the mausoleum.

"We take care of our dead. That's what being a Ghede means."

Michael started to say something but stopped. Cemetrie turned to face him. "What is it, boy?"

"I was just wondering…" He swallowed hard and searched Cemetrie's face. Gray eyes harder than the stone around them stared back, unyielding but patient. Still, Michael chose his words carefully. "Is everyone in your family as…compassionate?"

Cemetrie let out a low chuckle. "You've met my brothers, seen how they behave. What'dya think?"

"I think there's a lot I still don't understand about them or you, or…"

Cemetrie gave him a knowing smile. "*Ah.* But this ain't 'bout me or my brothers, is it?"

Michael shook his head. Cemetrie went on. "How about this? I'll answer you, one for one. You ask. I'll ask. Deal?"

Cemetrie's knotted hand reached out, offering, *waiting.* Michael swallowed hard. The last deal he'd made with a Ghede had resulted in leaving New Orleans. Now, he'd been back less than twelve hours and he was considering making another. He rubbed the center of his chest.

Michael took a slow, steadying breath and shook his hand.

"How is she?" Michael asked.

Cemetrie shrugged. "Half in, half out."

"What's that mean?"

"*Ah, ah.* My turn," the Baron said. "Where you been?"

"Swamp." Michael considered leaving it there, but this could take all day if they both kept to cryptic one-word answers. He went on. "I've been learning about hoodoo and the earth. Trying to figure out my path, or any path, really."

Cemetrie nodded and motioned for Michael's next question.

"What do you mean she's half-in, half-out?"

"Just that. She ain't loa but she damn sure ain't human, and it's creatin' more chaos than good."

Cemetrie stopped walking and scratched the base of his chin. "If you're in the mood for learnin', take a little listen."

Michael followed his eyes to the western edge of the cemetery where the tops of the buildings rose beyond the high wall. He heard the traffic like a swift rush of distant water punctuated by the long trill of a trumpet.

It wasn't unlike staring at the malachite. The longer he held his eyes on the space around the horizon, the clearer he could feel it coming into focus. But instead of seeing the desert, he heard people, like a hundred televisions on different channels. Crisp, clean voices in the Garden District sang alongside the muddled accent of the deep bayou, and they all said the same thing. *Jiji, please...*

Michael's voice felt light in his throat. "They're *praying* to her." He looked back at Cemetrie. "Not just the boys. All of them."

"Aye. And you know prayers are a powerful thing, answered or not."

Michael listened for a minute longer, piecing out individual wants and needs from the crowd. Each time they began to soften, they would rush back with new weight. Deeper want. More *need*.

"How could one person even *begin* to answer all of them?" he asked, but Cemetrie said nothing.

Right. Not his turn.

"Where you headed?" Cemetrie asked.

"Honestly, I'm not entirely sure," Michael said. "I still need to talk to her, if she's willing. That should give me a better idea of exactly where I fit in all this, and where I'll go."

"She has your soul on a string," Cemetrie reminded. "You go where she says you go. To Hell or otherwise."

"She already did that. I left."

"All the more reason she may do it again and not leave you an option."

Michael nodded his understanding. "Hell hath no fury. Don't think I haven't considered it."

"Considering it's one thing, puttin' yourself in the crossfire is another entirely. Now, as head of household, I can't promise to keep her from guttin' you, but I can be convinced to speak on your behalf."

Michael put up a hand to stop him. "I'm not exactly looking to make a deal with one Ghede to stop another."

"Ain't about stoppin' her. Like I said, we care for our charges, and she ain't mindin' hers."

Without noticing, Cemetrie had led them to one of the few actual graves in the cemetery. It sat on a high hill that had obviously been placed just to defeat the water table and keep the casket from pushing its way to the surface. The dirt was still loose and wet. Michael squinted into the sun to see the headstone.

"Reginald Dupont," he read aloud. "He just died a few days ago."

"Damned hippies. Whole lot of them movin' for green burials nowadays. Muckin' up the whole show." Cemetrie jabbed the tip of his cane into the soil. "Come on then, you damned fool, show yourself."

A brick of dread formed in Michael's gut. The dirt tumbled away from the foot of the cane, disturbed by whatever was moving underneath. One hand broke from the top soil followed by another. If it was meant to be a green burial, someone missed the memo about the decaying speed of polyester. Dirt clung to his navy sleeves and then to his face as Reginald Dupont made his way to the surface of his grave.

Michael staggered back. "Jesus Christ!"

"Kind of like him, yeah," Cemetrie said.

The corpse continued his slow but steady crawl forward. When his torso was half-out, Cemetrie poked the tip of his cane into the dirt again.

"Settle," he commanded.

Reginald's movements slowed, but he seemed to be fighting against it.

"I said, settle down!"

Cemetrie's power flexed again as he drove the cane

deeper into the mud. The light, the air, even the breeze in the grass stuttered and died. Michael found a clean breath inside his gris-gris bag as he focused on the feather. Cemetrie struggled for a moment longer before finally giving up, and Reginald resumed his own exhumation.

"See what I mean? Like a damned jack-in-the-box, these things!"

Michael tipped his head, considering Reginald and then Cemetrie. He extended his hands and felt the sun's warmth against his palms. It took a minute to find the difference in the air and the heat, but slowly Michael began to separate them in his mind.

He peeled back his own fear and doubt as well as any other lingering reservation he had about right and wrong. He wasn't trying to bury a man alive. Reginald was no more of a man than the rabbit had been an animal. The natural order of things had seen its soul in one direction and its body in another. Thought crystallized into action. Reginald stopped struggling. Michael pressed his hands down against the air, and the zombie began making a slow retreat back into the ground.

Cemetrie cocked his chin against his shoulder, clearly troubled.

"You been learnin' about more than the earth," Cemetrie said. "What else you got in that bag of tricks?"

A cold slice of fear ran through Michael's gut. He had no intention of showing a Baron, certainly not one as powerful as Cemetrie, the contents of his gris-gris bag. But if he refused to answer, would he be compelled by their agreement?

A smile passed over his lips.

"It's not your turn," Michael said.

"Go on then, boy. Ask your damned question."

Michael shook his head. "No. I'm good."

Cemetrie's lips parted to expose the black soot in the gaps between his teeth. It was a look meant to inspire retreat or, at the least, compliance.

"I answered your questions, as per our agreement," Michael said.

Cemetrie spat into the grass. It withered and died, leaving behind a bare circle of earth.

"*Eh!* You and she belong together."

Though clearly meant as an insult, Michael smiled. "I'll tell her you said that."

"Might also tell her to take care of her business," Cemetrie said as he gestured toward Reginald's grave. "Or maybe you want to earn yourself a little bargaining chip and take care of that for her. Either way, ain't just Mr. Dupont needin' help back in the ground."

He set the straw hat on his head, tapped it into place with the cane, and turned on his heel. As he marched off, his voice echoed from farther in the cemetery.

"A good Catholic boy doing hoodoo. What is the Delta coming to?"

Nineteen

After making two laps around the Quarter, the rum was finally creeping out of Danni's system. It was Laurent's scent that clung to her now, as if he'd planted himself between her muscle and bone. Or maybe he hadn't, and she just wanted to believe she'd been spelled instead of perfectly aware of what she had let him do to her.

She rounded the corner at Rue Royal but came up short when The Baron Samedi appeared in her path.

"You run and you run, and yet you get nowhere, *cher*."

His gray suit coat was open, leaving his smooth, blue-black skin naked from waist to throat. A painted half-skull started at his chin and ended at his nose, leaving his amber eyes undecorated, burning, but still very frightening.

Danni glanced down the street. Only a few of the art galleries on either side of the street appeared to be open. Fewer still had made it outside for the day. If anyone else noticed him, they knew better than to show it.

His fingertips coasted against her skin, but the

lingering touch was colder than ice water dumped down her back.

"You look positively radiant." Samedi lifted his hand to his lips and sucked her sweat from his fingertips. "And you taste like rum. How delightful."

Danni stared down the length of her outfit. The only thing she'd had clean were a pair of ragged sweat pants and a shirt from last year's Mardi Gras parade, both of which were soaked with sweat and rain.

"I look homeless."

"Mere costumery," he said and swept her hand to his lips and laid a quick, hot kiss against her knuckles.

The stickiness vanished from her skin and so did the clothes. A suit formed in their place. It was the color of fresh-water pearls, the texture of corn silk, and cut to fit tightly around her hips and breast. It also matched his. She started to shake her head and realized even her hair was dry. She checked her reflection in a shop front, and saw it swept back from her face and pinned into a smooth, up-do of black curls. He'd even added make-up.

When she took a step forward, her ankle twisted and pitched her forward into his arms. She glared at the black stiletto on the end of her foot.

"Give me back my tennis shoes. Now!"

"Well then you really *will* look ridiculous. Coffee?"

He snapped. A pair of French doors opened where there had only been brick a second earlier. An iron garden table rolled out and righted itself as two matching chairs galloped to join it. Danni instantly thought of *Fantasia*, but the creature holding her was no Mickey Mouse.

He gestured toward their seats but didn't wait for her to join him.

"*Garçon!*"

Joto was frowning as he rolled over the threshold with two demitasses in his lap. Danni felt sick to her stomach.

"Might as well do what the man says," he said glumly.

Danni dropped into a chair while Joto wordlessly dumped several heaping spoonfuls of sugar into Samedi's cup and then finished it with a dash of cream. The Baron swirled his finger and a tiny whirlpool opened inside the coffee.

Joto gestured toward Danni's cup. "I don't know how you take it, so…"

Danni only shook her head. Samedi took the first sip off his cup and then set it back on the saucer with a soft clink.

"Curious thing, humanity," he said. "You feel real sympathy for him, and yet you do nothing about it. Why is that?"

"What choice do I have?" she asked through gritteeth.

"None." He stirred the top of his coffee again. "I was simply asking, Ghede to Ghede."

"Including me in your ranks now?"

Samedi pressed his lips together and released them with a soft sigh.

"What choice do I have?"

"Oh, I'd say you've been doing a pretty good job of

keeping to yourself recently. How are things at the Crossroads these days? A little quiet, I imagine?"

"You took twenty-six souls out of *thousands*. Don't get cocky."

"And Cemetrie? How's he?"

It stung, but she'd meant it to. Cemetrie had taken a lot more than twenty-six souls off his hands, and claimed the title of Head of Household in the process.

Genuine anger flashed across his eyes. "Now you're just being rude."

He stripped the hat from his head and balanced it on one knee, stroking the length of the feathers on the brim. His smile eventually came back, but at only half the radiance it had been.

"You have the temper of a Ghede, I'll give you that."

She slammed her hand against the table and both cups jumped.

"Then how about giving me a clue as to what I am supposed to do with the rest of this? I turned water into flower petals last night for Christ's sake!"

Joto's eyebrows jumped, but Samedi looked unimpressed. He lifted the cup to his lips again and asked, "What kind of flower?"

"Magnolias. What does it matter?"

His amber eyes flicked to Joto as they exchanged knowing glances.

"Cemetrie had it guessed as a rose," Joto said.

"*Qu'il fit*. He did, indeed."

Samedi patted the inside edge of his jacket. He

withdrew a postcard and tossed it on the table between them. The photo was a collection of cypress covered in thick Spanish moss, but the water was so dark it was almost purple. She read the gold cursive across the front.

"What's *Jou Mon Mouri*?" she asked.

"Tomorrow, *cher*. You're expected."

"No, thanks."

She tossed the card at him. Samedi tossed it right back.

"No choice."

He jerked the hat off his knee and stood. His body pulled into it until all that was left were his fingers clutching the brim. The hat fell to the sidewalk and then disappeared in a cloud of ash.

"Good to see you, too," Danni mumbled. She turned to Joto. His smile spanned ear to ear.

"What are you not telling me?" she asked.

Joto clapped her on both shoulders as laughter lifted his voice a few octaves.

"Magnolias! They're your *odè natirèl*, your natural scent. And, honey, you smell like royalty. Suspect the old boy wasn't quite ready to hear that just yet. Anything else happen last night?"

At least nothing else she wanted to tell him. Danni shook her head and let her eyes drift over the table. She stopped on the postcard. Something about it felt strangely familiar, for a swamp.

"Where is this?" she asked.

"Saint John's Bayou. Ghede turf. You don't show tomorrow night, you got a lot bigger problems than trying to get white folk to foot the bill for your orphanage."

"I really don't know how many more times I can tell you this, but–"

Joto's smile vanished. "Yeah, yeah. You don't want none of it. I got that much. But not wantin' don't make it not true. So, since I ain't gonna come up with a way to shake you free from your power in the next twenty-four hours, it probably wouldn't hurt you to do some workings before the *Jou*."

"Workings?"

"*Answer some prayers*," he said pointedly. He reached back behind his chair and then dropped a half-folded copy of the *Times-Picayune*.

The headline read: *Attack Occurs at Church Trunk-or-Treat*. It went on to mention an elderly woman had been knocked to the ground after what witnesses described as a filthy, homeless man ran through a parking lot.

"Police have no suspects, but they believe the man could be linked to the unexplained attacks earlier this week," she read. She looked up at Joto. "What unexplained attacks?"

"About a week ago, people started reporting attacks. At first, just a couple of college kids saying they were jumped by some guy that smelled like rotten meat. Cops figured they was drunk or something. Next time was a couple of Japanese tourists, said they were rushed by something they called *kyonshi*. Means living dead.

"Then I get a call this morning from a lady up in the Garden District. Said she was handing out candy last night when a real big kid came to the door dressed up like a zombie. Took her a minute to realize it was her husband."

Danni blew out a long breath. "So, some tourists get spooked and a guy plays a prank on his wife and suddenly I have to do, what? Mount up?"

"Her husband died three weeks ago. Cancer."

Danni laid her forehead against the table.

"Zombies," she mumbled. "Wonderful."

"Got another phone call this morning, too," Joto said. "From Sister Ned."

Danni lifted her head. "Is that so unusual? You do have a common interest where Michael is concerned."

"Twenty-four years I've known that boy, and there ain't one time I can recall that Sister Ned thought to speak to me first."

"And why was today so special?"

"Because she wanted to talk about *you*. Any idea why that might be?"

Plenty. Still, Danni shrugged. "What'd *she* say?"

Joto scrubbed his hand against the stubble around his mouth. "She's worried."

"She's a nun. She worries."

"Yeah? Then how come Gabriel turned up on my doorstep this morning asking me if you were dead? About the only reason he could figure you'd no-show last night after you promised to take them out for candy."

"What did you tell him?"

"Exactly what you tell a kid. The truth. That I didn't know, and I hadn't seen you. But you owe me sixteen bucks for one of them St. Jiji dolls, because that's what it took to get him to stop wailin' in the middle of my shop."

Danni spread her arms wide, crossed one leg over her knee, and shrugged. She'd never been comfortable in anything other than jeans and a t-shirt, but she had to give Samedi credit. The suit moved with her and formed a clean line from her knee to her ankle.

"Put it on my tab, yeah?"

Joto stared at her. "Yeah. And Sister Ned's right. You're all out of sorts." He gestured toward the newspaper. "I wrote down the widow's address there. Might want to go pay her a visit, at least offer her your condolences."

He backed away from the table but stopped when they were shoulder to shoulder, eye to eye.

"You decide you want some help with whatever else is going on, you give me a holler. 'Kay?"

Twenty

Turn left, count to thirty, turn left again. Repeat.

It had a rhythm to it as long as no one got in the way. Michael circled Danni's apartment with no idea what to say and less of an idea if he should even try. It was the same thing he'd done last time he was here. If it hadn't been for the roses wilting in the seat he wouldn't have stopped then.

The relief he'd felt when she wasn't home still weighed on him and kept him driving around the block. It was Cemetrie's words that made him consider what could happen if he stopped. There were just too many variables, and without a clearer idea of her state of mind, he could have been taking his last drive altogether.

Turn left, count to thirty. Rep–

A flash of red and white stepped off the curb directly in front of his truck. He slammed on the brakes. The red was long, flowing red hair. The same red hair he'd last seen at Del's store in the swamp. He threw the truck into park and climbed out.

"Catherine! It's Catherine, right? I almost hit you," he said.

The white in his initial vision was a dress the color of café au lait. The matching stiletto heels put her eye to eye with him. Catherine smiled as she pushed a pair of mirrored sunglasses down the bridge of her nose.

"Well, if it isn't the mysterious stranger! What are you doing here?"

"I'm moving back to town." He glanced back at Danni's apartment. "At least, I'm hoping to. Are you okay? Did I...umm...you look, that is...you look lovely."

"Thank you. And I'm fine," she said. "Not even a wrinkle. Close thing though, huh?"

"You're telling me. I didn't even see you."

He didn't see her car either, which meant she was on foot, though probably not for long in those heels.

"Do you live around here?" he asked.

"Looking for a friend, actually. Hoping she would have lunch with me." Catherine wet her lips. The soft, lilting accent dropped out of her voice. "Would you like to be my friend? For lunch, that is."

Michael swallowed hard and nodded.

"I know just the place," she said.

Thankfully, Catherine suggested they walk. He had no desire to explain the condition of his truck, much less the entirety of his belongings in the bed. He parked in an adjoining lot and met her at the corner.

"Are you sure you want to walk?" he asked and glanced down at her shoes. "I mean, those can't be comfortable."

She slipped her arm inside his. "This will do nicely. So, tell me everything there is to know about you."

A blush warmed his cheeks. "Not much to tell, I'm afraid."

"Oh, now I don't believe that. Let's see…" The weight of her eyes and the proximity of her voice only made him blush more. "You're about thirty-four?"

"Thirty-five."

She nodded and continued. "Your accent says you're a native, but then what's a good Catholic like you doing unmarried?"

Michael glanced at his hand where it rested against her arm. Right. No ring.

"I'll give you not married, but how did you know I'm Catholic?"

"The newspaper in the swamp. You flipped all the way to the back page to read a story about nuns, so I'm going to say you're a Mount Carmel boy."

"Maybe I was just reading the paper," he suggested.

"Maybe I was just guessing."

The sidewalk ended abruptly at an orange construction barrier. On the other side, a cement truck dumped fresh concrete into a form. The men lifted their heads from their work and blew sharp whistles in her direction. Catherine either didn't notice or was too accustomed to them to care. Her attention stayed trained on the side of Michael's face even as she stopped and motioned him toward an open doorway.

"The Joint?" he asked. "Are you sure you want to go in here wearing white?"

Catherine grinned at him. "Mind your own shirt."

The sweet smell of barbecue and slow-roasted beef was so thick he could practically taste it. It took him a second to place the earthier scent inside it. He pulled out a chair for her. The cool waves of her hair fell across his hands, and suddenly it was *all* he could smell.

He cleared his throat and moved to take the chair across from her. "I haven't been here in *years*. All new digs now. Real tables, chairs and everything."

"All new grease stains, too. You know the rules," she said with mock seriousness. "If it ain't messy, you're doing it wrong."

A heavyset black girl brought menus to their table, but Catherine reached out and patted her arm.

"Just bring us two baskets of the special, won't you?"

The young girl didn't even nod as she turned and walked back to the kitchen.

"New place isn't exactly friendlier," Michael said and then brightened. "So, did you buy the boat?"

"We worked out a deal," she said. "But I'm having it brought up here. You were right. Too much nothing in the swamp."

"There's only so much peace and quiet a body can stand."

"Truer than you know, Michael. Truer than you know."

Their food arrived in red plastic baskets, accompanied by oversized plastic mugs of tea. They were both quiet while they ate. Michael paused once or twice to check her face. Take away the barbecue sauce and the checked table cloth, and she could have been a lioness tearing the meat off the bones in delicate bites, yet she wasn't wearing any of it. He frowned at the sauce speckled across his shirt.

Catherine finished ahead of him and sat back. "So, what does 'hoping to' move back to town mean? Looking for work?"

Michael nodded. "Though I'm not too worried about that at the moment. Something'll come up. First, I have to find a place to live."

"Perhaps I can help. I have a guest house near the back of my property. It's really not much, but I don't use it. I only hesitate to offer because it hasn't been cleaned out in a while." She pulled a card from her small clutch. "My address and number."

Michael scrubbed the sauce from his hand with several napkins before reaching for it. Their hands touched. A small electrical charge raced up his arm and across his chest. The hair on his neck stood up, and he dropped the card. It fluttered down into her plate.

"I-I'm sorry," he stuttered. "Clumsy of me. Static, I guess."

He pinched the corner of the card and tugged it away from the pool of barbecue sauce.

"This is very kind of you." Michael rubbed at the dull ache in his chest as he turned the card over in his fist. "This is... you live in the Garden District?"

Not just the Garden District. The 1500 block of Harmony, which, as long as he could remember, had only contained one house. Most of the homes in the Garden District were part of walking tours. 1500 Harmony never had been. The wall that surrounded it made sure it would never be.

"Correct me if I'm wrong, but isn't that the old Daye Plantation?" he asked.

Catherine lifted a single eyebrow, reached across the table, and tapped her fingernail against the name at the top of the card. Catherine *Daye*.

"Oh," Michael said.

He considered telling her that he and Joey had attempted to scale the wall once when they were boys. His childhood memory recalled the slick limestone as flawless and hard. They never made it farther than the first few feet. While the mystery of finally seeing it excited him the same way it always had, his adult mind knew what walls like that meant, to the people outside as well as in. So, he said, "I wouldn't want to impose."

Catherine frowned hard.

"What I mean is I can't afford much in rent at the moment," he said.

The smile crept back into her voice but never reached her eyes. Her hand dove into the clutch and returned with a slim, silver case.

"Don't worry about it," she said. "You clean it out, we'll call it even. Believe me when I say it would be nice to have someone around. Cigarette?"

He shook his head but watched as she lit one for herself. The first cloud of smoke was thick and smelled faintly of cloves before she sucked it in with a sharp breath.

It was much lighter on the return trip.

She held up the smoldering end. "A parting gift from my husband. I always hated the smell, until he was gone." She exhaled again. Another stream of smoke disappeared when it reached the lazy rotation of the overhead fan. "I imagine he and his new girlfriend will be *very* happy together."

"I'm sorry to hear it," he said.

Suddenly the car, the boat, and the overtly flirtatious behavior made a lot more sense. Michael stared at the card in his hands.

"This would be very helpful, but I'm not sure it would be appropriate," he said.

"Because I'm recently divorced, or because I'm a woman?"

Michael swallowed but didn't answer immediately. Catherine cocked an elbow against the empty seat beside her and continued.

"Do you know what is inappropriate, Michael? My family and I spent our lives giving to this city. Schools, hospitals, orphanages. *Everything*. And for a while, my husband and I were *the* power couple of New Orleans. Then, he trips over some rotten little whore and the empire we built turns to ash."

She tapped the end of her cigarette over the pile of licked-clean bones and stood, rising with a cloud of smoke. She tucked her clutch underneath her arm.

"The address is there on the card, should you change your mind."

"Shouldn't I give you a lift back?" he asked.

Catherine was already gone. The screen door swung back and struck hard against the jamb. He stared at the business card and swallowed the lump in his throat, but all he could taste was her perfume.

Twenty-One

Ruth Cazneaux's hair was more salt than cinnamon, and her voice more sadness than fear. She took up all of the double-door on a house that looked like it had been dropped out of *Gone with the Wind*.

Billowing cushions of orange and red mums crowded the banquette closest to the street while wisteria and ivy competed for claim to the second floor balconies. Center to it all was the misty eye-widow, whose weak sobs only deepened when she saw Danni.

"You're going to think I'm as crazy as the rest of them!" she cried.

Danni searched the grand foyer behind her. A place that big had to have maids, right? It looked empty.

"Can I come in?" Danni asked. "Maybe make you some tea?"

Ms. Cazneaux waved her across the threshold and then farther down the hallway beyond. "The kitchen's that way, dear."

The kitchen matched the rest of the house. White

pine cabinets spanned the length of five of the six walls. The last led into a breakfast nook that could seat at least twelve. The marble countertops were bare except for a neat row of hand-thrown crockery in descending size. The last one read: TEA.

Danni scuttled around for a few minutes, finding cups and saucers and finally a tray to set them on. She carried it to the adjoining parlor where Ms. Cazneaux was sitting in a wingback chair dotting fresh tears with a linen handkerchief.

"Oh, thank you, you dear girl. How perfectly sweet you are."

Danni settled across from her. "You called a friend of mine this morning. Joto?"

If the name rang a bell, Ms. Cazneaux's face didn't show it. Instead, she reached for a pair of tiny silver tongs and dropped three sugar cubes into her tea.

"Jasper and I were married for forty-three years this past May."

She dug around inside a canvas sewing bag beside her chair and returned with a thick photo album. She passed it into Danni's hands and began to work through the pages one by one.

Forty-three years passed in three painfully slow hours. Somewhere around one o'clock, Danni's arm went numb, forcing her to adjust, which started year twenty-six over again.

Ruth and Jasper had nine children. Jasper Junior, Marie, Laurine, Julian, Samuel, Della-Sue, twins Charlene and Charlie, and Rae. She'd also miscarried four others.

She and Jasper loved to travel and garden, though where they found the time, Danni couldn't guess.

Jasper was a fourth generation cobbler and a first generation American, borne of French immigrants. He was ambitious, which was one of many things that attracted Ruth right from the beginning, and in 1984, a cute little shoe company owned by a man named Nick bought Jasper's design for cloud shoes, which had a pocket of air in the center of the sole.

It didn't take Danni long to figure out Ms. Cazneaux was talking about Nike, and Jasper's shoes had been the prototype for Air Jordans.

The sun was slipping toward the horizon when they reached Jasper's final days. An orange glow had filled the parlor, drawing long, somber shadows across the floor.

"He struggled for so long," Ms. Cazaneaux said with a sniffle. "I just couldn't stand to see him like that anymore. So, I got his favorite pillow from the upstairs guest bed room. He always said it just slept better than any other pillow he'd ever found. We bought it at a little linen shop just outside Beeker, Indiana. We were on our way to Columbus, Ohio to see our daughter—"

"Della-Sue," Danni said.

Ms. Cazneaux's face lit for a brief second. "Yes. Della-Sue. She's my sweetest girl."

"But a bit of a busy body," Danni finished.

"Oh, so much. Girl couldn't keep a secret if you sewed her lips shut with a dull needle." She took a slow sip of tea. "So, I took Jasper his favorite pillow. And then I smothered him with it."

Danni lost grip on the photo album. "I'm sorry. Did you just say…"

"I smothered him. He was mostly gone anyway, I just helped him along. It isn't wrong. In fact, not doing anything is just cruel. You'd do the same, too, if your husband was dying. Oh, uh, what's his name, dear?"

"Who's name?" Danni asked.

"Oh, your husband's."

"I'm not married."

For the first time all afternoon, she eyed Danni with clear suspicion. "By your age I'd already had five children. You're almost too far gone to hope for one that doesn't come out retarded."

Danni kind of wanted to laugh. Then cry. Then scream. But she just sat there, unblinking, stunned.

Finally, she cleared her throat and asked, "So, when Jasper showed up last night, do you think he was here looking for revenge?"

The widow pursed her lips and looked out to the street. "You know, I suppose he probably was."

Twenty-Two

1500 Harmony looked exactly like Michael remembered. He followed the high wall all the way around the block, feeling just like he had as a child. The only difference now was he wasn't just a kid from the Ninth Ward trying to get a peek at how the other half lived. He had no place else to go.

Michael shook his head at the thought. That wasn't entirely true. After lunch with Catherine, he'd made six more trips around Danni's apartment before deciding she wasn't home anyway. He'd try again tomorrow. Still, none of that stopped him from returning to the convent. He had no doubt Mother Superior or Joto or even Zed would offer him everything he needed. So, why *had* he called the number on Catherine's card? Pride? He shook his head again. That wasn't exactly the truth, either.

A pair of arched gates marked the entrance. He pressed the intercom button. The gates swung inward as the scent of honeysuckle and lilac rolled out to greet him. He shifted the truck and pulled inside.

The tires crunched up the cinder driveway past rows of granite statues, but he noticed quickly they were a little more than garden art. Each sculpted white body was nude, faceless, and locked in a perpetual embrace. He smiled inwardly. They spoke of true love and devotion, even without expression.

Michael's smile faded as he moved farther up the driveway. What started as tasteful nudes became progressively more obscene. He saw men on their knees, bound and broken as white-skinned women rode them, two or three at a time. He had a hard time not looking at them or feeling the horror they couldn't express, until finally he just wanted to be past them altogether.

The driveway reached a short brick promenade that led to a pair of massive wood doors. Ivy draped over the sweeping rooflines of a house that was even more imposing than the gate had been. Three floors of early colonnade arches and columns were whitewashed in their original style.

A bellman in a white coat waited at the edge of the stairs. His eyes were the color of spring grass, vibrant and wet. He reached for the truck's door handle before Michael had shifted into park.

"Ms. Daye is expecting you, sir," he said in a mellow voice that reminded Michael of an early Shirley Temple talkie, as if everything around him should have been black and white.

A split second later, the door opened and Catherine stepped out to greet him. Her feet were bare, but she still managed to look elegant in a simple, white cotton sundress.

Her hair bounced along behind her as if she'd recently brushed the curls out into loose waves. She trotted down the short stairs and kissed his cheek.

"I'm pleased," she said simply. She pulled back to see his face. "Something wrong?"

Michael glanced back toward the driveway, relieved that he could see none of the statues through the foliage.

"Your art is a little intense," he said.

She frowned. "I'm sorry if they bothered you. There's a separate entrance off the gardens you can use. You won't have to see them again. Maurice?"

The bell hop hadn't ever stepped away, but he did straighten when she said his name.

"Take Michael's truck around back," she said. "And make sure he's able to come and go as he pleases."

"Ma'am."

Michael watched Maurice and the truck roll back down the driveway. When it was out of sight, Catherine nudged her hand into his.

"Let me show you the guest house," she said.

He'd always imagined 1500 Harmony as big, but it seemed nearly twice as large inside as it did from the outside. He struggled to keep up as his eyes were pulled in a dozen different directions: tennis courts, a swimming pool, and even an adjoining sauna, all built from white granite.

Like the front, wide columns supported a massive balcony across the back of the house. The windows had been left open, sucking the sheer cream curtains out in the breeze. The minute he saw it he knew it was her bedroom, no doubt decorated in rich whites and reds just like her car and her outfits and *her*.

The path ended at a high trellis wall. Catherine continued through a narrow gap between the greenery, turning left and then right as she moved forward.

"It's like a meditation maze," he said.

"Exactly."

"I'm not sure I'll be able to find my way out."

"The trick is to concentrate and keep moving. Trust your instincts and the path will lead you to where you need to be."

Catherine's fingers caressed a ruby flower blooming from the garden wall. She turned the flower out for him to see and drew a deep breath. Color flushed across her cheeks but faded just as quickly.

"The Blackout Lily," she said. "They grew almost exclusively in Charlemagne's garden. He used to gift them to the artisans to make the most vibrant paint."

Blood-red petals curled out from a center of streaking black. Water, pooled at its heart, spilled down to the long, spindled tips. Michael wasn't sure what was more intoxicating: their smell or their history painted by the dulcet sound of her voice.

The entire trellis wall was covered in blooms. Just like the statues, the longer he watched them, the less lovely they were. Each needled tip rose and fell together, as if the whole wall was breathing. He blinked, but when he looked again, the flowers were only moving in a soft wind.

His truck was already parked in the cut out of a narrow driveway of the guest house. It was draped in moss and surrounded by gnarled, winding pine trees. Catherine pushed the double doors, letting clean natural light into the front room.

"Clear out anything that you don't want," she said. "Just stack it by the door and my men will haul it off."

The main room was one long expanse with doors at either end, and the ceilings were twenty feet high, accented by palm frond fans. Catherine guided his attention with her finger.

"The first door leads to a small kitchen, everything you should need. I had Maurice stock the cupboard and refrigerator. There is a small dining area as well, but let me show you my favorite room."

Michael heard distant, rushing water. The sound got louder as Catherine pushed back another set of double doors. Wood floors gave way to smoother river stones. A mirror ran the length of the wall above a green marble counter, making it feel twice as large as it was.

Michael followed Catherine around the corner. His jaw dropped open involuntarily. The river stones continued to a shallow pond surrounded by a rock wall, in which a series of setbacks formed natural places to sit or stand. A heavy waterfall rushed down over all of it.

"Want to see the fun part?" she asked.

She tapped a command into a recessed panel on the wall. A perfect summer storm erupted from somewhere high in the ceiling. The water splashed off the rocks into the pond that quickly rose to cover Catherine's feet.

Michael followed the flow of water in reverse, tracing the rivulets up across the muscled calves of her legs to the soaked bodice of her sundress. She raised her arms over her head, eyes sparkling.

Was it rude to stare, or not to? How about to drool?

"Breathtaking," he whispered. He coughed and tried to shake the fuzz from his brain. "But you're, umm, getting very wet."

"I had to change clothes, anyway. Places to be."

Catherine pulled her hair into a bundle and wrung out the water over the drain.

"I'm sorry to have kept you. You're right. This is amazing. All of it." His eyes stopped moving when they found her face. "*Beautiful.*"

"Glad you finally noticed. I'll show myself out, although I can't wait to hear what you think of the bedroom."

There was wicked glee in her smile as she pushed the trim beside the window. The entire wall swung out into the garden and then closed behind her.

Michael stared at the backlit panel on the wall and tried to find the sequence of keys to turn off the water, or at least turn it into a cold shower. Then, because she had mentioned it, he made the bedroom his next stop.

The four-poster canopy bed was big enough to sleep at least six people comfortably. A matching pair of dressers sat on either side, but everything he owned would easily fit in one drawer. His eyes followed the wall tapestries up to the center of the ceiling where they were bunched around a crystal chandelier. The effect gave the room the air of a Bedouin tent or a bordello somewhere in the Quarter.

The thought stayed with him as he moved back to

the main room. The late afternoon shadows played across the floor, but even that was a predefined effect, he realized. He stepped over it to read it properly.

Capon vive longtemps.

He followed the slivers of sunlight back up through the French doors to where the trellis wall had been trained into a mirror image of the shadow on the floor.

"The coward lives a long time," Maurice said from behind him.

Michael turned sharply and found the man standing in the door, just off the center of the light.

"I'm sorry?"

Maurice pointed to the words at Michael's feet. "*Capon vive longtemps.* The coward lives a long time. Ma'am said I should come down, see if you'll be needin' anything else for the night."

Michael stared back at the message on the floor. It felt oddly personal, if not intended solely for him.

"Has this always been here?" he asked.

"Long as I have," Maurice answered. "The Daye family motto, I do believe. Anything else I can do for you, sir?"

Michael shook his head. "No," he said, but then added, "thank you, Mau—"

But the man was already gone. Michael sat on the edge of an overstuffed divan and scrubbed his face with his hands.

He was a long way from the swamp, that was for sure.

Twenty-Three

Ms. Cazneaux agreed to let Danni sit on the front porch to wait for Jasper. She pushed the door tightly on the latch only to return a few minutes later with a crystal bowl heavier than all the candy inside it.

"Well, if you're going to hang around, you might as well just," she told Danni and headed back indoors.

The children came in waves. Popular costumes were tied at Iron Man and Spider Man for boys, and princesses and brides for girls. It was a subtle truth that seemed about as natural as rainstorms in the summer: all boys dreamt of being heroes, while little girls just wanted to be beautiful.

Danni bounced on the edge of an Adirondack chair and unwrapped a lollipop. What had she been when she was a child? She thought she remembered something about a mermaid, but dismissed it as a memory superimposed by the collection of Ariel's she'd already seen.

Then she began to wonder: what had Michael been? She knew he'd grown up in the Ninth Ward, poor and predominantly alone thanks to a single mother with a half-dozen problems of her own. Still, she tried to imagine what he might have looked like as a boy. Copper-red hair. Big, doe-eyes. Freckled face. She smiled. He would have made a great cowboy.

Another hour passed. The younger children tapered off and eventually even the rowdier groups began to subside. Exterior lights switched off, leaving her alone with the crunch of discarded wrappers tossed on the breeze.

When Ms. Cazneaux's light went out, Danni set the bowl on the patio and stretched. Jasper was a no-show, which meant she'd wasted the better part of the day listening to the history of the Cazneauxs for nothing. At least she could tell Joto she tried.

Danni stopped at the gate and looked back at the house. Maybe it was worth knocking, if only to let Ms. Cazneaux know she was leaving. She moved back to the door and lifted the knocker. The door crept open on its own. She reached back for the knife in her pocket and stepped over the threshold.

"Ms. Cazneaux?"

A clock chimed off the half hour farther down the hall. Danni made a quick sweep of the kitchen, the parlor, and all the adjoining rooms. Empty.

"Ms. Cazneaux? I'm walking through your house. Please don't jump out and hit me with anything."

She stared up the master staircase and added under her breath, "Or smother me with a pillow."

The stairs were marble, which made climbing them in silence easy. At the top, the hallway split off in two directions. Something thudded against the floor off to her left. Danni pressed her back against the wall and slid along as quietly as she could.

The eyes of the Cazneaux twins, Charlene and Charlie, followed her. *Because they were so photogenic.* Although Danni suspected it was more because Ruth liked to see them in matching outfits. The entire wall was covered with their photos and ordered by age, infant to adult, just like her crockware.

Danni peeked into the master bedroom. A tall, lanky shadow was positioned over the bed while Ms. Cazneaux's feet kicked wildly beneath the blanket. Jasper moaned, but it didn't sound right. His breath didn't quite reach his vocal cords and the only sound he could manage was a heavy gurgle.

Danni leapt around the door and ran at him, full speed. Her shoulder struck first, sending him cleanly into the wall. Ms. Cazneaux jerked the pillow from her face and gasped big gulps of air. She clapped her hands together twice and the lights blazed around the room.

"Son of a bitch!" Danni clamped her hand over her mouth and swallowed the rising gag. "I thought you said he died of cancer!"

"Oh, *Jasper.*"

Danni staggered back, eyes fixed on Jasper's face. Or at least, what was left of it. Her leg caught a dressing stool near the foot of the bed. She landed hard on her ass. The knife tumbled out of her hand.

Jasper was already on his feet and following her. The same stool caught him at the shin. Danni rolled, and he landed squarely on her back. She tried to ignore the smell and the sound of the air being sucked through the open cavity in the center of his face. Definitely not cancer!

"Jasper! Jasper, honey! Please!"

Whatever Ms. Cazneaux was doing only caused Jasper to flail more, pressing Danni down against the carpet. She clawed at the edge of the bed until her fingers found the sharp end of the blade. She clinched her hand around it, regretted it a second later when fresh blood made the handle slick, and then swept it back and drove the business end into the top of Jasper's head.

Nothing happened. Danni jerked the knife back and tried again. Still nothing.

"Oh, please stop! Please! You're hurting him!" Ms. Cazneaux wailed.

Danni pulled her arms beneath her, braced her palms against the floor, and drove up hard as she twisted. Jasper rolled away from her. Danni scrambled to her feet.

"What the hell happened to him?" she screamed.

"Well, about fifteen years ago—"

"No, no. We don't have time for that." She wrenched her hand down on Ms. Cazneaux's shoulders. "*Why* is his face like that?"

Jasper let loose of a wet roar, or as much of one as he could muster. His mouth just kind of hung, ineffectually, from his bottom jaw. The only thing that made it seem slightly less gory was the lack of blood. Whatever had been done to him had happened *after* he died.

"Oh, honey. You're hurt."

Ms. Cazneaux reached for him. Danni struggled to keep her back.

"He's way past hurt, lady. Just, stop!"

Jasper stopped. The knife stood out of the back of his skull, the handle caked with hair and thicker things. He swayed in place, but didn't take another step forward.

"Jasper," Danni said softly. "Come here."

He took one shambling step and then another. He was about to take a third when Danni issued another command.

"Stop."

He did.

"Put your left arm out."

He did that, too.

"Put your right arm out."

His right arm floated up from his side.

"Shake them all about." That, he did, too. "Okay, Jasper. Stop."

"What did you do to him?" Ms. Cazneaux demanded.

"What did I do to him? What did *you* do to him?"

"I-I just wanted a nice, open casket," the old woman insisted. "It's all I wanted. The last chance we would be together for a nice family photo. But Charlie, he just refused.

"The night before the funeral, he took Jasper's best shotgun. Oh, the one he got in Jacksonville. Mississippi, not Florida. They only made five-hundred of them, and Jasper loved his guns—"

"Whoa! Wait a minute. Are you telling me Charlie shot him in the face after you smothered him, which was *before* he really died of cancer?"

Ms. Cazneaux nodded. Danni looked back at Jasper and frowned.

"You poor bastard," she whispered.

Jasper gurgled.

Danni righted the foot stool at the edge of the bed and kicked a few other things out of the way, making a clear path to the door. She backed away a few steps, motioning Jasper to follow.

"But you can't just take him!" Ms. Cazneaux yelled.

"I can and I'm going to. And you should think about seeing someone, a shrink or a priest or something because *this* is not your biggest problem."

Twenty-Four

"You're lucky, you know? I wouldn't even be doing this if it wasn't Halloween."

Jasper slogged along down the center of the street on what Danni hoped was the fastest path back to his grave. If he heard, let alone understood her, she couldn't tell.

They crossed a few more streets and ended up at the white-brick wall around Lafayette Cemetery. Jasper stayed straight until he walked into it, then half-slid his way down to the iron gates. He bounced against them, letting them catch and toss him back into the street. Danni grabbed his shoulder.

"Hang on a second. Stop. Stop!" He stopped. "Okay, now move that way."

He staggered to the side, and Danni tugged on the lock. Surprisingly, it popped open and the gate swung back.

A few steps inside the cemetery the air shifted and vanished, sucked out and replaced with nothing. The Baron Cemetrie coughed beside her.

"Fine night for a stroll," he said, but it wasn't

spoken like an invitation to do so.

His white shirt was buttoned up to his throat and held closed by a silver string tie. He kicked back the brim of his hat, moved to the center of the path, and crossed his wrists over the silver shovel head at the end of his cane.

Danni pointed at the fence. "The lock was open."

"You're a harbinger of the dead, sister. Ain't a lock made by man that'll keep you off this ground. That'd be *my* job." Cemetrie flexed and stretched his spine. "So, what business you got here?"

"Zombie." Danni turned back to the gate and let out a frustrated sigh. "Jasper, come."

Jasper shuffled his way forward. Cemetrie extended the cane and stopped him with a hard push to the shoulder. His eyes thinned down to white slits as he inspected Jasper head to toe and back again.

"Get this *thing* out of his head," he said.

Danni set one hand on Jasper's shoulder and got a good grip on the knife. She tried to jerk it straight out the way it had gone in, which kind of worked. The blade pulled free with a wet sucking sound, but it caused Jasper's head to roll back so his only remaining eye was looking at her. His flapping jaws made incomplete sounds.

"Is he trying to talk?"

"That's what happens when you animate them with your own blood."

"I didn't animate him at all!"

Cemetrie frowned and stared at the shallow cut on her hand. Danni spat into her palms and rubbed them together.

"He attacked me first," she said.

"Just trying to find his way back home, I suspect."

"Well, he certainly found that."

"Not his house."

Cemetrie waved them both to follow as he moved deeper down the path. They turned left and then right through the tight maze of mausoleums. He stopped halfway down the next row where one of the stone doors was cocked against the lintel. The monogram above it read: CAZNEAUX.

"His *home*," Cemetrie said.

Jasper double-timed it to squeeze through the gap. A silver light flashed around the door behind him and went back into place, perfectly undisturbed.

"Does that happen often?" Danni asked.

"When conditions are right. *You* ought to be more careful."

She scrubbed the guck off her knife with the edge of her suit. There hadn't been time to change before heading to the Cazneaux's. While she'd been comfortable enough to have forgotten it, she just felt stupidly overdressed now.

"I told you, he attacked me. Besides, a zombie is a bit outside of my magic ability."

"Eh, we ain't in the business of raisin' them anyway. Now, you take their soul, lay them down proper?" Cemetrie snapped. "That's what being a Ghede is all about. Go on, try it out."

Danni's mouth went dry. "Try *what* exactly?"

He rocked back on his heels and opened his arms to the mausoleums around them.

"Got that pretty little knife and a whole kindergarten in your pocket. Why don't you give it a whirl? Go on, now. I ain't one to offer lagniappe often."

What exactly did he expect? Danni stared at the knife in her hands and shook her head.

"I don't know what I'm supposed to be doing."

"Because you're thinkin' about it. You have to feel it in your bones. Down in the cockles."

"Am I making a zombie or playing jazz?"

"You're takin' someone's soul, sister. Takin' them home. What do you think all this second line stuff is about? Good music to sleep to? *They're calling us out*, askin' us to see them on their way."

Danni chuckled. She'd lived in New Orleans almost ten years and still hadn't been to a proper second line. Zulu, the Muses, sure. But a real brass band march to a grave and back? The idea had always unsettled her.

Her fingers traced the blade of the knife, trickling over the runes etched into the handle. As long as she had had it, she'd never truly known what they meant. If she was a loa now, wouldn't they make sense? Shouldn't she be able to read them, or at least feel something of their meaning when she touched them? All she felt was cold, empty. Lonely.

She thought of Ruth Cazneaux and her subtle, Garden District madness. Alone in that house with four decades of photos of a man who, for all her faults, she loved enough to kill. It wasn't logical, but at least it made sense.

The blade began to warm against her palm. The

light swelled until it was all she could see. It folded in on itself and then died, but before it vanished completely, Danni swore she heard Jasper's full voice in her head.

Akeyi yo, Jiji.

A noise broke the ensuing silence, like a match head pulled over the strike. To her left, Samedi appeared in a red blaze of smoke and ash. LaCroix wasn't far behind and clouded together at Cemetrie's right.

"*Brothers!*" Cemetrie greeted.

LaCroix was the first to speak. His voice was more melodic than Cemetrie's, nowhere near as deep as Samedi's, and edged with irritation.

"We thought we might be missing something important. Didn't we, brother?"

"Indeed," Samedi growled.

His amber eyes were fixed on the knife. Danni blew out a shaky breath and took a step back, closer to the gates. She doubted she could outrun any of them, but it made her feel better.

"There's no need to be scared, sister," Cemetrie assured her.

Danni forced a smile. "Halloween. Lafayette Cemetery. Three Ghede. Can't blame a girl for being a bit on edge."

"*Four,*" he corrected. "There are four Ghede here tonight."

Though for whose benefit he mentioned it, she couldn't tell. While LaCroix seemed to take it as a reminder and sent a gracious nod in her direction, Samedi only spit.

"*Pitit fi bata!*" he said.

The words rolled around inside her brain, familiar but not. She knew they were Creole, and his tone suggested they were an insult. She just wished she knew enough to return them. As she wished it, the words came together inside her mind as if she had always known them.

"Wait a minute. Did you just call *me* a bastard?"

"Aye," Samedi said.

"I didn't ask for this! I don't even want it!"

Samedi laughed, loud and long. It cut off as briskly as it started, and his voice poured out against her skin like something liquid and hot.

"*Oh,* you want it, *cher.* The power of the Ghede has tasted you as surely as you have tasted it, rolled in it like a happy little bitch. You are as selfish and hungry as the rest of us. Your nuns know it. Your children know it. Michael knew it. And that's exactly why he left."

The knife lanced through the air even before Danni realized she'd taken the swing or heard the shapeless scream that accompanied it. A red line slashed across Samedi's chest. He staggered and ran his fingers across the wound. Blood, real blood, dripped down his fingertips.

LaCroix gasped. "*Mon Dieu.*"

Samedi snarled and pulled in a lungful of air. The buttons on his jacket sprung open just before he exhaled. The flame behind his breath quivered the air between them and landed hard against her chest. Danni choked and dropped to her knees.

"*Hold!*" Cemetrie yelled. "You two will not be makin' a mess of my grounds, ya hear?"

Danni waited for Samedi, while he seemed to be

164

waiting for her.

She nodded. "Agreed."

"Aye."

"Good. Now, I believe we all have a party to prepare for." Cemetrie waved a soft hand in the air. In the distance, Danni heard the shrill squeal of the gate opening again. "Sister, a good evening to you."

Even if it hadn't been her cue to leave, she had no more interest in staying than Samedi seemed in her being there. She gave him one last look and trotted away on the exact path they'd come in on. By the time she reached the gate, Samedi's voice had risen again, but this time it was a howl. It was sad, almost mournful, and filled her eyes with tears.

She knew that sound, that pain. That *loss*. She felt it every time she looked at the nail around her neck or thought of Michael.

Danni ran, and she didn't stop until she was back inside her apartment.

Twenty-Five

By evening, the tension had finally released from Michael's neck. The shower had helped, but the wine hadn't hurt either. Still, luxury felt strange, almost wrongfully indulgent. Or maybe that was just his conscience. He settled into an oversized leather chair, a glass in one hand and a thin book in the other: *The Seventh Book of Moses*.

He'd been reading for several hours, working to decipher the arcane take on Hebrew, but decided it would have been satirical in any language.

"The Terrible Hero," he read aloud. "Well, that's one way to look at it, I guess."

Catherine's hand slipped forward over his shoulder and withdrew the book. "How far did you get?"

Michael jumped. The glass tipped in his hand and the wine spilled onto the arm of the chair.

"I'm sorry," he said. "You startled me."

She swept a finger across the leather and through the spilled wine before sucking it between her lips.

"Mmm… Chateau Margaux. Not my most expensive vintage, but definitely one of my best."

Michael shifted in the chair and tried to keep his tone light. "How'd you get in? I thought I locked the door."

Catherine laughed softly and sat on the ottoman just beyond his feet. Her robe wasn't much more than two long, gossamer pieces of fabric tied at her waist. Beneath it, her simple black teddy was just long enough to cover the most intimate parts of her.

"Pour me a glass?" she asked.

Michael went to the kitchen but took a minute before returning. He flipped on the faucet and threw some cold water into his face. The haze cleared from his eyes, but the tension had worked its way back to his jaw. She wasn't the type of woman who went unnoticed. In fact, he was betting she was unaccustomed to being anything less than the center of attention. It was why she was here now, wearing *that*, that made it infinitely more difficult to accommodate her.

He made the slow walk back to the living room and handed her the wine.

"How was your evening?" he asked.

She swirled the first notes off the top and set her bottom lip against the paper-thin rim. "Boring. Yours?"

"Peaceful and comfortable, thanks to you. Your library is pretty extensive and eclectic." He picked up the book just to have something else between them. "This one certainly is a fresh look at some old knowledge. One I've been paying more attention to lately."

Catherine uncrossed and crossed her knees, one

over the other, but she never stopped moving. As soon as she'd settle, she'd shift again, and the slip barely moved with her.

"Since you stopped being a priest?" she asked.

He wasn't sure why, but the question surprised him, especially now.

She shrugged. "There are a number of people in the Quarter who still remember the good Father Michael. I only had to ask."

"You could have asked me."

Her smile switched off. "I did, didn't I?"

He supposed she had. He sighed. "It's not something I usually open with."

"I was the same way when my marriage failed. It took me a while to admit it, even to myself."

"Tell me about him," Michael said. "Were you married long?"

"Long enough for it to mean something. That it should have meant something. But I realize, I stopped loving him a long time ago, and I'm *far* better off without him."

Catherine twisted the glass by the stem, watching the wine coat the inside.

"Your turn. Why did you leave the priesthood?"

Michael chuckled and took a sip of his own wine. "I fell in love."

"What's her name?"

"Danielle," he said and then shook his head. "Danni. She'd probably kill me if she heard me call her that."

Catherine frowned. "She sounds lovely."

"You remind me of her," Michael said suddenly. Catherine's frown only deepened. "It's a compliment. She's fierce, powerful. Passionate. It's probably why I'm–"

He stopped and stared down at his hands before looking at her again.

"Why I'm attracted to you," he finished.

Her smile came back, cautious at first, but growing infinitely bolder as she slid toward him. Michael pressed his open palms against her bare shoulders.

"Catherine…"

Her hand made another sweeping pass through the puddle of wine and then rose to his lips. His mouth went dry. The moment seemed to span across several minutes of slow, internal debate before resolving to a half inch of forward movement. His mouth closed around her fingertips.

It was the same flavors, grape and flowers, caramel and acid but with an earthy tone that sent a spark through his senses. He leaned into it, drawing in one knuckle and then two. He pulled long and hard against her skin, thought he heard her gasp, but got lost in the feel of her free hand weaving its way into the hair at the back of his neck.

He pulled her fingers from his mouth and kissed the pulse point of her wrist. It throbbed against his lips, which only made him hungrier. Her free hand guided his mouth to hers, lips parted enough he could see the dark warm center of her mouth. He smelled the wine on her breath a second before he tasted it again.

Her tongue moved past his lips with certain skill,

like warm velvet against the roof of his mouth. Michael drew her into his lap, and felt her hair spill forward to cover their faces, a curtain pulled around them, blocking out the cooler air until all he could smell was her perfume. He cupped both hands against her bottom jaw, letting his thumbs run over her bare neck. He followed the lean lines of skin across her collarbone and pushed the straps down her shoulder.

He wanted to see her, all of her. It wasn't a logical desire so much as a vital one. He *needed* to touch every inch of her.

Waves of electricity burned from his lips to his toes and bounced back again, meeting a second wave when they both reached his chest. The shock ripped his mouth from hers. Catherine fell backwards and landed hard against the floor.

Suddenly, he was fighting for a full breath, but every effort sent pain spiking into the center of his chest. He leaned forward and tried to concentrate on breathing, in and out, until he could finally do it without saying the words. He pressed a hand against his mouth and found her smell.

Catherine glared at him from the floor, but when he reached for her again, she jerked back.

"I'm sorry," he said. "I-I didn't mean to…did you feel–"

"You throw me on the floor?"

She shoved herself to her feet and smoothed the wrinkles out of her slip. He stood.

"I am so sorry. I guess I'm not very good at this sort

of thing. And I think I gave you the wrong impression. I'm not, that is…you're beautiful, but—

"I'll go," he offered quickly.

She gave him an apologetic smile. "No, Michael. It was my fault. The wine."

The glass was empty, still rocking against the floor where it had fallen. He watched it seep into the thick carpet, too stunned to think of how to stop it.

His head swam. Catherine's face shifted in and out of focus until it was impossible to hold himself up any longer. He was falling, but it felt more like melting, pooling, and finally drifting across a slicker, softer heat. His face touched cool silk. A pillow. He heard rushing water. The bathroom. He saw the curtains drawn to the center of the chandelier, blacks and reds spiraling out just like the Blackout Lilies in her garden.

"Sleep," she said.

Sleep. He tried to repeat the word, but it faded long before it made it past his lips.

Twenty-Six

"I'm telling you Joto, Samedi looked stunned."

Danni waited for the signal to change at Decatur and Dumaine where the air was thick and sweet with the smell of pralines. She stopped at the back of Evan's Creole Candy in a cloud of kitchen exhaust, as much to enjoy the scent as scan the waterfront.

Joto sounded flat and far away inside the cellphone, but she didn't miss the note of worry in his voice.

"I'll bet he did."

"What's wrong now?" she asked.

"Nothin'. Nothin'. Well, somethin'. You drew blood, darlin'. He provoked you and you drew blood. That's just bad form."

"I can't help but feel like it's what he wanted."

"How do you mean?"

"I'm not sure. I got the feeling he was trying to get a rise out of me, to test my control."

"Shit, girl. The Ghede don't care about control. They care about power. Between them they possess thousands of souls. How many you got?"

Danni counted them off in her head. There were twenty-six boys at Queensland, another dozen dead in Bel-Koté. And now Jasper.

"About forty. I don't know. Maybe more. They're hard to count."

"Forty against thousands, maybe millions." Joto pulled the phone away from his mouth to whistle. "Point is, you're doing a lot more with a lot less."

"I still don't think I'm fit to go more than a few rounds with any of them."

"Speakin' of, where y'at?" he asked.

"I'm fine, Joto."

"No, I mean, really. Where are you?"

"Riverside Market."

"Fixin' some groceries?"

"No. I'm looking for where I ran into Bouchard the other day. He was dumping something into the water, I just don't remember where."

"Rule of land: you don't fuck with N.O.P.D.."

She chuckled. "I doubt whatever Bouchard is doing is in the best interest of the people."

"Well, listen to this girl, talkin' like a patron."

"You were the one who told me to do workings. I dealt with your zombie, now I'm going to go deal with a corrupt cop."

"Just watch your ass," he warned.

"Aye."

She punched the END button on the phone and sat on a bench overlooking the promenade. She fished around inside her pocket and pulled out a coin a little bigger than a half-dollar. It's gold face glinted in the sunlight, sending gold ribbons of light across the sidewalk. On one side, a man, and on the other, a serpent. She pressed it to her lips.

"*Psst*. Snake."

A voice drifted through her head, soft, slow, and feminine.

Yesss, mistress.

"Um, how have you been?"

Well, mistress.

"Good. Look, I kind of need your help. Can you get to the Mississippi?"

There was a hesitation, then: *Yes, mistress.*

Danni watched the river, debating if it was worth the effort or the risk. The snake was actually a koulev, a terrifying combination of snake and man...well, woman. And kind of hard to miss, given her size.

A glistening flash broke the surface of the Mississippi. Danni jogged down the shore, found a secluded place near the wharf, and tapped her hand on the top of the water.

The koulev coasted into the shallower waters. Her skin and scales expanded and contracted in a slow, undulating rhythm. She was kind of pretty, until she lifted her head. Even then, she wasn't ugly, just strange.

A thick, cartilage hood ran from the top of her head down the top half of her spine, a combination of a cobra and a water snake. Her mouth was a broad arrowhead of scaled bone with large pitted nostrils big enough to fit a hand inside. It was her chest that tended to the more human, containing the largest mixture of skin and scales.

Two yellow eyes searched Danni's face. She'd stabbed them out and left the poor thing blind only to regret it later, but it was good to see the damage hadn't been permanent.

Danni held the coin to her lips. "There were a couple of big crates that got dumped in the water, somewhere near a pier with lots of barges. Any guesses?"

The koulev tossed her head in the water a few times, but if she were sensing something or just playing, Danni couldn't tell. Finally, she reared up and her voice whispered through Danni's head.

That way.

Danni jogged alongside the bank. They followed the wharf down the moonwalk to where the park ended. A long cut-back bank that formed a naturally barrier to the shipyard. Danni cleared the chain link fence on her own, but the bank was too steep to climb down.

The koulev slid out of the water again and lowered her head so the widest part of her back was spread at Danni's feet.

"Are you sure?"

Yes, Mistress.

The koulev moved gently down the bank and then waited for Danni to step off. She lifted a hand to block the sun from her eyes and scanned the water again. It looked familiar. She kicked over a few small pieces of driftwood, bent down for a stick, but fell back when it grabbed her arm.

"Holy shit!"

The koulev whipped around, fangs bared on the stick, which was actually an arm.

Dead, she said.

"And yet, still moving."

Farther down the shore they found a leg, a few fingers and another arm. The last one was holding her sneaker.

"That is about the most frightening thing I have ever seen."

Danni caught the edge of the pier to pulled herself up, but felt herself pushed instead. She stepped off the koulev's head again and turned back to look at her.

"Do you have a name?"

Name, the koulev repeated.

"Yeah, something you're called?"

Sevi.

Danni frowned. "That means slave. Anything else?"

Dauphine.

She hesitated. "Were you human?"

The *whoop* of a police siren cut her off before she could answer. A police car pulled through the gate.

"Hide!"

Dauphine disappear with a splash. Danni ducked behind a long roll of rusted shipping cable. The dock shifted and popped under the weight of the car as it crept down the dock. The engine died. Bouchard stepped from the driver's side and yanked a woman out onto the dock.

Her turquoise dress was clean and pressed, but her skin was the a shade just past death, tinged purple around her mouth. Bouchard guided the zombie to the front of his squad car and waited. Another pair of footsteps joined him a few minutes later. From what Danni could see of him, the second man was Creole.

"Caught you a nice one, Oscar," Bouchard said. "She was just hanging around Jackson Square this morning. Left over from Halloween, bro."

Oscar grunted and moved up to inspect the zombie, and whatever he saw, he clearly didn't like. Bouchard grew impatient.

"What'dya say, bro?" he asked. "She should be good for at least fifteen hundred."

"Two-fiddy. Top."

"You out of your mind, bro? She's the whole package."

"I told you, *bro*, my buyer needs the young ones."

"She's young," Bouchard protested. "Forty, maybe fifty."

Oscar reached up to the dead woman's forehead, scrubbed something off her face, and worked it against his thumb and index finger.

"Mortician's paint. She be at least sixty."

"But she looks good for her age, right? That's got to count for something."

"Naw. Not to my boss."

"Maybe I could talk to him, then," Bouchard said. "Cut out this middle man bullshit. *Bro*."

Oscar chuckled, as if the suggestion amused him but should scare Bouchard. "You wanna meet *my* boss?"

"I've been bringing you primo shit for weeks. Think it's about time I move up."

Again, Oscar chuckled. "Yeah, let me set it up. Mean time? Get rid of this shit."

Bouchard cussed his way to the end of the pier, dragging the zombie along behind him. The woman followed with heavy steps, staggered, and fell. Bouchard's gloved hand snatched the back of her head and he wrestled her back to her feet.

"Get up, ya' bitch!"

He carried her to the edge of the dock, unsnapped his holster, and drew his gun. "Ain't got time to put you in a box, so..."

Danni stood.

"Bouchard!"

The gun came around as he did. Bouchard's surprise shifted to amusement.

"You don't learn, do you, Toussaint?"

Danni palmed the coin. "I just wanted to ask you a question."

"Yeah? What's that?"

"Do you like *snakes*?"

She tossed the coin into the air. It spun end over end, glistening white-gold as it reflected in Bouchard's sunglasses. He followed it over his head to the water. It stayed in the air and began to twirl.

Dauphine rose from the Mississippi, breaching up and out in the wide arc. Bouchard lost his footing and stumbled toward the end of the pier. With nothing else to stop his momentum, he grabbed the zombie, twisted, and tossed her at Danni. She fell fast, taking Danni down to the dock. Bouchard's feet raced past her as he leapt back to his patrol car.

Dauphine's sleek body piled over shipping crates and rigging with ease. She cambered back and hissed. Danni heard the wet *pop!* of her head striking Bouchard's windshield, then watched her crank back for a second strike. The engine of the patrol car roared, tires chirped and peeled as Bouchard fish-tailed backwards up the ramp. Dauphine stayed on him, but Danni called her back.

"Wait! Let him go."

She wiggled out from under the zombie. Dauphine slunk back down beside her and flicked her tongue over the corpse.

Dead.

"They're all dead," Danni said as she walked out to the end of the pier. She opened her hand to the air and called the coin back to her fist.

The muddy water churned below her, kicking up foam as it began to boil. She could feel the energy just below the surface, *dozens* of souls. And they felt her, too.

They rushed up to her hand, following the coin's path. It was an interesting sensation, to say the least. Danni grunted when they passed through her and followed them around before realizing they hadn't passed *through* her at all. Their voices echoed back from Bel-Koté, a fresh tier added to the already turbulent choir.

Danni walked back to Dauphine and stooped to where the zombie lay on the deck and snapped in front of its face.

"Hey. Yeah, you. Can you understand me?"

"Me," it groaned.

"What's your name?" Danni asked.

"Name."

Danni's eyes stopped on a gold wedding band. She said a silent prayer for the finger to stay connected before she tugged the ring free. The inscription on the inside was faded but still legible.

"Forever love. Carl and Agnes," she read.

"Agnes," the zombie moaned.

"Yeah, but Agnes *what*?" Danni looked at Dauphine. "Help me stand her up."

Dauphine used her head to push Agnes back to her feet as Danni kept her from going too far forward and into the river with the rest of them.

"You'd better get out of here before Bouchard comes back with a harpoon," she said. "I need to get her back home, whereever that is."

"Home," Agnes repeated, then began to walk, jerky but sure, in whatever direction that was.

Stranger things had happened, especially in New Orleans. By the time Agnes' unbroken march reached Treme, she'd massed a dozen tourists. Danni hung back, accepting tips when they were shoved into her fist and offering vague explanations to the locals.

"Performance art. She's trying out a new act."

It was enough for them, and eventually the crowd dispersed.

Agnes kept moving until she reached a burned-out building beside the I-10. Danni followed her through an alley to a fenced lot. Agnes leaned against it, pushing through a loose section like she'd done it a hundred times before. Inside, the ground was thick and brimming with plants, more vegetables than perennials. Agnes followed the narrow path between root plants and stopped at a large compost pile.

"Home."

Danni frowned. "That's a heap of trash, Agnes."

Something rattled behind a wall of tomatoes. Danni drew the knife and turned. A woman clutched a pale, dried gourd in one hand, while the other served as a shield for the two boys behind her. She smelled like oil and oxidized metal, a combination of fry grease and blood. Typical mambo. Danni could feel the power stuttering off her in thin waves.

The boys studied Danni with guarded expressions, seeming a lot more unnerved by her than Agnes. The older of the two leaned into the mambo's ear.

"Mama, I think that's–"

"Hush, boy," the mambo snapped. She angled her voice over Danni's shoulder. "Ma, s'at you?"

"Home," Agnes moaned.

"Yeah, ma. You're home."

Danni glanced back at the compost heap. "You buried her here?"

"Spent all I had layin' her out the first time."

She rattled the gourd again. If it was meant to be a warning, all it did was make Danni's face itch. She chased the tickle up her nose and into her hairline. The gourd rattled again.

"Stop that," Danni said.

She didn't. Instead, she raised the gourd higher and

gave it a hard shake. The tickle became a tingle and then a burn that smelled like scalded sugar. *Samedi.* If anyone, that gourd, or at least the power attached to it, belonged to him. Which meant, so did the mambo.

Danni stepped back, bowing her head and holding her hands out at her sides.

"Go on now, Carl," the mambo said. "Get your gran'ma. I got my eyes on this one."

Carl stepped out from behind his mother but no farther.

"I won't hurt you," Danni said.

He nodded, but kept his eyes on her as he tried to guide Agnes away, but her feet stayed rooted and her attention focused on Danni.

"Home," Agnes said again. Only this time, it was a plea.

Danni heard the desperation but *felt* her restlessness. This body, her body, was done. She wanted to go home.

Warm light worked its way across the blade. It was startling, just like it had been in the cemetery, but the less Danni feared it, the less she resisted, and the faster Agnes' soul passed into Bel-koté to mix with the wind.

Twenty-Seven

Danni side-stepped a large, wooden crate just inside the doorway of Sister Ned's office. There were six more just like it lined down the hallway. She could make out the words KITCHEN PLUS through the layers of shipping wrap, but nothing else.

"What is all this?"

"Gifts from our new benefactor," Sister Ned said.

She tossed an invoice onto her desk, directly in front of Mother Superior.

"Catherine Daye," Mother Superior said.

"That ought to help, don't you think?" Danni asked.

But they didn't. She could see the tightly drawn lines in the corners of their eyes, they were far from impressed. They were downright suspicious, though who owned more of the suspicion, her or Catherine, Danni couldn't decide.

"How much do you know about this woman, Danielle?"

"Enough to know she can afford it."

"And in exchange?"

"She didn't ask for anything. That was the point of the fundraiser, wasn't it? To raise funds?"

Mother Superior's lips tightened into a frown. "Not if it means we'll be licking her boots later."

"Spare me the proverbs, Sister, please. And what are you doing here, anyway? Shouldn't you be across town, shepherding something?"

"I called her," Sister Ned said. "Because you weren't here."

Danni rolled her eyes. "Look, if I want to take a night off, I don't see that I have any reason to clear it with you first. I left you in charge of this ship. Run it."

"We don't know who this woman is, Danni. Or where these things came from."

"She's an entrepreneur. Hell, you invited her."

Mother Superior exchanged glances with Sister Ned then said, "No, we didn't."

"I'll ask her about it next time I see her, but you know how it goes. You send an invitation to some CEO, they pass it off to someone lower on the food chain."

Sister Ned turned over another invoice. "Of Daye Industries? Sounds owner-operated to me."

Danni frowned. "Open the boxes. Use the shit. Stop feeding these boys leftover meatloaf and cold casserole." She reached past Sister Ned and tugged on the drawer handle. "Open it, please."

Sister Ned made no reach to unlock it. Instead, she folded her arms across her chest.

"*Open the drawer*, Sister."

"Not until I know what your intentions are."

They might have been able to keep her from Michael, but the nail, the piece of him inside it, belonged to *her*. Danni felt the throb of the nail, of Michael's soul. As she focused on it, the lock turned on its own.

"No lock made by man," she chuckled.

She looped the nail around her neck and headed for the door. She followed the hushed whisper of voices up to the dormitories. The boys were clustered around a tower of plain cardboard boxes.

"Are you just going to stare at them or would you like to see what's inside?" she asked.

Rene tucked his hands in his jeans and toed the floor. "Sister Ned say we can't."

Danni stormed across the room. The boys followed, whispering excitement as she split the packing tape and turn the whole thing over on its side. An avalanche of balls of different shapes and sizes rolled and bounced around the room. They travelled freely for a minute before being snatched up.

"Well, go! Take them outside."

They did, traveling in one exuberant herd until the room was empty.

Almost.

Danni toed a soccer ball up her leg and caught it.

"You sure you don't want to go play?" she asked Gabriel. "I'll bet you could kick this one clear to the Missi'sip."

Gabriel shook his head and kept his eyes in his lap. She dropped the ball and let it roll off into the corner.

"Are you still mad at me?" she asked.

"I wasn't mad at you, Jiji. I thought you were dead."

"And now you know I'm not. So go outside and play."

He shoved himself off the bed to stand at the window. "I want Father Michael to come back."

Danni pulled in a long, whistling breath. "Not a Father anymore."

"I want to talk to Father Michael!"

"And what do you want to tell him, Gabriel? That I forgot about Halloween? That I didn't take you trick or treating? What makes you so sure Father Michael gives a damn? *He's gone*. He left. And he doesn't want you or me or anyone else to find him."

The nail began to burn. Danni ground her teeth against the pain. Bile forced its way up her throat, filling her mouth and then her words.

"There are no happy endings in life, Gabriel. Eventually, you'll lose everyone in some way or another. Michael, Sister Ned, Rene, Maurice. Something much darker in this world will take them from you, or worse, they'll leave on their own. Get used to it."

Gabriel's breath grew shallow as his eyes glassed with fresh tears. Danni turned and started for the door.

"Jiji, wait!"

Halfway across the room, Gabriel staggered and fell. He landed hard, and his broken sobs chased her all the way out of Queensland.

Twenty-Eight

Michael woke to pain. Not the stiff, body ache from the small bed he was accustomed to. This was different, sharper, and seemed to ripple across his chest with every breath.

He sat up and dropped his bare feet off the edge of the bed.

"I'm too young for a heart attack," he said to himself.

But that was exactly what it felt like, as if his heart was missing every other beat. When he stood, the throb shifted from his chest to his head. Now *that* was a more familiar pain.

He stumbled into the lavish bathroom and found a bottle of aspirin behind the mirror. Heart attack or hangover, it would have to do. He shook three out into his fist, tossed them back, and used the same hand to scoop fresh water to his lips. His focus shifted to the reflection of the setting sun. How long had he been asleep? He moved back to the bedroom and glared at the clock. It was damn near six.

Somehow, he'd lost an entire day. He jerked on a fresh pair of jeans and a shirt, which instantly stuck to his lower back as he stepped from the cool darkness of the guest house.

A block away from 1500 Harmony, he was stopped by a line of parade floats being pulled back to storage. The light changed, but the flatbeds just kept moving through the intersection. Anxiety bunched his hands to fists around the steering wheel, and he struggled to relax them.

What the hell was wrong with him? He was milling over the source of his unrest when the last float eased through the light followed by a loose group of shuffling…

"Zombies?"

No less than a dozen. Michael scrubbed his eyes and leaned into the dash. From what he could tell, the float was a massive grim reaper. Lit up, it was probably impressive. A black drape covered its long body, shimmering in the later afternoon sunlight, but the only part that stood out now was the loose line of bodies, limp-stepping it past the end of his truck.

They could have been stragglers or costumed left-overs from a super krewe. He almost dismissed them completely, until he realized they were losing pieces along the way, and those pieces were continuing the march. A single hand scraped its way forward through the intersection.

Michael flipped on his signal and turned against the light to follow them, stopping every so often to snag a hand out of the roadway and flip it into the passenger side floorboard.

They travelled out of the Garden District and into a cluster of warehouses along the truckway. The floats began to peel off from the pack, moving across parking lots and into their respective dens. The zombies stayed with the reaper float as it pulled into a vacant lot and stopped. They shuffled forward and threw themselves against the back of the float.

A door opened under the reaper's armpit, and the driver dropped down to the ground.

"Hey! Cut it out! Ya'll know how much these things cost?"

When none of them responded, he reached back into the cab for a tire iron, cocked it back, but didn't swing.

"I ain't fuckin' with ya'll, now. Get out of here!"

Michael waved for his attention.

"You with these idiots?" the driver asked him.

"Not really. But maybe I can help?"

"I don't give a shit what you do, just keep 'em off my rig!"

A zombie at the head of the group stepped forward again. The driver swung the tire iron, and it connected. The sound was wet and hollow, like a watermelon dropped against the pavement. The zombie staggered but didn't fall, then continued forward. The driver stared at Michael, wide-eyed.

"Did you see… *Fuck!*"

The tire iron hit the ground with a sharp ping, and the driver took off on foot. The zombies continued to jostle and bump each other into the back of the float. The crowd parted enough for Michael to see why.

On the back of the float, just below the bottom riser of seats, Michael spotted a huge, painted *veve*. In fact, the entire thing was covered in voodoo markings, most of which he recognized as symbols specific to the Ghede.

"Leave it to Endymoin," Michael said with a sigh.

Then, he remembered Cemetrie's words. Maybe it wouldn't be a bad idea to take care of these and any others he could find, just so he could say he hadn't slept away the entire day. Besides, they were mindless, shuffling shells on autopilot. How hard could it be?

The sun had finally fallen behind the horizon. Michael took a deep, settling breath and held out his hands, trying to separate the heat in the air from his skin. It worked, just like it had in the cemetery, and the zombies stopped pitching themselves against the back of the float. Instead, their attention drew around to him.

One hadn't seemed so imposing, but under the scrutiny of so many cold, gray eyes Michael felt his focus begin to falter. His mind reached into his gris-gris bag for the piece of the portmanteau that had once held several souls. He let it take shape in his mind's eye and felt its pull.

The herd did, too, and began to shamble in his direction. Michael matched them step for step, moving backwards until he was at the rear of his truck. He kept one hand out, used the other to drop the tailgate, and slid up into the bed.

The lead zombie followed. His suit coat was well-worn long before he'd been buried in it. Thanks to the float driver, his indented head was now slightly left of center. It took a minute for him to wrestle himself over the tailgate. It wasn't so much of a climb as a desperate crawl until the others behind him pushed and toppled over him, using his body as leverage.

It was a tight fit, but eventually they all made it into the truck bed. Michael flexed his hands and curled his fingers upward. They dropped together. The truck bounced, but they ended up, more or less, seated.

Keeping his focus behind him while driving forward proved to be a little more challenging. Every so often, one of them would stand and force Michael to pull over and settle them again.

Even if he could put them all back in their graves, he still needed to figure out where they had come from. The best place to take them was back to Cemetrie. He was the Baron in charge of the cemeteries and head of the household. The problem was finding him.

Michael turned off St. Bernard Avenue and cruised through a densely packed residential neighborhood. He and Joey had found a park there one summer, full of brightly painted jungle gyms but empty of other children. They'd spent hours launching themselves from the swings and zipping down the slides, until Joey stumbled over the loose cluster of headstones tucked away at the far edge of the park. They'd never gone back after that.

It was a little more overgrown than Michael remembered. He jumped the truck tires over the curb, waited for the weight to shift in the bed, and eased down to the cemetery. The park was no longer empty.

Shapes moved around the broken row of

headstones. They changed directions and started toward the truck. Six became ten, then ten more. Michael hustled to crank his window up as they rushed forward and slammed into the truck on all sides. It was Night of the Living Dead, only here, the dead were as threatening as docile cows. Michael tried to open the door only to have it pushed back as more bodies swarmed against it. It was as close to the actual cemetery as he was going to get.

He jerked the gris-gris bag from his hip and dumped the contents into his hand. He wouldn't need much, just enough to get Cemetrie's attention. He decided on the feather and tried to envision the cemetery somewhere on the other side of the mob.

The light was minimal past the bodies around him, the air heated by his own breath. He felt the stirring whisper of wings in the back of his mind followed by the updraft that carried them. The feather vibrated in his palm. Outside the truck, the zombies began to moan. Michael wasn't sure what, if anything, they were trying to say.

A bolt hit him hard in the chest and involuntarily clamped his hand around the feather. He felt the quill break at the same time the zombies flew away from his truck and landed roughly in the grass. Michael's jaw dropped open.

The park was littered with bodies. Some still stood, but most were laid out in a perfect ring around his truck. The group he'd originally guessed at twenty extended to the far edge of the park in all directions. Men and women, young and old. Whole and... not so whole.

The collection of parts twitched in his floorboard. Michael reached over them, pushed out the passenger side door, and kicked them into the grass.

The smell smacked him in the nose, worse than all the Dumpsters in the Quarter during mid-July. He choked back a gag and struggled to pull the door closed again, but all it did was trap the smell into the cabin with him.

He staggered from the truck and quick-stepped it through the park, careful to set his foot in the grass and not *on* them as they struggled to stand again.

A zombie shouldered him from behind, pitching him forward into another. Four more moved in behind him. Whatever aimless direction they were headed now, they were going together, and Michael was going with them.

In less than a mile, it was clear they weren't aimless at all.

Twenty-Nine

Michael was gone, and he wasn't coming back.

It took saying it aloud to connect the concept in Danni's head to her heart. Now, it sat there like periphery knowledge. He didn't *want* to come back.

The nail swung from the hook beside the shower. Her eyes shifted to her reflection in the steamy mirror. She laid an open palm against it, tracing her face from cheek to chin, all the way to the angry gash the width and length of the nail in the center of her chest. The pain was grounding in a way that the grief hadn't been. She hadn't even tried to heal it, somehow already knowing she couldn't if she wanted to.

Catherine pulled in a long, hissing breath behind her.

"That looks like it hurt."

Danni snapped an arm around her breasts, drew the knife off the sink, and swung around.

"*Easy,*" Catherine said as she used the tip of her fingernail to guide the blade away from her throat. "Your door was open, and it's nothing I haven't already seen."

Still, Danni dropped the knife back into the sink and readjusted the towel around her waist to cover her chest.

"I wanted to see how you were," Catherine said.

Fresh sweat ran down Danni's spine. Her fist collided with the mirror. It split inside the frame, fell, and shattered into the sink.

Catherine chuckled. Her heels echoed off the tile as she closed the distance between them. Blazing, red hair fell freely around her face, seeming to move just a half-second behind the rest of her when Danni focused on it too long. The hard ribbing of her corset complimented her already perfect figure.

"I hear there's a party in the bayou tonight."

"Jou Mon Mouri," Danni said.

Catherine shrugged. "Could be fun."

"Let me get dressed."

She had nothing to compliment let alone compete with Catherine's outfit, so she opted for a simple, black tank top and jeans. She tucked the knife and the koulev's coin into her back pocket but hesitated when she reached for the nail.

"What's the story behind that thing?" Catherine asked.

"The Baron Samedi put it in my chest."

Catherine started to laugh but quickly sobered when she saw Danni's face.

"Why?"

"He's an asshole," Danni said. She looped it around her neck. "Let's go."

Catherine drove while Danni held on. By the time the Mustang coasted into the lowlands of Bayou St. John, Jou Mon Mouri was already a yellow glow in the underside of the trees. Drums beat from somewhere deeper in the swamp. Catherine idled down the engine.

"Ready to see what you're made of?" she asked as she ran a fresh coat of red gloss over her lips in the rearview mirror.

Danni started to answer, but the words died when Catherine's lips met hers. Her kiss was chaste but sweet, tangled with the heady scent of mud.

Danni's head spun. She tasted power, old, thick, and blinding in its intensity. Gravity bled out beneath her as she felt herself being lifted and then falling. The drums grew louder and voices joined them.

"*Ghede. Ghede. Ghede.*"

When Danni opened her eyes, she was standing in the center of a low stage. Fire flashed at all four corners of the conclave, lighting the bodies in motion beyond the stage. They dipped and turned random paths through the dirt as they chanted.

Catherine was gone.

Danni staggered backwards and ran into Cemetrie.

"*Bonswa*, sister. Gotta admit, I was beginning to think you wouldn't show." He scanned her head to toe and frowned. "Your outfit could use a little work."

Cemetrie, on the other hand, looked resplendent in his gold and silver surcoat. White satin gathered around his cuffs and throat. It was a far more complex ensemble than she'd ever seen him in, yet still managed to be natural.

He rocked back on his heels. "Since this is your first Jou, allow me to explain the rules."

"*Rules?*"

"By entering the circle, you commit yourself to this house, and swear yourself to our pact."

Danni's eyes tracked a fat, white line that had been painted a foot from the edge. Cemetrie cracked his cane against the wood and the circle flared.

"Inside this circle we Ghede lay down our petty rivalries, our ambitions, and join hands as brethren."

Danni screwed up her face. "Some kind of peace summit?"

"If ya like. Though peace is bloodless compared to amnesty between loa," he said. His eyes thinned as an icy warning chilled the air between them. "But a fate worse than death to any who would seek to violate these rules."

Cemetrie strode across the stage and spread his arms out to the crowd. The chant became his name.

"*Cemetrie! Cemetrie! Cemetrie!*"

It seemed no effort at all for his words to reach out and overpower them.

"Brothers and Sisters! Jou Mon Mouri is upon us! This is our night! Let the Ghede present!"

The chant began anew.

"*Samedi! Samedi!*"

It rippled across the audience, rising to a crescendo as Samedi marched across the stage. His coat stretched across his chest and fanned out into long, white brocade tails. His dark skin blended with the night so the entire outfit looked hollow until he lifted the brim of his hat. His amber eyes burned with madness behind his painted skeleton mask. He conducted the chorus with a driftwood cane, swaying from side to side like a conductor of the damned.

LaCroix appeared out of thin air, dressed in screaming shades of reds and greens. He greeted Danni with a warm kiss to her cheek.

"He thinks he is the one they have come to see," he growled as he watched Samedi prance. "I so hate to disappoint him."

LaCroix's ebony cane shot into the sky. Fire flew from its tip, drawing ornate runes over the heads of the crowd. The flames rushed out before exploding into colorful fireworks.

People swooned, falling into the arms of whoever was near them. Excitement became tangible joy, and the weight of it collided with competing chants for both Baron's.

Danni pitched forward, shouldered aside from behind. She fell to her hands and knees, looking up just in time to see Catherine striding across the stage. Danni couldn't even remember what she'd been wearing in the car, but it wasn't this. Couldn't have been.

Flames burned and flowed around her like a cape, and yet anywhere her skin was revealed, the fire flattened out around her. Her hips rocked in long, sweeping gestures that seemed two parts feline, and one part snake.

Samedi met her center stage. He captured her around the waist and drew her into him. Their kiss was long and sensual, like lions licking off the blood of a fresh kill.

Samedi's face contorted around hers, then *into* it, as his painted white mask spilled over her face. She broke away from his mouth, laughing. Below them, the crowd let loose of an enthusiastic scream.

Danni struggled to her feet.

"Who the hell are you?" she screamed over the crowd.

Catherine's eyes burned across the stage like something toxic and fatal. She lifted her arms to the crowd.

"Jou Mon Mouri, who am I?"

The crowd exploded in response. Their chants thundered through the air and shook the stage beneath Danni's feet.

"Brid-gette. Brid-gette! BRID-GETTE!"

Thirty

The force of the voices hit Danni like a thunderclap.
Bridgette?

Samedi's *wife*?

A buzz started in the base of her skull and worked
its way down her spine. Bridgette had lied. The why hardly
mattered. She was a loa and nothing about that could be
good. The only option Danni had now was to run, and she
was just about to when Cemetrie reappeared in a cloud of
cream-colored smoke.

"Little Sister. Our people await you."

"You've got to be kidding me."

His eyes blazed so hot she could feel the heat on her
face.

"Oh no, *cher*," he said. "You have never seen me
more serious. Your followers await. Do *not* disappoint
them."

She turned back to the roaring crowd, but her eyes
travelled to where Bridgette was stroking a lazy hand
against Samedi's chest. While the motion appeared languid

200

and soft, she couldn't help but notice the wince inside the Baron's painted smile. Bridgette's eyes flared when they caught hers.

Danni's mind went in several directions at once. It was a solid mile of swamp in any direction. Lake Pontchartrain was her best bet, to the east. There were more snakes, but also Dauphine. Decided, Danni pivoted toward the edge of the stage, but Cemetrie was already there to stop her.

"I'm not going to tell you again. Present!"

His cane flashed forward in the air beside her head, pointing her back to the conclave. The cheers faded to a muted hush, until all that was left was the beckoning weight of their eyes.

Danni raised one arm. The chant began to build again.

"JIJI! JIJI! JIJI! JIJI!"

Jou Mon Mouri swept over her.

She tasted sweat and sand, blood and earth. She felt every individual heartbeat. Mambo and houngan. Men and women, the children among them. Her awareness reached out to every corner of the gathering, then into the streets and beyond the city lights. Every living and dying thing screamed her name, and Danni answered them. Not as the frail being she was, but as a Ghede.

Samedi, LaCroix, Cemetrie and even Bridgette joined her. The circle flared around them again, and where their powers had been divided, they were now limitlessly one.

Danni saw their histories, their successes and

201

failures, as sure as if she'd experienced them first hand, racked out in dazzling bursts of a language she knew hadn't been spoken in a millennia.

In turn, they explored her short mortal years. Her first steps. Her first crush. Her years in prison. They gazed with wonderment at what she knew of humanity, and where she thought she should feel embarrassed, she only felt the liberation of being blissfully undone.

One song bled into another. Fantasies became realities, flash-burned across her mind like ignited spider webs. Different versions of her history played out to multiple possibilities. What if she hadn't come to New Orleans? Met Michael? Fallen in love with him? The Ghede showed her. Questions asked and answered, one after the other, faster than she could reason.

All the choices she had made, was making, and would make, expanding to overwhelm, but coming to one unavoidable end. Her attention ricocheted on a thousand memories, split around a single second in time: the moment Michael first kissed her and gave over a shard of his soul.

The Ghede would have always found her. Michael's soul had only accelerated the process. And possessing it not only gave her control of his life, but his death. And *that* was the real power of the Ghede.

Death.

Danni was caught somewhere between the half-life of one vision and the next when a shrill scream broke their connection. The circle parted and fell.

She heard the hard thump of several bodies against the stage, followed by her own when she landed on her hands and knees. She was drunk on the power rushing through her, but it was already beginning to draw back, leaving her feeble and impossibly small compared to what she'd just experienced.

Only Bridgette appeared unaffected. She stood in the center of the circle, her hands sweeping the air up into her face at the same time she inhaled.

Cemetrie worked his way to his feet and cracked his cane against the stage.

"What have you done?" he demanded.

"Only what your carelessness allowed, old man," Bridgette hissed.

Danni followed her long finger into the brush line as the first of several hundred shadows became faces. Dead, white eyes reflected the firelight as they tromped mindlessly toward the open grass.

The living crowd broke and ran deeper into the swamp. The zombies staggered on until they struck the sides of the stage, parted, and continued their forward stampede.

"Do something, Cemetrie!" Samedi screamed.

Cemetrie's cane flashed forward again, this time tossed overhand into the mass of zombies. It pierced the ground, sputtered, and died. The herd stomped over it without so much as a pause.

Cemetrie spun around to Bridgette.

"You disgrace this house!"

"And you should have stayed where you belonged, gravedigger!"

Danni tried to stand. Bridgette swiped her hand

through the air, and the concussive force flattened Danni against the stage.

"I'll be with you in a moment, girl."

Fire flared across every nerve ending each time Danni tried to breathe. Her bones ached, and the weight on her back kept her pinned, unable to do more than listen to the conversation occurring around her.

"This was not the way to settle this!" Samedi screamed.

"She is not one of us!" she hissed.

Lacroix's voice was plaintive but firm. "Bridgette, this is Jou Mon Mouri."

Bridgette spat. It landed beside Danni's face and melted through the floor.

"You limp, uninspiring old fools may be content to let our house fall again, but I will tolerate it no longer!"

Bridgette clapped once. A detonation started between her palms. Lightning spired down to the center of the stage. It arced out to touch LaCroix, Samedi, Cemetrie, and finally Danni.

Pain ripped across her body. If she screamed she couldn't hear it. She was weightless and free for a few seconds before slamming into the ground. There was no sensation attached to the fall, and that, her mind told her, was more dangerous than anything. She had to stay conscious, at least open her eyes.

When she did, all she saw was a gold coin in the center of a black field. She tried to focus on it, make sense of its placement in the moment. The harder she tried, the more confusing it became. It reminded her of something, but every time she reached for the word, it fell apart. She wished Michael was there to explain it. Make sense of her irrational need to hold it. She reached for it. Missed. Tried again and touched it.

"Where are you?" she whispered. "I'm... dying."

Thirty-One

The zombies were unstoppable. Michael fought desperately to stay on his feet and not lose sight of the head of the line. They crossed streets and yards, plowed over fences, and trampled each other when they fell. At least the moaning had stopped, and aside for a few dragging steps, they were a peculiarly silent bunch.

They slowed when they reached the inlet waters of St. John's Bayou. Michael searched the skyline beyond the levee. Firelight reflected against the low clouds. Distant drumbeats chased the light, followed by a chorus of chants too far away to make out.

The terrain changed just over the rise of the levee. Swamp grass and patches of thistle grew from clumps of upturned earth, while stagnant water pooled in lower places along the batture. Mud sopped his boots and pushed underneath his pant legs. Michael resorted to using the bodies around him for balance. At least they had no problem maneuvering through the mud.

Proximity brought the voices of a much larger

crowd into context.

"Jiji! Jiji! Jiji!" they screamed.

He could barely see her through a haze of mist, but he could definitely *feel* her. Her body spun so fast in the center of a low stage it made him dizzy. Michael shouted her name but knew she couldn't hear him. He couldn't even hear himself.

He pushed himself forward, climbing over mushy limbs to the head of the mob. Samedi, LaCroix and Cemetrie were also on stage, doing a softer version of Danni's reel. The crowd, the trees, and the air itself spun with them.

The only still thing in the entire bayou was Catherine.

Her green eyes narrowed as they swept out over the crowd. Michael felt his brain stutter-start as he tried to make sense of her placement in the moment. Then, her lips parted, and the skull painted over her face became a malevolent grin.

A trickle of warmth formed beneath Michael's nose. He reached up, touched it, and found blood. The crowd's chants shifted to shrill screams at the same time Danni's frantic whirling stopped. She dropped to the stage with a hard thump. The three Barons staggered and fell with her.

Another round of screams sent a ripple of pain across his chest. It seemed to be having the same effect on the zombies, and the one closest to him let out a wet roar. The living crowd lost cohesion, turned, and ran. The herd of zombies rushed forward to meet them.

Lightning spiraled down from the sky. The first bolt

struck Catherine before fracturing out to the others. Danni flew over the crowd in a blur of black. White orbs burned inside his eyes for several seconds, and when he could see again, nothing made sense.

The world around him was on fire: the ground, the trees, the zombies, what was left of the stage. Heavy, smoke hung in the damp air, but he could smell the burnt hair and charred flesh.

Bodies shifted and broke beneath him, living or dead, he didn't know. It didn't matter. Danni mattered. He followed the direction she'd gone, climbing, falling, and finally crawling until he found her.

She lay motionless at the lapping edge of the swamp. He pulled himself to her, found her hand, and brushed his lips across her broken knuckles.

"Danni, please."

She didn't answer. Didn't move. He lay his hand over her gaunt cheek. Her breath shuddered out into his palm, light and ragged. He forced himself up from the mud, aware that he needed to move her but unsure if he could even stand.

"*Mike!* What the hell are you doing here?"

Joto shoved his wheelchair over the rutted ground but froze when he saw Danni. "*No.*"

"I have to get her out of here!"

"Ain't anywhere to go, man."

Michael followed Joto's eyes out to the edge of the swamp. The fire had traveled the line of trees and rose into a wall. The people who hadn't escaped in the initial onslaught, now ran panicked and frightened, slamming into each other before finally falling back as the smoke overwhelmed them.

The flames parted. The koulev broke through the inferno and threw a blind strike at the scorched earth. Michael didn't remember it being quite so big. Or as fast.

It moved across the clearing with impossible speed and rose up over Michael. He threw an arm over his head, grabbed for his gris-gris bag, and pictured himself behind the boulders in Arizona. The snake's head bounced off the air and slammed into the ground beside him. It shook off the collision and pulled back to strike again.

Michael tightened his hand around Danni's fist, and a gold coin tumbled out of her palm. He held it high above his head.

"*Wait!*"

The snake paused and lowered its head. It blinked one slitted yellow eye, considering him, before its cold, lilting voice rasped through his head.

Let me, it said.

The narrow end of its tail worked into the loose earth beneath Danni, while the koulev used her nose to nudge her body away from the ground. Scales shifted and shaped themselves into a shallow cradle.

Fire crackled and sent licks into the air, stealing Michael's breath. He wrapped his sleeve across his face.

"Can you lead us out of here?" he yelled from behind it.

The koulev seemed to nod and dove headfirst into the tree line. Michael took the handles at the back of Joto's chair.

"Normally, I wouldn't do this…"

"Drive on, brother!" Joto yelled.

The snake flattened the path ahead and Michael followed, shoving Joto along behind her. The smoke thinned and the air cooled as sound shifted to the steady hum of frogs. Finally, they broke through a deep thicket of mangroves and into a clearing. The koulev piled itself into a coil but kept Danni's body cradled in the center.

Joto swallowed audibly. "Is she…"

A long, hard cough rattled up Danni's throat. She sat up, dazed. Michael took his first deep breath in several minutes and reached back for Joto's shoulder.

Danni set one foot against the ground and tested her balance before sliding off the koulev's back. Michael saw her eyes find his, but felt something wither inside him when they continued past him to Joto.

"What did she do to me?" she asked in a raw whisper.

Joto held up his hands. "I don't know."

"*What* did she do?" Danni said again.

"Honest, Jiji. I don't know. From where I was sittin', everything looked normal. Barons presented, then Bridgette, then—"

Michael cut him off. "Bridgette?"

"Tall red head. Lightning bolts from her fingertips," Joto said.

"*Bridgette.*" Her name echoed up Danni's throat as a harsh tremble. "I'm going to *kill* her."

Michael had little doubt she meant it. Still, he reached for her.

"Maybe you should sit down," he said gently. "Your ribs are—"

Showing. The skin and underlying muscle was split across her side. Her pale bones glistened in the moonlight, but Danni only stared at it, tipping her head side to side, as the wound began to stitch itself closed. Michael watched and waited until her raw insides were only smooth, pink flesh. It was still impressive, no matter how many times he'd seen it.

"How do you feel?" he asked.

"How do I *feel*?" she growled.

Joto rolled backwards a few feet. "Um, Mike?"

"You've been gone two months and the first thing you can think to ask is, *how do I feel*?" Danni asked.

"Seriously, Mike. You might want to step back," Joto warned again.

He tried. But for every pace Michael put between them, Danni stalked forward. Her hands opened at her sides. Cold ash spread around her feet, seeming to boil off her in heavy, choking waves. The sharp lines of her cheekbones deepened until light no longer reached the hallows beneath her eyes. A skull.

"*How do I feel?*" she asked again. "How do you think I feel? I *feel* like…"

Her words trailed off. She turned and searched the darkness. Whatever she was looking for, it made her frown. Her breath caught, and she lifted a hand to the base of her throat.

"Where are they?" she whispered.

Michael looked back at Joto, but he only shrugged.

211

"Where are *who*?" Michael asked.

Danni ground her fists against her temples. "No! No, no, no!"

She stumbled in one direction and stopped, looked up at the sky, and screamed. Michael pressed his hands over his ears. Eventually, her air ran out and the scream became a hard sob. She stumbled forward once more.

Then, she ran.

Thirty-Two

The bayou ended and the street began, but the transition from mud to pavement was imperceptible under the *whur-whur-whur* of blood hammering inside Danni's ears. When she broke from the tree line, she was six blocks from the orphanage. Too far. It was too far. And she couldn't hear *them*. Rene. Jean-Paul. Maurice...

Gabriel.

They were gone. How and why competed for answers that only confused conventional rationale. If they were dead, she should have still felt them in Bel-koté. And those voices she could still hear. It was only the living ones who had broken from her.

She cleared a drape-cable border between gravel alleys in one swift vault. Ahead, Queensland was backlit with a dewy, red glow. She skidded to a stop in the light of a street lamp. Officer Bouchard kicked off the bottom stair and met her in the center of the street.

"I should have put a bullet in your head a *long* time ago, Toussaint."

His elbow shot out, too close and too fast to avoid. It landed against her eye. Grit bit the heels of her hands when she landed at his feet. Bouchard hand snatched the back of her head and yanked her face up to his. The barrel of his gun dug into her temple, but she couldn't see it, only feel the tremble of his hand as he pressed it against her skull.

"Enough!" Laurent barked.

An open, leather vest left his muscle-bound chest exposed as he stepped down from the top of the stairs.

Bouchard relaxed his grip but didn't withdraw the gun.

"I said, *enough!*"

"She and I have unfinished business," Bouchard said.

Laurent stooped to place his mouth beside Bouchard's ear, but even Danni felt the searing heat in his breath.

"Your business is at my mistress's pleasure, *monsieur*. And that pleasure is she be alive."

Bouchard frowned and tossed her back to the pavement.

"We'll have our day soon, Toussaint."

Danni struggled to her feet. The longer she stood in the shadow of Queensland, the harder standing got. Even the wet air felt like a weight in her lungs.

Laurent's dark eyes softened. He laid the back of his hand against her cheek, but the sensation traveled deeper, calling out the memory of his skin pressed to hers.

"I can still taste you, *amoureux*. I wonder, can you

do the same of me?"

Danni knocked his hand away. "You weren't that good."

His attention shifted as Michael's truck pulled up the street and stopped.

"Ah, *le garçon d'amant*," Laurent purred. "Joining us at last. And he brought a friend."

Joto hopped himself and his chair from the bed of the truck to the street. Michael moved toward them. Laurent seemed excited by the idea. A warm wash of power leapt off his skin, but Danni lifted a hand in the air above his chest.

"I still have enough power to wipe the street with your face," she warned.

Laurent studied her fingers and smiled. "The power, perhaps, but not the courage."

The door to Queensland opened. Sister Ned's thin, silvery hair fell freely over the shoulders of her simple dressing gown, as though she'd only recently been pulled from her bed. Tomas wrestled her over the threshold. She fought him and even got in a few solid smacks before he grabbed her, lifted her, and carried her down the stairs. Laurent drew Sister Ned from Tomas' grasp and passed her to Michael.

"Cantaloupe," Laurent told him.

Michael took Sister Ned's shoulders and guided her behind him before looking back at Laurent.

"Beg pardon?" he asked.

"Your woman." Laurent nodded his chin at Danni and ran his tongue across his top lip. "She tastes like sun-warmed cantaloupe, in case you were wondering."

Danni kept her eyes on Laurent's back as he climbed the stairs again and took up a post beneath the overhang. The red mist clung to the windows, steaming them from the inside, out. Bridgette cocked her hip against the open doorway.

Danni rushed forward, but some unseen barrier slammed against her chest. She tumbled backwards. The pavement raked across her skin, but the pain went deeper, beyond her flesh and bones. It roared across Bel-Koté as a howling wave, uprooting trees and grass, tearing apart the sky until Danni could feel nothing else but her world turning to dust.

"Amazing, isn't it?" Bridgette asked.

Her heels counted off the steps until the sleek tips of her black heels were inches from Danni's face.

Danni twisted her face up from the ground. Bridgette extended her hand and sent a visible ripple across Queensland.

"All that time you spent trying to get out, and now, you want back in."

"Catherine?"

Michael. Danni tried to focus on his face. Her hand grasped for the nail around her neck.

"You look a little tired, Michael. Did you sleep okay? Bed wasn't too soft, was it?"

Danni tried to make sense of her words and the collision of several truths. His soul fluttered in her palm and then vanished.

"Michael?" she whispered.

"Has been in town for some time," Bridgette answered. "You didn't know? Oh. Of course you didn't. You were too busy meddling in the affairs of *my* family."

Danni struggled to find enough air to speak.

"But C-Cemetrie said the Jou was—"

Safe. It was supposed to be safe because a 'fate worse than death' awaited anyone who would violate their circle, and Bridgette had. So, why weren't the Barons here, now, exacting their revenge?

Bridgette made an angry sound, a cross between a growl and a gasp.

"Did you really believe in besting my husband you were immune to all of us?"

Bridgette snapped. A hard wave of power shuddered out to touch the windows of Queensland. The steam slid away and Danni's eyes found Gabriel's instantly. He clutched the leather folio to his chest, mouthing words she could barely make out through the mist. Bridgette's laughter peeled over the street.

"Oh, don't worry, *Jiji*. Before I turn them out properly, I'll need to break them in."

A sob broke from Danni's lips. Another followed, harder and deeper. It left her breathless. The compressing pain pulled the last bit of strength from her muscles, dragging her down to the cold, hard ground at Bridgette's feet.

"This is what it means to be broken," Bridgette told her.

She snapped again and Gabriel's folio appeared in her hand. She flipped it into the air. The pages fluttered and fell, ink bleeding and then vanishing as the light drizzle of rain became a downpour.

"And *this* is what it feels like to be forgotten."

Thirty-Three

Sometimes light hid more than it revealed. Like Mother Superior's angry expression when they arrived at her door. She took one look at Michael, then let her eyes fall to where Danni's body was cradled against his chest. She ushered them into her office and left them there.

Michael lay Danni on the couch and sank to his knees beside her. Her face was slack, motionless beyond sleep. What small breaths she took were ragged, infrequent. He brushed the hair back from her face and felt a cold ripple run down his fingers. *That's what death feels like*, his mind told him, but his heart refused to draw the same conclusion. She wasn't dead. She couldn't be. She was still breathing!

Yet, from the moment she had dropped to the ground at Bridgette's feet, Michael had felt a darkness growing inside him, a heavy, sour shape that made the bile burn in the back of his throat.

The door opened behind him with a soft click as Mother Superior returned with Sister Levine.

"Michael," she said softly, "you have to step back."

But he couldn't. He wanted to scream at the quiet, make the room less still, if only to hear something as loud as the pain inside him. Sister Ned took his shoulders and eased him back to standing, but he couldn't feel it. All he saw was Danni's face moving farther away.

"She looks…" His voice choked out before he could finished the words. He tried again. "Is she?"

Sister Ned gave him a painful look. "I don't know. All the more reason for us to get out of the way."

Us. She meant him and Joto. Sister Ned knelt in his place between the other two sisters. He tried to hear the quiet conversation that passed between them but quickly gave up to exhaustion.

He sat on the edge of a high-backed fabric chair, its rich patterns lost in the shadows of the meager lamps. The floor beneath his feet had always been so warm and comforting; heavy dark wood in patterns as old as New Orleans. Older. Now they were another wall, another pressure pushing against him like the darkness beyond the faint lamplight, walling him in.

He flexed his fingers and stared at his hands. His clothes stank of ozone and fetid water, another layer over the gore already crusted to his skin, blood from things he never wanted to see again, not even in his mind's eye.

Joto set a reassuring hand on Michael's shoulder and didn't let go until Sister Levine sat back on her heels, frowning.

"I've got a thready pulse," she said, "but her lungs sound bad."

"What about the boys?" Mother Superior asked Sister Ned.

Michael shot her a heated look.

"We're all concerned about Danni," she said, "but the boys must come first."

"Catherine Daye," Sister Ned said. "She has them."

"Catherine?" Joto and Michael asked at the same time.

Joto whirled around, looking from Michael to Sister Ned and back again. Finally, he asked, "You *both* know her?"

"She made several large donations to the orphanage," Sister Ned explained. "We tried to talk Danni out of it, but she was adamant we keep them."

Michael started to speak, but Joto overran him. "And, just so I got this all sorted, that's the same lady who we all saw at the orphanage, tonight?"

Sister Ned nodded.

Joto turned to Michael. "And you know her *how*?"

Michael felt their collective attention shift to him. He kept his eyes on his hands, wringing them together until they ached. The pieces slowly came together; from the first time he'd seen her in the swamp, to her sudden appearance in front of his truck, up to last night when she had kissed him.

Michael took a deep breath and settled on the easiest explanation he could.

"I've been staying in her guest house."

Joto whistled and ran a hand over his mouth.

"Well, her name ain't Catherine, it's Bridgette. And

she's never been the type to come at you from the front. She waits, lets you get cozy, get your guard down. She's a—"

"*Predator*," Michael finished. The word growled out of his throat. He pulled his eyes up from the floor to look at Joto. "What else have I missed?"

The three of them exchanged glances, Joto looking to Sister Ned and then Mother Superior. The sisters shared a few silent seconds as they decided who should speak first. Eventually, Mother Superior stepped forward.

"This has been a trying time for all of us, most of all you," she began.

Michael held up his hand to stop her. "*Don't* talk to me like I'm fresh out of seminary, Mary Constance, I'm not in the mood. Tell me what happened."

Mother Superior unfolded her hands and let them fall at her sides. It was a battle stance, one Michael recalled seeing only once: the day before Katrina, when the National Guard tried to force them to evacuate, and she had refused. He'd stood with her through the ensuing chaos, but it made him angry to see the same hardness turned on him now.

"Fine," she said. "I warned you. I prayed that I was wrong, but I did warn you Danni wouldn't stay committed to any of this once you were gone."

Growing anger filled his voice. "You sent me off to the swamp just to test her?"

"I sent you to Father Brantly to help you find your way. What path Danni chose in the interim was hers and hers alone. If she wanted the help of this community, she needed to prove her dedication to this parish, to the boys, and to herself."

The room was still until Joto's deep-chambered voice broke the hush. "No. She didn't."

Mother Superior stared at him, shocked then annoyed as her eyes narrowed to slits.

"Were she a person, maybe so," Joto said. "An ex-priest, probably. But she wasn't either. She's loa, Sister. A god to her people sure as any you might see fit to worship."

"Who are you to compare anyone to Our Almighty God?" Mother Superior demanded.

"By your book? A sinner." Joto pointed at Michael. "Don't forget, I've been hangin' around this boy as long as you have. I've had my Bible lessons, and what I took from them was this: good is good and evil is evil. Jiji wasn't evil, neither was Danni.

"But you picked at every choice she made, whether at the orphanage or in the streets. She threw away all she was for those children, but that wasn't enough for you. You wouldn't let her be Danni *or* JiJi, no matter what her followers were praying for.

"Now, you been in N'awlins long enough. Do you know what Bridgette is?"

"Historically," Mother Superior said with a shrug, "another specter of death, same as the rest of the Ghede."

"*Historically*," Joto said, "she was nothing more than a pregnant slave when she took her first soul. Her own child, if you can stomach that. Any other time, in any other place, she would've probably died doing it. As it stands, it's what made her into a loa, but it's *belief* that has allowed her to become one of the most powerful and violent queens in a millennium. And now, believe in her or not, she has your orphanage."

"Are you inferring *I* hold some blame in this?" Mother Superior asked.

"You all do!" Joto snapped.

His eyes swept around the room before stopping on Michael. "She has a piece of your soul for Christ sake! It doesn't get more real than that!"

Michael finally stood, needing to end the debate as much as he needed a task, a direction. Something to put his hands around, even if his only option was Bridgette's throat.

"Tell me what to do," he said.

"Ain't nothin' you *can* do," Joto answered. He glanced back at Danni and shook his head. "Pray, maybe."

"The best suggestion I've heard so far," Mother Superior said.

For the first time in his life, it was exactly what Michael *didn't* want to do. Still, he watched as Mother Superior rejoined Sister Levine and began to pray over Danni.

Sister Ned stirred but didn't join them. Instead, she cried softly under her breath while she shuffled through the damp stack of pages collected in her lap. She peeled them apart delicately, laying them out against the floor as if she was struggling to preserve something precious.

Michael knelt beside her. "What are these?"

Sister Ned sniffled and tried to wipe away her tears. "It's so stupid, but it's all I have left of them."

Michael smoothed one against the floor and traced the crayon pressed into the page. Where had he seen that design before? The image came back to him. Graffiti in the Quarter; angel wings around a four-point magnolia. He eased the stack from Sister Ned's lap.

He remembered seeing them fall from Bridgette's hands, remembered wondering what they were, before being overcome by everything else. It was strange, but it soothed him to feel the weight of the letters pressed into the pages and see her name scrawled in careful cursive.

"What about this one?" he asked as he pulled the bottom page from the stack.

"That's Gabriel's handwriting," Sister Ned said. "What does it say?"

Michael turned it into the light and read aloud:

"Jiji told me a secret today. She said love is complicated, but when it's right, it's the simplest thing in the world."

Michael let the page drift away from his hand and stood. He brushed past Mother Superior, scooped Danni into his arms, and ran.

Thirty-Four

To anyone else, the swamp was silent, nothing but the sound of nature buzzing in the high grass. It was the first thing Michael had noticed, too. He'd since learned to listen to the chatter, hear their voices for what they were. And they were pissed.

The truck tires dropped off the pavement onto the dirt track with a heavy thump. It bounced Michael up to the roof. It also lifted and dropped Danni's head against his thigh, reigniting his painful awareness of her dead weight beside him.

Bull frogs croaked long, harsh warnings that only seemed to grow louder and longer as he neared Zed's cabin. When he opened the door, crickets and cranes and the steady, alarmed hoot of an owl joined them. Competing rhythms signaling one message: *danger*.

He ignored them, scooped Danni from the passenger seat, and staggered down the dark path to the cabin.

Zed was already leaning against the door frame,

slicing birch wood into a pile of long curlicues at his feet. Inside, the fire was stoked and waiting for company. Still, he frowned.

"And here I thought they were playin' a damn trick on me again."

He circled his finger in the air and the racket of swamp creatures faded to a whisper.

"No, I said. Michael knows better. He wouldn't dream of bringin' a loa into our swamp after everything I showed him about why we keep ourselves to ourselves, and let the Ghede alone. And yet, there you are." He dropped down the short stairs and narrowed his eyes on Danni. "And there *she* is."

Michael shifted her in his arms, pulling her deeper against his chest.

"Please, Zed," he begged. "I don't know where else to go. I don't know what happened, and I don't know what to do."

"So, instead of telling me what you don't know, how 'bout telling me what you do."

Zed motioned him up the stairs and into the cabin. Once Michael had settled Danni on the cot beside the fire, he gave Zed the quickest recap he could. The zombies, Jou Mon Mori, Queensland. Bridgette. The old man listened, nodding every so often as his eyes stayed on Danni's face.

"*Bridgette*," he said when Michael was finished. "Damned terror, that one. She get you, too?"

"You could say that."

"Though not nearly as good as she got your girl, here." Zed held his hand under Danni's nose, felt for the pulse in her neck, and stepped back. "Hand me that box on the mantle."

Michael stood to retrieve it. It was a little bigger than a match box but worked just the same. Zed pushed out the side and withdrew two thin pieces of cord. He tossed one at Michael's chest.

"Don't have to be too tight," he said. "But left over right, every time."

Zed wrapped the cord around Danni's wrists and finished it with a rolling hitch. Michael wanted to ask but didn't. Instead, he mimicked the knot around her ankles.

"Where's that knife of hers?" Zed asked at the same moment both their eyes found it in the top of her waistband. Michael slipped it carefully away from her skin and held it out.

"No. You hang on to that," Zed said. "It's the only thing that'll break those knots now. When you release her is up to you. But you best be sure. You let her loose too soon? Well, she ain't gonna hurt *me*."

Michael nodded and pushed the knife deeper into his pocket.

Zed stomped around the small cabin. He slammed a fat candle into the center of the working table, yanked herbs down from the rafters, and tossed a handful of coins into the sand, muttering the entire way.

"Damned foolishness… damned love… God gave this boy's brain a good stir, that's what he did."

Finally, Zed stopped and crossed his arms.

"All right, Michael. Ready to meet your maker?"

"I'm sorry, what?"

"I'm assumin' you brought her here to save her. *And* I'm assumin' no amount of argument from me is gonna stop you from doing the dumbest thing in the world to achieve that."

"And *I* assume you're not joking when you say I have to die to do it."

The old man nodded once. Still, Michael hesitated.

Zed pointed a hard finger at Danni. "In one hour that body will stop breathin' and the woman you know will be gone. Hard to say what might be left, but if Bridgette had a hand in it, I'm gonna guess whatever it is won't be pretty.

"Now, you wanna stop that from happening? You're gonna have to take a walk and find her. To do that, you have to go where she can but we can't, the heart of her power."

"Bel-Koté."

"That what she calls it?" Zed shrugged. "Whatever it is, you can't go there while you're still breathing."

Michael nodded his understanding. Danni had once done something similar to get to the Crossroads. It had taken Michael giving her CPR to revive her.

Still, he stared at her for a long minute. How many times had they walked this line? Cheating death, exchanging one soul for another. A harder question rose in his mind. When would their luck run out?

"Second thoughts?" Zed asked.

"Seconds, thirds. Fourths," Michael said. "When I do find her, how will I bring her back if I'm dead?"

"Leave that to me."

Of everything Zed had said so far, that made Michael feel the safest.

"Got that nail of yours?" Zed asked.

"It's not my nail, it's hers." Michael withdrew it from his pocket and dropped it on the table beside the candle. "Or maybe, it's ours. If I'd taken the time to figure that out, none of this would've happened."

Zed dusted the sand on the table into a smooth canvas and began to draw. "Go on," he said.

"I let my mouth run away with something my ego couldn't handle. I was headed to see her, stopped for take-out. Bought a bunch of balloons and a little stuffed monkey. Old parade throws. Silly gestures, you know? After what we'd went through, I cherished the lightness.

"When I came around the corner to her apartment, she was standing in the window, watching for me. I waved. The wind caught the balloons, shoved them in my face. I must've stepped off the curb, couldn't see squat for a second. But I heard the truck.

"Next thing I know, I'm on my ass on the other side of the street. Me and the monkey are covered in lo-mien and the balloons are flying away."

"You fell?"

"No, she *pulled* me. The truck, it was a big sucker. She saw it before I did. Used the nail to yank me out of the way. Saved my life, but scared the hell out of me. I didn't handle it very well."

Zed stopped drawing. "You got angry."

"I got stupid. Yelled, stomped off. Probably slammed the door. I came out here the next day. We haven't talked since. Not until tonight."

"Well, she saved your life, now you're gonna return the favor. Come 'ere."

Zed took Michael's hand and turned it over the flame. He shook a long green ribbon out of his pocket and wound it around Michael's wrist. The throb began in his hand almost immediately, worked its way up his arm and into his chest, dull but aching. His vision bent around the edges, pulsating in time with the gradual slowing of his heart, as if he was feeling his body and his soul separating from each other. He glanced up at Zed and realized… *he was.*

A thousand questions surfaced at once. Zed addressed them all.

"What you're feeling is my mojo, not yours. I'll be able to see you, hear you. But I can't help you, not until you're ready to come back. Just nod if you understand."

Michael couldn't have answered aloud if he wanted to. His chin dropped forward once, but he didn't have enough strength to lift his head. Just pulling in enough air was a struggle.

"Good," Zed whispered. "Now, if you get scared, try to get angry instead. It'll help keep you moving. Don't stop moving. Not for a second. Time will be different there, but I can't say how fast or slow. Just don't stop moving, whatever you do."

When Michael was a child, he had competed with his brother to see who could stay underwater longer. It was exactly how he felt now. The weight of the water pressing down on him, the stippled cement of the city pool below.

The pressure and the fatigue, followed by the spots in his vision. Only here it was the cabin floor at his back and Zed's power above him. Around him. *In* him.

Michael let his eyes slip shut, smelled chlorine, and died.

Thirty-Five

The air was wet against his skin. Even as Michael realized it, he felt the sweat roll between his shoulder blades. His eyes opened to long, hanging shadows that became clumps of moldy plant life. Overhead, motionless, gray clouds hung like they'd been nailed into place.

Don't stop moving, he reminded himself.

He walked forward, only because he saw no other direction to go through the thick, blanketing fog. The path led down through the undergrowth to what looked like a stream, but the water didn't move. The surface scum filled the air with rot and decay. Dead willows crowded the water's edge. He pushed past their limp branches and into a small clearing.

"Hello?" He waited. "Hello?"

It was like shouting into a cardboard box, flat and hollow, barely extending beyond his own ears. He followed a broken bridge across another stagnant stream.

A second path appeared out of the darkness, but not for long. The fog only allowed him to see three steps ahead, and were it not for careful steps, he would have ran headlong into the massive oak blocking the way.

Michael felt his way around the rough bark alternating with the dank slime of tree moss under his palms. For a second, the moss took his mind back to the cold crushing weight of death above him. He jerked his hands away. Jagged limbs and pointy leaves stabbed against his back. He leaned forward, away from the sudden sharp pain and shuddered.

He felt more than saw the area behind him open up, a sense of space at his back. When he turned, he could make out more shapes. The canopy overhead was thinner, but it took a few moments to make sense of the flat angles and thin struts in the dim light. A swing set, a teeter totter. A playground?

A playground should have meant children. Laughter. Noise. *Something.* He started across it with short, hesitant steps. The canted shape of a merry-go-round tottered over the gravel. He reached out to stop its rotation, but the metal seared the inside of his palm, blistering hot even though the air around him was dank and cold.

He put his hand out again. The metal radiated heat. He moved to the slide, tried again, and found the same thing. His eyes searched the ladders and jungle gyms, forts and monkey bars.

A dozen places to play, but not one safe to play on.

He moved toward a break in the trees where a rolling shade of darkness rose into the still sky.

"Where there is smoke…" he said to no one and started down a rocky path toward it.

The path bent and switched back, turning around on itself a half dozen times. Each time he kept straight on, once or twice crossing his footprints in the ash and mud.

The air warmed, just as thick and humid but growing so hot, Michael was sure the sweat on his face was going to boil. The path, such as it was, topped out at the edge of a ravine. Remains of a giant fire filled the valley below him. Smoldering ash drifted down to cake the earth. Michael stood on the lip and wiped his brow. Something was moving through the ash. Several somethings.

A ragged line of grays and blacks shuffled toward the center of the pyre, pushing sticks and limbs and branches into it. Feeding it. He saw no flames, but the pile seemed to be consuming faster than they could stoke it. Fresh horror filled his gut. They were *children.*

Michael ran down the path, staggered by jagged roots and limbs. He tripped, fell, and found himself at eye level with a boy who couldn't have been more than four. His eyes were blank, the skin on his cheeks stretched thin and pale beneath the layer of ash covering his body. His voice was high and thin, like a puppet inside a tinny metal box.

"You don't belong here. You should go."

Another voice came from deeper in the smoke.

"You should go."

This one was older. He stepped in close enough for Michael to see him: a teenage boy in ragged jean shorts and a threadbare t-shirt. More faces appeared behind him, more voices joining in.

"You should go," they said in unison until the

chorus reduced itself to short barks. "Go. Go. Go. Go."

"Who are you?" Michael shouted against them.

The only answers were the same short commands. "Go! Go! Go!"

"Where is Danni?"

"Go!"

The pile smoldering in front of him stretched out in jagged peaks, and the air grew so thick every breath was a battle. Michael felt his skin beginning to blister against searing heat, but the only clear path was behind him, back up the jungle wall. The children surrounded him.

"Go! Go! Go!"

Michael raised an arm to cover his face and ran straight at the fire. Within steps, he was slogging in ash up past his knees. He shut his eyes against the heat and prayed to stay straight.

His pace slowed. The ash rose above his waist. *Don't stop moving!* his mind screamed. In another step, he was up to his neck, and then the weight sucked him under. He used his last burst of energy to free his hand and drag himself forward.

Each motion became its own mission. A foot, a few inches, an inch, maybe less. Until suddenly, there was no more resistance. His hand stabbed empty air, reached out again, and dug into loose earth. He let loose of a loud scream as he pulled himself free.

The sky above him was a solid bank of gray. He gasped and gulped the cooler air, struggling to find a rhythm and a few more breaths.

Then, it began to rain. The first few drops clumped

in the ash. He lay there, too tired to move, with just barely enough energy to enjoy the sudden drop in temperature that came with the downpour.

Some of the ash washed away, the rest embedded itself in the fabric, cementing itself to his skin. He rolled over and pushed himself to his knees. It took another breath before he could rise up off his hands.

"I'm not giving up!" His voice was ragged, a shout not much better than a whisper. "Kill me or take me to her! But I'm not giving up!"

To his surprise, the rain stopped. The darkness in front of him eased enough to show him a path. He staggered to his feet and followed it. A hundred steps farther gave way to a final clearing. Michael stopped at the entrance and stared.

A massive chair hewn from white birch sat in the center of a smoldering field. Long, pale branches spread out of the back like a porcupine, tipped with sun-bleached skulls.

Danni hooked her bare foot over the armrest. Her white dress was charred, hem to seam, and her black hair was loose and moving, independent of the still air. If she breathed, he couldn't see it. But she was watching him. Blue eyes glowed like ice caps backlit by dawn. The painted half-skull on her face drew hollow shadows below her cheeks. The voice was hers, but not. Twisted, cloying, and coming in on all sides.

"It's a dangerous thing to enter this place without invitation."

A thin wave of her hand produced a fresh billow of

gray smoke from the ground beneath her. She vanished, lost inside the swell, only to cut through a second later.

The smoke clung to her, moved *with* her, and with each step, a fresh scorch mark in the shape of her bare foot stayed behind. A low chorus of voices began to hum, but their words were too far away to hear.

Danni turned out her wrists and spread her palms to the air. Her head dropped back to expose the creamy, clean line of her throat. The sky unfolded and the sound grew sharper, clearer as she swayed to the off-key melody of a lullaby.

"Jiji come to me tonight. Watch over me until morning light. As darkness falls and shadows loom, we welcome you into our room. Rest your bones beside my bed, lay a kiss upon my head. If I should die, before I wake, I give to you my soul to take…"

The last line echoed over itself. "My soul to take…"

"Danni?"

The song faded away. She twisted her head so he could only see the profile of her face.

"Not here."

JiJi. Right.

Michael stepped toward her again. "What happened to the children?"

She laughed, but even that sounded sick. Madness flashed in her eyes then faltered, pulling her face into a much more neutral expression. She drifted away, farther down the slope of the hill to wander across a wasteland of fire-gutted furniture. Mattress skeletons and seatless chairs, plastic rocking horses, melted and sinking into the mud.

"We have to get out of here," he said. "The boys need us."

"The boys have their patron. And I have this."

"Danni, this place is crazy!"

She sat on the back of the rocking horse and stroked the singed ends of his mane.

"Not madness. *Misery*."

Michael turned away, gesturing toward the decaying plants and trees. "I remember this place. I remember it green, filled with sunshine and warmth. The laughter of the children. You made them happy. Made them safe."

The horse rocked back and forth beneath her. He watched her face for recognition but only found stillness, sadness.

"Danni, I won't leave without you," he said finally.

"You'll leave," she said. "Eventually, you'll go. You didn't want to come back. You were—"

She hesitated, closing her eyes and reaching toward his chest. Her fingers settled in the place above his heart.

"Angry."

"I was afraid," he said. "I'm afraid now. But I'm here, and I'm not leaving without you. Whatever Bridgette has done to you. Whatever I've done, I was wrong. I will never leave you again."

He looked into her eyes. "If you're staying. So am I."

Something flickered in the corner of his vision, a flash of glittering white against the dull, gray clouds. Danni followed his attention skyward. Smoke pillared up from the earth to intercept the streak of white, but it dipped and dove between attacks as it sailed toward them. A white crow.

Danni stood and shook her fists at the sky. The crow stilled for a moment before finding the updraft. It dove one final time and opened its clutched feet. A long, green ribbon fluttered down into Michael's fist.

Zed.

Michael wrapped one end of the ribbon around his wrist. Danni started after the bird, but Michael caught her elbow. He slipped the other end of the ribbon around her wrist and pulled her to him.

"Hold on."

Thirty-Six

"Am I a good teacher or what?" Zed cackled.

"You could have mentioned the nausea," Michael answered from the floor of the cabin.

He blinked the gumminess from his eyes and sat up, but the room spun. It took him a full minute to find his bearings and a minute more to stop marveling at the air filling his lungs.

Zed held out his hand and pulled him to his feet. His knees felt warm, but not quite whole enough to hold his weight. Zed waited for him to find his balance.

"Careful now, you just spent ten minutes in what could be the afterlife. Wasn't real sure when you were going to stop mucking around in the dirt."

"Thanks for getting us out of there," he said.

"Don't thank me yet. We don't know what good it's done you. She may decide to go right back."

Michael followed Zed's eyes to where Danni was flexing against the knots around her wrists.

"We can't stop her?" Michael asked.

"Not for long. Shoot, those things don't hold, we may have to settle on keeping her from trying to kill us. I'm going to get something to clean her up."

Michael sat beside her on the bed. All the pale harshness was gone from her face. Her skin glowed in the warm sunlight as he watched her breathe, soft and easy, her lips slightly apart. Her brow knit with confusion when she pulled against the knots again.

"Danni?" he said cautiously.

She jerked upright and tossed him off the end of the bed.

"Let me go!"

She twisted her wrists together, pulling so hard he could hear the wet pop inside her joints. Her frustrated growls became more frustrated screams, but to Michael's surprise, the knots held.

She fell back onto the cot, sobbing before going deathly still. She closed her eyes, slowed her breathing, and went ridged.

"Yeah, that's not going to work," Zed said as he stepped through the door again. "Doors to Bel-Koté are closed. You're stuck here for the time being."

He set a bowl of water and a cloth on the floor beside Michael.

"You can't do this to me!" Danni screamed.

"That's the point," Zed said. "I shouldn't have been able to. And yet, here we are. Why'd you suppose that is?"

Danni ignored him and began to pull at the knots around her wrists again.

"Those are The Devil's Shoestrings," Zed

explained. "Struggle all you want, but I wish you wouldn't. Fixing broken bones is just gonna slow things down."

She slammed her hands against the mattress and looked at Michael.

"And you're going to *let him*, Father Stand on the Sidelines?"

Zed laughed. "Father Stand on the Sidelines. That's a good one." He sobered. "You *are* talking about the man who just crawled through your personal hell to find you."

Danni opened her mouth, but Zed's arm shot forward, snatched the bottom of her chin, and closed it for her.

"Listen to me, loa. This isn't about him. It's about you and what you let happen to a lot of people who didn't do nothing but love you."

Michael watched as her anger bled to sorrow and back again, ricocheting between the two emotions in the time it took to take a breath.

"Why are you doing this to me?" she sobbed.

Zed's voice softened. "Because it needs doin'. Get her cleaned up. I'll start supper."

Michael knelt next to her. He flattened the damp cloth on his palm, focused on the fire agate in his gris-gris bag, and blew a long breath over the cloth. The water warmed, but when he reached to wipe the mud from her face, Danni jerked away.

"*Don't* touch me."

She backed herself away from him until the space ran out, trapping her in the corner. Michael took a deep breath and moved toward her. He worked in silence, taking the dried grit off her face in slow, methodical passes. Each time he lifted the cloth, she'd relax but go rigid when he reached for her again. When he had cleaned off as much as he could, he sank back against the floor and sighed.

"That's going to have to do for now," he said. "When's the last time you slept?"

Before she could answer, Zed pushed the door back with his foot and carried in a cast iron pot and three bowls. He dumped two on the table and the third on the floor at her feet.

"Probably 'bout the last time she ate."

He spooned a thick stew from the pot, slapped it into her dish, and hung the remaining portion on an iron arm inside the hearth.

"That smells like alligator shit," Danni sneered.

"Close. Tail. Come on, Michael. Get it while it's hot."

Zed stuffed a spoonful into his mouth then spoke around it.

"What was it?" he asked. "Last thing you ate? Do you remember?"

When Danni didn't answer, Zed shook his head. "Didn't think so. Michael, what happens when you burn power and don't feed the body?"

"The power burns you."

"Right in one," Zed said. "You're using every bit of power you got just to drag your bones around, girl."

"You don't know *anything* about my power!"

Zed chuckled. "I knew your power before it blasted its way all over the gulf. All you did was get in its way. But that's how life works. Sometimes folks get what they don't earn. It's what they do next that makes them matter."

He chewed through another mouthful, wiped his lips, and turned on the stool to face her.

"Danielle, you got you some wicked enemies, people who don't want you dead. They want you to hurt for all time. That's cuz' they scared of you. Thing is, they got no reason to be until you stop being so damned scared of yourself. Now, I mean to help you with that, so, shut up and eat."

Surprisingly, she did. Michael glanced up from his bowl ever so often, watching her chew through delicate bites as if the sensation was foreign, almost painful.

Michael cleared down the table, moving through the motions by rote. Washing out the bowls, rinsing and drying them before tucking them back into the cupboards. It was good to be back in a place he felt useful.

Zed knelt in front of the fire while Michael cleaned the working table, acutely aware of Danni's eyes picking over each motion.

"Well, aren't you two cozy," she grumbled.

"Jealous?" Zed asked. He stood and dusted the ash from his hands. "Nothin' to be ashamed of. Means there's still a part of you that cares for him, deep down, which might do you both some good."

"Is that what this is about?" she asked. "You're going to teach us that love conquers all?"

Zed sniffed a laugh, but his face was full of pity. "No, darlin'. Can't say I could teach anyone so bitter how to love again. Now, it's common practice around here to say prayers before bed. Any you'd like me to say for you?" He waited. "No? Good enough. I'll come up with something. Sleep tight."

Danni leaned back and stretched across the full length of the bed, making it clear there was no room left for Michael. He grabbed a blanket, slid down the wall, and worked the stiff boots off his feet.

Michael watched her drift off to sleep while half dozing himself. For just a moment he saw her, not as she was, but as she'd been when he would have seized any chance just to watch her sleep. Soft long breaths and quiet little noises, the most beautiful thing he'd ever known.

Then, when true sleep started to take him, she cried out. His eyes snapped open. Her head made small twitches from side to side. The fading firelight played with the shadows across her face, but whatever her dream was, it wasn't happy.

As carefully as he could, he stretched out beside her. She stirred and turned into the crux of his arm as her breathing smoothed and deepened. Ten deep breaths and she'd be out, and he'd return to the floor.

He made it to six before he was asleep.

Thirty-Seven

A scream ripped over the swamp. The sound chased Michael out of the cabin, *hunting* him through the blue light of the following evening.

Where the day had started with the warmth of waking up next to her, it hadn't stayed that way. Shortly after breakfast, Zed had taken him outside to offer an ominous warning.

"Let today happen. You might get scared, even angry. But whatever you do, don't try to stop it."

The first hour had been intense, watching her face contort around an endless supply of pain, drenched in sweat and sick with fever that would no sooner cool than it would spike again. The next twelve had been petrifying.

Michael paused in anticipation of Danni's next broken shriek. The air stood silent for a second, then–

"*MI–CHAEL!*"

While the first part started strong, the end faded out on a gut-twisting sob. Michael nearly lost his grip on a wad of linens in his arms. His sanity? He was almost certain that was gone.

When he was seven he'd caught chicken pox. Sister Ned had insisted on moving him into some of the dormitories at the school to expose the other children. At first, it'd been a welcome reprieve from the double-swinging door at home. The sisters doted on him, brought him chicken soup, coloring books, and pink lotion to soothe his skin. But by evening, he was alone with the whimpered cries of the sick children around him, thinking then knowing, he had caused their pain.

He felt the same way now, moving across the grass with less than determined steps as his name was raked out across his skin. A gag rose in the back of his throat. He dumped the sheets into the grass, bent over his knees, and retched.

Zed watched him and stirred a bubbling cauldron with a long paddle.

"How can you be so calm?"

"Panic doing anything for you?" Zed asked.

Another scream cut through the swamp. Michael winced.

"I don't think she can take much more of this."

Zed waved the steam off the top of the pot into his face. "Don't ever think she ain't a bit as strong as you are."

Michael swallowed and nodded. "Right. I know. She's a–"

"*Woman,*" Zed finished for him. Something thick and dark went into the pot, followed by the Mason jar it'd been stored in.

"God built them to endure the most excruciating

pain there is to offer," Zed said. "She can take it."

"I just don't think I can take much more of witnessing it."

"Might want to reconsider that if you plan on starting a family one day."

Had he thought about it? Only in the distant, shapeless way he'd considered so many things with Danni. Of course he wanted a family. But wanting was easy. It had proven far more difficult to express that want, let alone act on it, and now part of him feared he wouldn't have the chance.

"What vexes you, boy?"

Michael shook his head. "I should go back."

"She's gentled down for the moment. Probably dozed off. So, go on, tell me."

Michael pulled in a deep breath.

"After Jou Mon Mouri, there was a man, at the orphanage. He said she tasted like—"

Zed waved him off. "I got the idea. She cheated on you."

"That's just it. I can't decide. We haven't actually ever…"

Why was this so *damn* hard? Michael stared at his hands, flexing his fingers to fists. What promise had he given her? Short of a few stolen kisses that, upon reflection, had been guarded, at best.

Then there was Bridgette. He remembered the thrill of drawing her fingers between his lips, the first real sip of passion he'd had in months. What had followed made a strange sort of sense now, knowing who and what she was.

But he hadn't known that when he let his mind consider, *seriously consider*, every single pleasure she offered.

Splashes of hot liquid hit his hands and jerked his attention back to Zed.

"Uh-uh. Ain't no sense in going there now. When she's right again, you ask her. Get the answers you need, then decide what you can live with knowing."

Danni's voice was winding up again. Michael stared back at the cabin, exhausted. "She sounds like she's dying."

"I imagine a bit of her probably is, but it's a part of her needs killin'."

He lifted the sheets from the grass, set them on top of the water, and used the paddle to pressed them beneath the surface.

"To a loa, emotion is its own kind of power. It's got its own weight, shape. Sometimes that means lollipops and rainbows, other times its a fifteen car pile-up on the I-10. Probably worse for her since all she's got to draw off of is those kids.

"Children see the world with purer, clearer eyes. Night and day. White and black. Right and wrong. It ain't til you're older you pick up watered-down habits like melancholy or apathy. So, what she gets is raw, unbridled joy, but also—"

Danni's renewed screams sliced off the end of his sentence.

"Terror," Michael whispered.

"Probably that, too."

Michael shook his head hard and reached into his pocket for the knife. "I have to untie her."

Zed threw down the paddle and jerked Michael around to face him.

"And let her go back to that hell-pit she called home? You and I both saw what that place was, what it was doing to her. Don't you get it? *This* is just a manifestation of the same thing."

Zed drove a hard finger against Michael's chest. "If you can't stay your heart, then stay your hand. The question ain't, do you love her? It's, do you love her enough to keep her from harming what she's duty bound to protect?"

He released Michael roughly, tossing him back a few feet before repeating a familiar warning.

"Let today happen. Worry about the rest tomorrow."

Thirty-Eight

Danni was vaguely aware of Michael as he moved back into the cabin. Liquid pattered across the floor, dripped from the sheets soaked in the dull tea that did nothing to ease her suffering.

At some point she'd grown aware of exactly what was happening. What it all meant. The Jou. Bridgette. Losing the orphanage. Then disappearing into Bel-Koté. It hadn't been a quiet place, but it was safe. Free of the pain she felt now, the agony of knowing just how much she had lost.

"Let me go back," she begged. "Michael, *please*."

She wanted the grief to end. Wanted so badly to feel the cleansing rush of anger and the steadiness in her grip. Not the endless waves of torture ripping her apart from head to heart.

Something soft and wet touched her lips. Water ran down her chin, but she gulped what she could, feeling his hand on the back of her neck as the other pressed the sponge against her mouth.

He whispered something, over and over. A prayer, or a chant. Some new rhythm on an older song, perhaps. She caught ones syllable and another on the refrain.

"Let today happen," he said.

Agony reignited when he set the wet sheets at the foot of the bed.

"No, please," she sobbed. "No, no, no…"

He did it anyway, unfolding them across her so they clung to her legs, her chest, the bottom of her chin. The swamp doctor's poisons seeped into her skin, leaching out the heat and replacing it with an itchy, vile dampness.

She fought him with what strength she had left. What blows connected hardly seemed worth the effort it took to make them. Her wrists and ankles ached from the rope and burned where the underlying flesh had been worked raw.

Michael sank to his knees and pressed his warm mouth to her ear.

"I am so sorry," he began. "If I could take your place, I would."

Tears fell freely down her cheeks. "If you knew… what this…felt like… you wouldn't."

"Somewhere inside you, you know I'm telling the truth. Find that. Hold on to it. When you can't?" He lifted her conjoined hands and cupped them against his mouth. "Hold on to me."

An hour might have passed. She couldn't be sure. She coughed hard, spraying the edge of the pillow with brackish, gray fluid. *Ash.* She watched it wick into the fibers, willing whatever pain that gripped her into something hotter. Less fragile.

Her mind wandered across her childhood and back. Stale, lifeless memories not worth the skin they were written on until her thoughts traveled to more recent events. To how she'd felt with Bridgette at *Ville Noire*.

What had disgusted her at the time, captured her imagination in the moment. Possession. Submission. Domination. She imagined herself bound and hanging from a hook in the ceiling, struggling away from the lightning strikes of leather across her skin. It all made sense, laying there, bound to the cot, her lover at her feet.

Michael's eyes were fixed on her hands, which gave her a few minutes of quiet reflection on his face. There was a refined smoothness to his features. So much control; something she'd always attributed to his years as a priest. But even after he'd left the church, he'd regarded her with the same careful restraint. It was everything she wanted to break in the moment.

Whether he sensed the shift in her or just her body moving under the sheet, he sat up and released her hands.

"*Do it,*" she prodded.

He patted a hand against the bedding. "Yeah, you're right. This one's practically dry."

The sheet slipped off her skin in a teasing wave. Her body flushed with a different kind of heat. Michael reached across her to exchange her pillow for a fresh one.

She arched into him, pressing the line of her breast into the hard warmth of his chest. He froze but didn't move away. One knee pressed to the bed, a hand on either side of her head, he looked down, confused.

"Danni, what—"

She lifted her head and crushed her lips against his. He moaned into her mouth. She moaned back, using what little grip she had to catch the front of his shirt, pull him down, and deepen the kiss.

His body's response was natural, predictable, but no less advantageous. She used friction to do what her hands could not, inching her skirt further up her thighs until it was only her bare skin grinding against the front of his jeans. She laid a line of wet kisses against his pulse and felt him shudder against her tongue.

"I want you," she whispered into his throat. *"Please."*

She thought she heard him agree, knew she did when his hands found her waist, sliding over then gripping softer, fuller flesh.

"Whoa there, you two!"

The weight of his body vanished. Zed held Michael by the back of the neck.

Michael swatted his hand away. "That wasn't necessary."

"Your other option was a bucket of cold water."

"How about privacy?" Danni spit.

Zed chuckled and moved past Michael. She bucked her head side to side until he caught her chin.

"I suspect you probably ain't over this quite yet. But if you are, and you're celebratin', I'll leave you be."

Danni spit into his face, but Zed's gloved hand caught it. It started to sizzle a hole through the leather. He stripped it off, ducked away before she could gather enough mouthful for a second blow, and tossed the glove into the fireplace. The fire flashed blue over red over green before finally dying.

He glanced back at Michael. "You might want to give her the rest of the night."

"Let me go!"

Danni twisted and bent with new strength, stretching the limits of The Devil's Shoestrings until they creaked with tension.

"Now, does that look like the woman you know?" Zed asked.

"She was... we were just—"

"Oh, I know what you were *just*." He clapped Michael on the shoulder. "It's a hard lesson to learn, son. It ain't magic, but it might do you some good. Sex can mask a lot of things, but none quite as cleanly as anger. You be careful what kind of rage you're getting into bed with."

Danni snarled and spit at Zed as he made his way out the door. Her fury fell to impassioned pleas.

"Michael, please. I need you. *Please*."

He scrubbed a hard hand over his mouth and knelt beside her again to push the hair back from her face.

"Wanting you is easier than breathing. Loving you? Sometimes I have to hold my breath."

He stood again and took the dry linens with him, ignoring her screams the entire way.

"Michael!"

"MICHAEL!"

"*MI–CHAEL!*"

Thirty-Nine

A vibrant, pulse of life pulled at Danni's skin. She let it trickle over her senses and saw the room. The cabin was quiet beyond the whispered hush of wind passing through the grass. What daylight filtered through the edge of the door was brilliant and white. She could *smell* it. She could smell everything. The damp wood of the cabin, the ashes in the fireplace, the sunlight. The nail.

She sat up. It hung on the far wall. The floor creaked under her foot. The sound came with an image of the split in the back side of the board. It also pulled her eyes down to her unbound ankles. Her wrists were free, too. When had that happened?

As she took her first few shaky steps, she discovered they weren't shaky at all. They were solid, sure, as if she had walked the floor her entire life and knew every splinter to avoid.

The floor, the bricks in the fireplace, each grain of sand on the wooden table. She could feel them as real as her own skin.

She laid her hand against the door. The wood was warm and beyond it, the sun was even warmer. It pulsed against her hand, and she chased it, out across the wetlands, into the sky, and to its center.

The light flared and filled her vision, blotting out all shapes beyond the narrow overhang.

"Wait," Michael said from somewhere ahead of her. "Take my hand."

She felt it before she saw it, held out toward her. Her mind followed it back as the rest of him took shape just below the stairs. He was startlingly handsome in a simple pair of blue jeans and an open button-down. Long days in the sunlight had brightened his hair to the color of new pennies.

Danni let her gaze drift across his face, down the hard edge of his jaw, to the open throat of his shirt. She swept a hand through the hair at his temple.

"It got longer," she said. "I like it."

He smiled. "Then it stays this way."

His hand slid beneath hers, just light enough to hold but still let her move at her own speed.

"Go slowly," he warned. "We were in the dark for a few days."

"Days," she repeated. "How is that possible?"

"Zed has this thing he does with time. It's weird, but it helps."

She pulled in a fresh lungful of air and held it. The smell of the swamp flexed and bent inside her chest, and when she exhaled, she watched each individual scent travel back to its origin.

"Something's not right," she said. She pulled back a step toward the cabin. "I can't, I mean, I *can* feel everything. I can *see* everything. The cypress trees, the water, the mud. There's a really hungry looking alligator somewhere in those tall reeds."

Michael followed her finger out to the edge of the swamp before turning back and considering her with a soft smile.

"It's called full sight. Zed's been trying to teach me, too, but I'm a little slow on the uptake." He nodded toward a hornets' nest at the top of a tree. "He says when I can guess how many—"

Before he finished the sentence, the answer flashed over her mind.

"Seven-hundred and sixty-three."

"*Impressive.*"

"I can feel them," she whispered.

The stutter of their wings, the frenetic rush of their bodies moving through the air...

"This might help," he said. Michael turned her hand over and laid the knife into her palm.

The frantic buzz smoothed and faded, replaced with the voices of Bel-Koté. Michael watched her, nodding as if he understood its effect.

"It's a conduit between you and the souls you control, or so I'm told."

"More insight from your mentor?" she asked.

"Zed was a priest. He retired from a parish near here. Says he spent his days since then exploring other paths to the truth."

"That doesn't explain the magic," Danni said. "How he managed to yank me out of Bel-koté. He shouldn't have been able to do that, Michael."

"Maybe you wanted to leave."

"I didn't," she assured him. "And I'm still not sure I don't want to go back."

Still, she turned the knife over and slid it into her back pocket. Michael tugged on her arm.

"Come on, I've got some things I'd like to show you."

She pulled him back. "Michael, wait. I…"

Whatever she thought to say died as he came back to her, certainty as fleeting as her breath, which seemed a lot harder now that she was outside in the fresh air and light. The scent so uniquely his clung to every sensation leaving her shaky and completely overwhelmed. The moment stretched out until finally, Michael pressed a palm to her cheek.

"I'm feeling my way through this, too."

He slowly led her around the cabin. She looked out into the marsh grass, within easy reach of alligators basking in the sunlight. A snake lifted its head as if sensing their presence, then slipped off in the other direction.

"Zed has an understanding with the locals," Michael explained. "They don't eat us and we don't litter their yards."

Michael led her past a small garden and into a slightly larger orchard, guiding her steps over some of the fallen fruit.

"We've cleared only what we needed to work. Well,

I only did a little. Zed's been living here since before we were born. Sometimes I think he's older than the swamp itself."

Danni turned a slow circle, pulling in long breaths as she worked her eyes over the trees. For an answer she'd wanted so badly, it felt strange to see now. Finally, her eyes made it back to his face.

"Would it have been so hard to at least tell me?" she asked.

"Looking back? No. At the time? I was lost. I wasn't me anymore. And every time I turned around you were turning away."

She opened her mouth, but he raised a hand to stop her. "I know. You had a lot of people pulling at you. But, suddenly, nobody was pulling at me. I was drifting—"

"You were jealous!"

"No. I was alone."

"No," she fired back. "You were sulking!"

"I was doing nothing, *was* nothing," he said firmly. "I had to fix that."

"I still don't understand why that required you vanishing from my life. You promised me, Michael. You gave me your word, but once your collar was off, you didn't have anyone holding you accountable to that anymore."

"I didn't walk away, Danni. You pushed me, remember? You reached into my chest and shoved me across the street."

"I did it to save your life!"

"Yeah, but what would you have done it for the next

time?"

The anger burned like liquid metal in her veins. She stomped down the grass to meet him.

"Do you think I had some design on becoming a loa? A *Ghede*? The only reason I did any of it was to protect those boys!"

Michael's eyes narrowed. "And look how well that turned out."

His words struck hard and met the anger building in the center of her chest. Danni followed the path of the sun, but this time, she pulled it forward, into her. The patch of earth around them began to smolder. Grass withered in the quivering heat as blackened clumps of Spanish moss fell from the trees.

Her feet left the ground, but not by choice. Suddenly, she was upside down, flung sideways, and over the swamp. Michael followed. His eyes widened a split second before he slammed against her. They both dropped into the murky water.

Danni made it to her feet before him. Zed looked back from the shore, where they had been moments before. His hands were open, summoning the water at the same time he cooled the earth.

"Let's go then, witch doctor," she snarled.

She kicked off the slick bottom of the swamp and cleared the water in one bounding leap. She was on solid ground for less than a second before being blown backwards again.

"You want to come at power, girl? You best come fully armed!"

"I'll show you armed, old man."

Danni pulled the sunlight into a ball of blistering heat between her hands, but before she could release it in Zed's direction, she was knocked underwater again.

"We can do this until your fingers prune, if'n you want!" Zed said. "But you're not coming out until you learn how to do it together."

Zed's arms rose into the air. Water rumbled somewhere behind them. A wave rose, pressing forward through the thick line of cypress trees. A wave swarmed over them, rushing toward the shore.

When it receded and Danni made it to her feet again, the earth around Zed was already showing signs of new growth. Small sprouts of green spread out from the center of the orchard.

"And when you do come out," he hollered, "stay the hell off my grass!"

Forty

Two hours later, Danni was still soaked.

They'd decided it was impossible *not* to get wet if they were still standing in the water, and resorted to balancing on two cypress stumps while trying to avoid the rest of it. However, stopping Zed's wave was not going as planned.

For the ninth time, it rose above them, blotting out the sun and then the rest of the swamp. Danni cringed and heard Michael hit the base of a tree before rolling off into the water. She held on a second longer before being driven back to join him. When she stood, Michael was spitting blood from a fresh cut inside his mouth.

"*This* was better than staying in New Orleans with me, huh?" she asked.

The water was already swelling into a new wave. She slogged back to the stump and climbed on top. He followed doggedly, swiping mud from his eyes.

"I am exhausted," he panted.

"And I'm pissed! I want dry land and a bath that

doesn't smell like rotten fish. I've got power, Michael. We just need to use it!"

He sagged against the stump. "Your power is too hot. You can't control it and neither can I."

"Then what exactly *can* you do?" she hissed.

"Come down here, please."

Grudgingly, she jumped down beside him. "And now I'm back in the water. Good plan. Real good plan."

Michael placed his hands together, fingertip to fingertip. Air rushed down, flowing between his palms as he began to pull them apart. The water shifted with them, folding back until he and Danni were standing in a small pocket of muddy earth.

The water rippled around them, held in place by his power. Suddenly, the smell of Damascus rose and myrrh made more sense. She hadn't been able to place it until that moment. *Church.* Whatever he was drawing from was his own, not hers, and deeply rooted in his history.

She turned her attention to the wall of water bearing down on them. It was a force on its own, but with Zed's strength at its heart, there was no stopping it.

"I don't know what to do!" she said.

Michael's voice was tight with strain. "Don't let me get wet."

The wave reached its crest and fell. At the last second, Danni pulled in a long breath and released it toward the surge. It shimmered past Michael, traveling out as a perfect circle. The wave fell around them, but thankfully, not *on* them.

The water receded but didn't begin again. Michael

staggered and fell to his knees. The portion of the swamp he'd been holding back rushed around them both. Danni scanned the shore. Zed was nowhere in sight.

They slogged back to the grass. Michael stopped, just out of the water, and pulled off his boots. She started across the grass but within three steps began to sink. She spun back to Michael.

"Wait!"

But he was already beside her, sunk up past his knees.

"He said stay off the grass," Michael groaned.

Danni pulled against the sucking mud. Struggling only seemed to take her down faster, and she was buried to her waist in under a minute.

"You got any bright ideas for mud?" she asked.

"Not yet. Give me a minute."

"That's about all we've got unless we can figure out how to sink slower."

"Sink slower," Michael repeated.

His eyes glazed and then fell shut. She smelled incense again, but it had lost its intensity. Still, the mud beneath her feet shifted and solidified. Whatever he was doing, lifted her, inch by inch, until she was free.

Michael sagged forward.

"There," he wheezed. "You should be able to reach the shore from there."

He was right. She hesitated and looked back at him.

"You're still stuck."

Michael shook his head. "Too tired. Just go. Get Zed. Tell him I'm done for the day."

It didn't seem fair or right to just leave him. Instead, she reached for his face. Michael pulled away.

"I'm fine, go."

"Michael, *please*."

Danni reached for him again. Her fingers brushed over the tension in his jaw before pulling herself down to him. On the surface, it was a chaste kiss, but instead of pulling away, she blew a soft breath into his mouth, much like she had done with the wave. She felt it unfold inside him, the collision of one kind of magic against another.

She withdrew and whispered, "Try now."

Michael flew up and out of the mud, continuing over Danni's head until he landed some yards away, on his back, at Zed's feet.

"Well, look at that. You grew me a tree," Zed said.

Michael craned his head back in Danni's direction. The broad-reaching branches of a magnolia tree spanned across the white sky. She laughed beneath it and a few petals shook free, dusting the ground at her feet.

Michael stood and stared at the tree and then her, his mouth agape.

Danni gave him a small smile. "*Impressive.*"

"Well, what'd we learn today?" Zed asked.

"She can protect me while I'm conjuring," Michael said quickly.

Zed nodded and then looked at Danni. "You could have left him. Come got me."

She turned her hands up to the branches of the tree. The blossoms swelled and doubled in size, along with the tree.

"Didn't need to."

Michael's mouth dropped open again, but Zed only crossed his arms and asked, "Because?"

"I can lend power when he needs it."

Zed nodded once, seeming pleased for the first time since she'd met him. He turned, walked back toward the cabin, and called to her again.

"Didn't have to kiss him to do it, though!"

A blush crept into her cheeks, and she ducked her face away from Michael's eyes.

"Yeah. I know."

Forty-One

By the time dinner was over, Danni had decided alligator, prepared any way, was disgusting. Michael, though struggling to keep his head up, still managed to find the bottom of his bowl. He stood and reached for her dish, but she stopped him.

"It's okay. I got it," she said.

His steps across the cabin were heavy. Danni smiled when she realized he was asleep before his body had fully settled into the mattress. She quietly collected their bowls, rinsed and set them beside the sink, then headed outside.

So far from the city, the nighttime sky was black, punctuated by bright stars. She knew how they felt, burning to be part of something great. She stretched toward them, feeling the pulse of life humming against her skin. Snakes, gators, fish, lizards. Even Michael, and...

Zed.

"It's a sign of hope, you know. Reaching for the stars."

"Hope?" she asked and tossed a wry look over her

shoulder. "Or insanity?"

Zed moved up beside her. "Even crazy people got dreams. Don't stop them from wishin' they'd come true."

She crossed her arms and considered him for a long quiet moment.

"I can almost hear them. Michael's. Yours…"

Zed frowned.

"I said *almost*," she said with a smile. "It's like hearing someone through a mountain pass. They're there, I just can't make out the words."

"Do you remember being able to hear them back in New Orleans?"

Danni nodded.

"When you go back, you're gonna be able to hear them again. You can't ignore them and be who you are. It'll drive you mad."

"I didn't see how interconnected everything is. The water, the grass, the sun." She looked up again. "The stars. They're all part of the same…"

The words fell apart as she tried to shape them, replaced by others she didn't know.

"*Dotasyon*," she said. "What does that mean?"

"Eh, the idea gets lost in translation, but essentially, what you're talking about is what it means to be a loa. Bel-Koté, the souls in it. Part of you *is* that power."

"And the other part?"

Zed reached up and pinched the meat of her arm.

"Ow."

"That," he said. "Your body. It's why Michael had to find you, bring you back, and get you straight again.

Once that flesh is gone, you're stuck with what you got, as raw and real as anything."

The longer Danni thought about it, the less frightening it seemed.

"Still, much as I'd like to say this is only about you," Zed continued, "it ain't. This is about the Delta, those kids, and…"

Danni blew out a slow breath. "Bridgette."

"In a word."

"I can feel her, too. She's strong." Danni eyed Zed softly and asked, "Can you?"

"Not me, happy to say. If I can feel her? She's hunting me."

"When I think about what she could be doing to Gabriel, the other boys…"

Danni spread her hand over the water. It swirled and erupted into a boil. Zed extended his hand as well, moving over the patch of ground between them. He shaped the dust and melded it with the steam. The gray cloud rose and coalesced into a figure. She recognized Bridgette's face immediately: sharp, angular features, burning eyes. She was tall and lean, even here, pacing an inch above the water.

"What do you feel when you look at her?" Zed asked.

"Anger."

"And?"

That one was harder to admit. "Fear."

"Good girl." He motioned Bridgette's statue forward, walking her to the edge of the water, inches from

Danni's face.

"Anger always comes from fear," he said, "but it doesn't have to end there. Nothing is so useless that *something* can't be made from it. Nothing is so precious that it can be made permanent. And the same power that made Bridgette, has now chosen *you* to take her place. She came from darkness. She can be returned to it."

Zed ground his fist into his palm. Bridgette's image shuddered and collapsed. "Ashes to ashes. Dust to dust."

Danni watched the dirt collected on the water's surface. The soft current rocked it in and out from the shore, breaking it apart once and then again until they were gone.

"Until then, remember," Zed said, "don't matter how big a body thinks their powers are. The world is bigger. Takes some patience to keep it in tune. But, hey, nobody knows what all you can do yet. Why should you?"

"Michael always did," she said, "even when I didn't. He saw something in me and I trusted it, relied on it. When he left, I didn't know what to do."

"And now? You think you can trust him again?"

Danni shrugged. "I don't know that he trusts me."

"Trust?" Zed chuckled and took her by the shoulders, turning her to face the cabin. "You're the star he's still reaching for."

He left her alone with her thoughts and the sound of Michael's dreams. She followed images of the boys running across the cool grass back to the cabin. Gabriel and Jean-Paul, Rene, and the others, fed through Michael's thoughts, his prayers. His hopes.

Michael stirred against the pillow. His face was still, but a little more careworn than she recalled. She ran a finger over his cheek, tracing the outline of his smile. The nail was still hanging on the far wall. She held her hand out, called it to her, and then tucked it into his fist. Danni eased down against the bed beside him and smiled against his chest.

His dreams shifted. The children evaporated from his mind and she saw herself, reflected in his eyes. Once, a long time ago, necessity had forced her into a white, collared shirt and a tartan skirt. Against black hair and white skin, she made one naughty Catholic school girl. That was how she saw herself now, although the skirt was a little shorter than she recalled, and the heels were definitely new.

In his dream, Michael circled around behind her, pulled the curve of her hip against him, and let his hands travel a path they knew by instinct alone.

Forty-Two

Softness and light.

Michael was in Bel-koté, but not the Bel-koté of darkness and ash. The truly beautiful place it was.

The sunlight filtered down through the trees and cast a soft orange glow against his eyelids while Danni's silky black hair tickled his face. It smelled of rich magnolia blossoms but beneath it, her skin. He knew this dream. Knew the strength of his arm around her, and the pleasant weight of her body tucked against his.

His hand traced the line from her shoulder down her arm to linger on her warm, naked hip. A tingle raced up his fingers and into his brain. His breath caught when she nestled deeper, and a thicker, more authentic pressure rose against the back of her thigh.

His attention lingered on the glide of her flesh, silk on steel. He flexed his arm, pulling her tighter against him. His lips softly touched the nape of her neck before dragging a line of kisses across her shoulder to the places the amber sunlight failed to reach.

Deliberate breaths blew cool air across the planes of her skin. Her smooth, delicate palms covered his. She guided his touch up to her breast. Instinct told him to squeeze softly, then harder as her murmur became a moan. His hands brushed her nipples, fingers pinching and tumbling over stippling flesh as she rocked into the sensation.

Danni turned in his arms and her mouth found his. His groan grew into a plea of hunger and want. He drank her in, but caught himself laughing when he smelled oranges, somehow knowing his memory would always recall the way she'd tasted the first time he'd kissed her.

Bottomless kisses quickly became coaxing games as she raked her teeth across his bottom lip. Their mouths opened for a deep, long embrace before she led him down her body.

His tongue caressed her hard nipple in swift circles. He started to move farther down her body, but she stopped him, drawing him back up to settle between her thighs.

Confusion flashed against all other sentiments, locking him into place as his brain struggled to catch up. The sunlight spread across her face, lifting and shifting the warmth he remembered into more solid, *living* lines. He'd had this dream before. It wasn't new.

Her actual presence in it was.

If he thought to ask how, it vanished when her lips parted, beckoning him forward with a quick flash of her tongue. His thoughts dizzied when he smelled the sharper, headier scent between her thighs. Danni held one hand against his jaw as she kissed him, using the other to guide him inside her. He rested there, letting her body adjust before he started to move.

Each thrust was slow, deliberate, but intentionally so, an agonizingly wonderful movement dedicated to feeling every sensation. He watched her face, memorizing every expression that just seemed to border on pain until he could no longer maintain their rhythm.

Michael's back arched. Slow and deep became utter abandon. Still, they moved in harmony, their breaths keeping pace, building tension, and rushing toward the edge.

His head dropped against her neck, kissing the same line across her shoulder as their movements slowed. She wrapped her fingers in his hair and guided his mouth to hers again.

He felt her breath exhaled against the back of his tongue. Then her power. Like the day before, it unrolled inside him. Fresh fires ignited, burning a path down to where they were still connected. She twisted and rolled him onto his back.

Danni stretched above him, arching up as her head fell back. Her body was like a cold-forged blade, balanced on its midpoint. Laughter sang from her pale throat. It vibrated against his skin, tickling the places her hands couldn't touch. He reached for her again, but stopped when he felt something hard in his fist. He forced his eyes from her face to the nail.

He looked back at her for explanation but she laid one finger against his lips and pulled the other, the one with the nail, against her heart. That gesture, combined with the motion of her body, drove him over the edge.

Michael blinked. He opened his eyes to the cobwebs on the ceiling and the first croak of frogs somewhere deeper in the swamp. He tried for a smooth breath, but the best he could manage were shallow pants. He shifted against the bed, letting his body adjust to the difference between where he'd been, where *they'd* been, and where they were now.

Instead of his normal, waking tension, he felt boneless and warm. Danni was curled against him, but she was also beginning to stir. He stared down the length of her body, then his. Still clothed.

Her eyes fluttered open. She stretched and shifted into a yawn before giving him a salacious look.

"I need to break you of this habit of rising with the sun. But we can continue here, if you'd like."

He opened his hand and dangled the nail between them.

"Are you giving this back to me?" he asked.

"Do you want me to?"

He shook his head. "No. Never. And certainly not after…"

A blush flooded over his cheeks, and he bowed his head, unwilling to look her in the eyes. She pulled his face up to hers again.

"I didn't want you to think that I pulled you there. You needed to be there of your own free will, and you were. *Dear god*, you were."

He blushed again but this time felt both of her hands on either side of his face, soft but insistent.

"I love you," she said.

His eyes snapped up then, fixed and unblinking. Danni pressed her lips together, blushing herself.

"Funny, isn't it? I never said it before, but I could have. Probably *should* have. By the time I thought to, it was because I wanted you to stay, and that seemed worse than using the nail. I'm sorry."

She dropped her hands from his face and kicked her legs over the edge of the bed. "It's one of many apologies that I probably owe you. For that and…"

The words died before they made it to her lips.

"What was his name?" he asked quietly.

Danni stiffened for a second. "Laurent."

"And he's one of Bridgette's slaves?"

She nodded. "I wish I could say that I wasn't thinking, or that she had me under some kind of spell, but I can't. She has this magnetism about her, as if saying 'no' isn't an option. Even then, I'm afraid I just didn't want it to be."

Michael nodded. "Before you saw me at Jou Mon Mouri, Catherine… *Bridgette*, had offered me a place to stay. I don't know why I took her up on it." He paused and took a deep breath. "My first night there, she came to my room."

"You slept with her?"

Michael shook his head. "Thought about it. Wanted to, maybe. I did kiss her. I'm still not sure why, but I was afraid I'd never have the chance again."

The harder he tried, the less it made sense. He didn't want Bridgette, and was only attracted to the parts of her that reminded him of Danni.

"Bridgette uses her power to draw out what you fear," she explained. "I think part of me knew why you left. I was afraid of it, too. It's easy to have someone who can't run away from you, but it also means you're never really sure if they want to be there."

"I do," he said softly, then more firmly. "*I do.*"

They sat quietly. Danni watched the sun creep over the horizon while Michael watched the nail.

"I have to go back," she said eventually. "Will you go with me?"

Michael pulled her mouth to his. He kissed her warmly, deeply, and then rocked his forehead against hers, leaving only enough space between them to speak.

"Even if you didn't ask."

Forty-Three

"If you want to take on Bridgette, you're going to need a plan," Zed said.

"Got anything in there that might help us?" Danni asked.

Zed dumped the contents of a leather satchel on the table and caught a jar before it rolled off the edge. He tossed a few loose ends across the pile. Chicken feet, a pigs hoof, something that once belonged to a reptile.

"What, this? This is lunch."

Danni swallowed a gag. "Well, I can't just walk back into Queensland. Whatever barrier she put up made sure of that."

Zed nodded. "It's her domain now. You have to be invited in."

"Then how are we going to get the boys out?" Michael asked.

"I said *she* had to be invited in," Zed said. His finger shot out at Michael. "Not you."

"Oh, no," Danni said. "I'm not sending him in there

by himself. Did you get a hold of Joto?"

Zed nodded. "He said Bridgette's got the whole place on lockdown. Priests posted up at every door."

"The boys?" Michael asked.

"Ain't nobody seen them. Joto says there's a lot of construction going on, too, 'cept the whole place still looks the same."

"Then what's she doing?" Michael asked.

Danni closed her eyes, remembering Ville Noire. "*Excavating*. Her club, the whole thing is miles underground. She's probably doing the same thing to Queensland. What about the other Barons?"

Zed dragged a heavy chair away from the wall and sat. "LaCroix and Samedi are off licking their wounds. Still got a few corpses kicking up dirt in the Quarter, but Cemetrie seems to be puttin' his attention to that. Better late than never, I suppose."

Danni nodded. "Cemetrie's not strong enough to be head of household. I felt it, at the Jou. That's why the zombies were rising. The Ghede wanted him to relinquish his position. They were, that is, *we* were trying to decide who it should go to."

Zed frowned and shook his head. "You're forgetting something."

Danni closed her eyes and tried to picture the Jou. The wild crowd, their screaming chants. It all flooded back in a rush, but where she'd only heard her name before, she now recalled their prayers, their pleas. Their want.

"They were letting the people decide," she said slowly.

"A time honored and *fair* way to make such a choice, don't ya' think?" Zed cackled. "Well, don't hold us in suspense. Who'd they pick?"

Danni considered it. She paced the floor of the cabin but pushed her awareness beyond the walls and into the swamp where the air was cool against her skin. She traveled farther, where dirt roads turned to pavement, two lanes to four then more as they raced into New Orleans.

She felt Bridgette first, a pulsating heat like the wind off some arcane furnace. Danni could see the width and shape of her shadow, hung over the city, pressed down by its weight as it grew. Bridgette was smothering the people's prayers with her conceit.

"She's trying to shut them out. Not like I did. She can hear them, hear their pain. She *enjoys* it."

Danni turned her attention back to those voices. They responded with her name. Bridgette's veil flexed, turning the opaque image of a city into a flat, black wall. She sucked in a sharp breath and snapped her eyes open on Zed.

"That isn't who the *people* are asking for. You knew this the entire time?" Danni demanded of Zed.

"So did you, more or less."

Michael looked to Zed, then back to Danni. "You?" he asked. "You're Ghede head of household?"

Zed pushed himself up from the table and drew a fresh glass of water from the spigot. He set it down in front of her. "Drink that."

She did, slow at first and then gulping until she was breathless.

"You a'right?"

"What's wrong?" Michael demanded.

"Just opened herself to the squall a bit, felt her people. Didn't you?"

Danni nodded shakily.

"Easy to get overwhelmed."

Michael pressed a warm hand against her neck. He worked his thumb against the muscle, urging the tension to release. Calm spread across her shoulders and down her spine. Her thoughts drifted along the objects littered across the table.

Besides Zed's there was another pile, a small scattering in front of Michael's usual seat. A blackbird's wing. A lump of compressed coal. A sliver of white bone that had come from the box Cemetrie once used to contain the souls she and Michael sought; the game that had brought them together.

Wait.

Her eyes raked back over the table, but the pile wasn't there. She twisted to see Michael's face, then farther down to the bag tied at his hip. He offered her a soft smile and brushed his hand against it.

"Gris-gris bag," he said.

"There's a piece of a bone box in there. The portmanteau that I broke."

"Uh, yeah, I…"

Zed let out a long, low whistle and stepped back to put a few feet between them. He wagged a finger at her.

"You, uh… just pick that out of his head?"

"I guess. I mean, he was rubbing my neck and I

thought I saw it on the table, but then I realized it was—"

She stopped, more concerned with Zed's apparent shock then how or why. "What? What did I do?"

"It's fine, Zed," Michael said. "It was probably my fault. I was using it as a focus, but I probably wasn't shielding right or something."

Zed shook his head. "Nah, shielding ain't shit. I told you about that bag, boy. That's your mojo, your magic. Ain't nobody, loa or otherwise, can see in it without your say so."

Danni searched Michael's face for understanding. "I didn't mean to. Honest."

"Move away from her, Michael," Zed said. "I have to know."

Michael hesitated. "Give me your word you won't hurt her."

Zed's eyes stayed on Danni as he nodded once, and Michael stepped away from her. Zed shifted and dropped his hand to his own gris-gris bag.

"Go on then. Tell me what's in it."

Danni looked pleadingly at Michael. "Am I supposed to be able to or not?"

"Not," he said, "but don't worry about that. Just tell him what you see."

Her first instinct was to focus on it directly. There was nothing particularly special about it. The deflated leather sack, the braid of dark cord twisted around the puckered top. She followed the line of Zed's hip up to his eyes.

The tanned skin around his mouth was full of a

lifetime or two of experience. The longer she stared, the clearer she could see the marks of each expression. Emotion folded into his face, lines like well-worn paths he'd travelled from birth to death and back again. Anger. Grief. Happiness. Sorrow. *Wonderment.*

She saw it. A flash of silver, starred out to six points, four rounded, two flat like the head on a nail. It glinted under a light sourced from no certain direction. Danni tipped her head, considering its size, its shape. Its weight.

"It's a jack," she said and looked at Michael. "A steel jack. Like children play with." She saw it again, brighter, clearer, and added. "Or *played* with."

Spoken aloud, the words pulled the angle out wider, allowing her to see into a different room. It was a slat-walled shack, much smaller than the cabin. Just enough space for a lumped mattress, the fireless hearth, a squat table and two chairs. Clear, white sunlight filtered through the window, illuminating the dust motes around the child on the floor. He opened his hand and released a red ball. His arm darted out and swept the jack into his palm as the ball fell then bounced once before being caught again.

"Watch, mama."

He repeated the game. Up, snag, bounce, catch. "Onesies."

At the wash basin against the wall, his mother smiled at him warmly.

"That's good, Zedekiah. Probably need to get you a few more if you want to count higher."

Zed shook a mop of blond curls. "I can pretend."

The ball went up. His hand came out, snatching the solid jack then another empty place on the floor. Catch. "Twosies."

Danni watched the sadness leak over Zed's mother's face. She dotted the tears from the corners of her eyes before mustering a smile again.

"You're a smart boy, Zedekiah. As long as you have your imagination, you don't need anything else."

The room began to fade, drawn back until all Danni could see was Zed's older, creased face, watching her. Waiting. She couldn't help but smile.

"You were cute as a kid," she said.

Zed didn't answer or so much as blink.

"Come on, old man, you let me see that one."

When he finally did speak, the weight of several competing emotions filled his voice.

"If I was going to *let* you see anything in this bag, it would not have been that."

He pushed himself away from the wall, but hesitated before he sat again. "What is it they call you in the city? The judge?"

She nodded. "Jiji."

Finally, Zed sat but she could hear the creak in his bones. "You're far more dangerous than that. You could break a man with the things you see. Tread lightly, *maman*."

Danni bristled. "I'm no one's mother."

"You're everyone's mother now. Ignore that, and you'll be right back where you were a few days ago." He footed out the chair across from him. "Now, sit down and lets figure out how we're gonna crush the viper in your nest."

Forty-Four

"You're *sure* this is the only way?" Michael asked.

His eyes followed Zed as he moved window to window, checking the locks, and drawing the shades.

"You think I want to show this son of a bitch where I live? Took me a decade to put up the barrier to keep him out. Believe me when I say, she wants to talk to her brother, this is the only way it can happen here."

Zed extended his hand. "Better give me your gris-gris bag for the time being."

Michael unhooked it from his belt and dropped it into Zed's hand. For something he'd only had a short time, the vacancy on his hip made him uneasy.

"It'll be yours again," Zed said. "When I say so."

"I almost feel bad we did this to her a few days ago."

"Then you understand why it's necessary now."

Michael nodded. Zed tucked Michael's gris-gris bag inside his own and went back to the careful task of drawing straight lines of salt on the window sill.

"What are you doing?"

"Makin' damn sure he can't walk out this cabin."

Michael paced a circle in the floor and then sat back down. He stood again when he heard Danni's footsteps trotting up the stairs.

"You find it?" Zed asked her.

"Exactly where you said it would be." She lifted the hunk of limestone from her side and set it in the middle of the table. "I'm curious, though. Who puts a cemetery in the middle of a swamp?"

"Another tale for another day. That gonna be big enough?"

"I'm not sure it's a question of size so much as that it *is* a headstone. And I wasn't going to lug the entire thing past that alligator."

"I told you to take a bag of marshmallows," Michael said dimly.

Danni held his face between her hands and kissed his forehead, his nose, and then finally his lips.

"It won't be for long," she said.

"What if he says no?"

Dani shrugged. "Then he says no."

"What if he says yes?"

"Then we deal with that when we have to."

"What if he–"

"Michael, we don't have to do this," she said. "We can come up with something else."

His hands settled on her hips, thumbs brushing the skin just above her waistline as he buried his nose in her hair.

"If I could hold you, I'd be okay."

She laughed softly against him. "You really want your hands on me while Samedi takes over your body?"

He pulled back. "Yeah, maybe not."

She eased him down into the chair but kept her hands on his shoulders as she looked to Zed again.

"Peppers?"

He rattled a cluster of loose pods, still lava red even after they'd dried. He tossed them onto the table beside Michael and reached for an unmarked bottle in the uppermost corner of the kitchen cabinet. He wiped a hand across it, clearing the dust from the glass.

"I was saving this for who knows what."

Danni took it but caught his weathered hands between the bottle and her own. She lifted his knuckles to her mouth and brushed a kiss across them. "Thank you."

She motioned toward the nail around Michael's neck. "I'll need that."

Cautiously, he slipped it over his head and passed it into her hands.

"You're sure this is going to work?" he asked again.

"It's Samedi's nail. It was his conduit to me when it was buried in my chest, should work the same the opposite direction."

"*Should*," Michael repeated, his mouth suddenly dry.

"It'll be like falling asleep," she explained. "And when you wake up, I'll be right here."

He nodded. Danni turned the nail over in her hand and bounced the head against the stone. It made a soft *ping* inside the cabin, and yet Michael still heard it echoing off against the cypress and glades.

Ping.

The sound reverberated out into the swamp then shifted, falling in on itself. It resonated and doubled, a cymbal crashing against its mate. Michael pulled in a big lungful of air.

Ping!

Danni watched Michael's chest expand, but just as she expected him to exhale, his head slipped forward against his chest. She held her breath, watching him, until finally, Michael eased back in the chair.

No. Not Michael.

It was his face, but not his expression. Gone were the subtle, soft lines of his smile and the hint of constant worry in the center of his brow. What stared back at her now was much harder, darker. Deadly.

"*Cher*. So good to see you."

It took her a beat longer to adjust to the sound of Michael's voice played over the Baron's more sinister presence. Samedi turned a hand over in front of his face, inspecting Michael's skin.

"Can I assume you're responsible for this?"

"Yes," she said.

Samedi stood, flexing his shoulders and bouncing a few steps.

"I'm not a particular fan of the skin tone, but he's reasonably strong. Healthy." Michael's green eyes darkened as they scanned Danni head to toe. "*Virile.*"

"Don't get used to it," Zed said. "You're not staying."

Samedi pivoted. "Father Brantley. Still livin' in squalor, I see."

Zed glanced past him to Danni. "Get on with it."

"Yes, *cher*. Let's."

He rushed the short distance. Maybe it was because he was wearing Michael's face, but Danni reacted a split second later than she should have. Samedi carried her backwards into the wall, pinning her hands above her head as his tongue slid against the line of her throat. It was a confusing sensation. While her brain knew it wasn't Michael, her body didn't. She arched into the warm, wet brush of his voice against her ear.

"I can smell your desire, *cher*."

"Get off me!"

Danni jerked her knee up into his groin. He staggered backwards, gasping as much as he was laughing.

"Careful, now. Don't want to break your toys."

"I didn't call you here to play. I want to make a deal."

Samedi's laughter stayed breathless as he sunk back into the chair.

"Your deals don't tend to work out well for either of us. Nor do you stick with them. In fact, I–"

He stopped, his eyes fixed on the peppers and the rum sat out beside him. "For me?"

"Tribute," she said. "From one Ghede to another."

Samedi rubbed a hard thumb against the top of the bottle. "You *are* serious."

She closed the distance between them, taking a glass from the shelf along the way. She held it in one hand and took a liberal swig off the top of the bottle. Samedi watched her with Michael's eyes as she swished it around her mouth, spit into the cup, and offered it to him.

He was quick to accept, even quicker to swallow and pour himself a second glass.

"This body has no head for liquor. Talk fast."

"Joto told me you were cursed once, something called a *débouyé-a.*"

Samedi swirled the rum around inside the glass. "What of it?"

"How does it work?"

"Do you mean to unravel my dear wife, *cher*?" He clucked his tongue. "That seems a bit petty, even for you."

"I want my children back."

"Your children?" He laughed, sharp and loud. "*Your children*? To my recollection, they were mine long before they were yours. You think I'm going to help you steal them again? You been out in this swamp with madmen too long."

"The people named her head of household," Zed called from across the room. "Aren't you duty bound to do what she asks of you?"

"What is duty if our would-be queen cannot *enforce* her will?"

"Fucking Ghede," Zed grumbled.

Danni reached for the bottle and poured a few more fingers into his glass.

"I only want Queensland," she said. "You can't tell

me Bridgette doesn't have something else you want. What I'm offering you is a way to replenish The Crossroads."

"You mean, after you tear Bridgette apart, you want to give me her leftovers? Gutter-sluts and street-corner tricks?" Samedi spit at the floor. "*Ou se yon move moun fache.*"

"I'm not crazy. Not anymore." Danni stood and sighed. "But if you're not interested, fine. I can't force you to make a deal. Go."

"Now, *cher*. Don't act hasty. We're negotiating." He pushed out her chair with his toe. "Go on. Sit down. Conversate."

A quiver of heat formed at the edge of Zed's fingertips, as if he was heating some unseen element just to ease his tension.

Danni withdrew the chair and sat. Samedi busied himself with the peppers, wedging a thumb inside and stripping off long, dry pieces before shoving them into his mouth. Michael was going to feel that later.

"Tell me about the curse," she said again.

"That slave girl. It was her fault."

"I know the story. How does it work?"

"You heard a story. You didn't hear *my* story."

Samedi poured another glass and propped Michael's feet on the table.

"Had me a plan. Old de'Larousse had been playing the big dog on the island of San Lucia, making all my people jump. '*Master this*' and '*master that*'. Making them think they had it good, that he was gonna feed them, clothe them, and bring them the white man's God.

"Ignorant fool traded me a cornerstone off his house for a couple small favors. All he thinks 'bout is the next dollar, don't even see his own unmaking coming with the new moon. The people gonna dance, they gonna celebrate and sing to *me*! And that big house gonna bury him right where he stand."

Samedi walked his index and forefinger over the tabletop. "And then that little Emeka came around, talking about how Bridgette, my sweet Bridgette, had been spending her days looking at white men and nights with the master. Talking about how she don't see how I can stand it, getting less attention.

"So, I entertained little Emeka, gave her a night's pleasure. *And what a night we had*! Up all night, down again, through the barn and out into the field. Laying with each other, playing with each other."

Danni spun a lazy finger in the air. "I get the point."

Samedi's voice fell a few octaves. "Come the next morning, she had something that belonged to me."

"De'Larousse's cornerstone," Danni said with a growing smile. "She tricked you."

"*SHE DIDN'T TRICK ME!*" He pounded his fist into the table. The glass jumped. "*Non, cher*. That girl and her master got ahold of some *powerful* magic."

"Bridgette."

He nodded. "A test of my loyalty, she said. My fidelity. And I failed. *Mon Dieu*, was she angry. She punished me, which was her *duty*, as my wife." Samedi shot a quick glance at Zed. "See the difference?"

"Was Joto right, though?" Danni pressed. "You lost

your body?"

"Lost? *Mais non.*" He leaned forward over his knees. "She ripped me to pieces, starting with my favorite part."

His hand clutched the same spot on the crotch of Michael's jeans. The amber glow in his eyes intensified as he drew out every word.

"It is your last earthly possession, *cher*. Once it is gone, the only thing that will sustain you are the souls you take."

A shiver started low in her gut and worked its way up her spine. She forced herself to take a long breath before speaking again,

"So, what happened after Bridgette killed you?"

He shrugged. "I went away, made my amends to earn her favor again. And when I came back, I burned that plantation to the ground."

"But wasn't de'Larousse dead and gone by then?"

"His children weren't," he growled. "I wiped out his name."

Danni chuckled. "For a Baron, you're *such* a guy."

"Mind your tongue, *cher*." He fanned a hand against Michael's chest. "He has so many things he wants to do with it, yet."

"Just so I have this straight, Bridgette took your body, then your power, only to give it back when it suited her?"

"My wife enjoys pain, and inflicts it on anyone under her hand. Me, my brothers, we do our fair share, but not like Bridgette. She's a snake, probably the one who gave Eve the apple. And we've never seen her fit to care for children. So you can bet, them boys are suffering. She'll keep them that way for a while, until their bodies are broken, then she'll sell them off, one by one, and you will *never* find them again."

He stared down at the empty glass, eyeing Michael's reflection, but seemed suddenly unsettled.

"It ain't our way, you know? We Ghede might be death, but death is as much of life as anything. And it's against that nature to harm a child."

Danni started to remind him of all the harm he'd already brought to the same children but thought better of it. Eventually, Samedi sat back.

"I'll take your deal. But know, just because you steal them back, don't mean I'm done with them. I will have them again."

"You'll try," she said. "Tell me how the brick works."

"It isn't the brick that matters, *cher*. It's who has it. You'll need the cornerstone from the orphanage. Good luck gettin' your hands on it. By now she's got it in her belly with the others."

"Others?"

"Ville Noire. Belle Marseille, places she's got tied up for her pleasure. We all do it, *cher*. Swallow the stones. We are our houses. They are in us."

Which meant she'd need to get close to Bridgette. One problem at a time.

"Visit your brothers," Danni said. "Tell them my plan. I'll distribute powers evenly after Bridgette is dealt with, but they can't move against me."

Samedi nodded once. "And your word is good on that?"

"Better than yours. But, if it helps..."

She laid the knife against her hand and made a quick slash, pulling a fresh line of blood to the surface. Samedi didn't hesitate to extend Michael's palm. She tried not to go too deep. The cut opened and she laid hers against it. They shook once, but when she tried to release him, Samedi pulled her into his lap.

"An accord such as this deserves celebration, don't you think?"

He rocked his hips up, but she pushed him back against the chair.

"We're done here."

"I'd say we're done when I'm done. You still have something I want." He slipped a hand under her shirt to the curve of her breast. "Pretend I'm your boy. Makes no difference to me."

Danni flashed panic-filled eyes at Zed, but only saw his patient nod. She looked back at Michael's face and ran a thumb against his lips.

"There you go, *cher*," Samedi urged. "Kiss me."

She nodded and leaned in, pressing her lips against his. She held there before moving deeper into Michael's mouth. She tasted Samedi's sweetness, the faint hint of burnt sugar, and drew it down her throat. She held it for a minute before blowing it back into his mouth and deeper.

Michael jerked back, gasping. A hand clamped down on her hip. The other rose to clutch her throat, but there was no strength in either of them. She watched the fire in his eyes fade, washed away by a deep spring green.

"Why are you in my lap?" he asked.

Danni laughed and kissed his forehead before helping him untangle himself.

"How do you feel, Michael?" Zed asked.

"Like I got mugged in a bar." He started to stand and winced. "Why does my groin hurt?"

"Sorry," Danni said. "At least I didn't stab you."

Michael frowned at his bloody palm. "You didn't?"

She pulled his hand up to her mouth and spit, working saliva into the wound until the cut closed. Michael opened and closed his fist a few times.

"Did we get what we needed?" he asked.

Danni gave him a quick recap of her conversation with Samedi while Zed swept the lines of salt away from the window. By the time she was finished, so was he, and Michael had only one question.

"How are we going to get you close enough to Bridgette?"

"You're going to pull me," she said. She laid the nail in his palm and closed his fist around it. "Just get the boys out. It'll be my fight from there."

"Not alone, it won't," Zed said quietly.

Danni turned to face him. "I can't ask you—"

"You're not."

Zed dusted the remaining salt from his hands and reached past them for the bottle on the table. He took a long drink, spit into the glass, and then passed it into her hand.

Danni held it to her lips, keeping her eyes on Zed as

she swallowed. The barrier between them fell, and the distant whisper of his voice became an allegiance as solid as all the bedrock below their feet.

Akeyi yo.

Forty-Five

Michael pressed his face against the window of the van for a clearer look at the back of Queensland. Storm clouds banked in from the gulf, blocking out the stars and filtering the moon so everything was bathed in half light and shadows. There were no fences, no guards. Why bother? No one in their right mind brought trouble to Bridgette's door, let alone her backyard.

"I mean really, Mikey, how many great rescue stories start at the thrift shop?" Joto asked.

Michael reached under his shirt to scratch the middle of his back. "This one did, leave it alone."

"The bad guys wear black. We wear black," Zed said.

"And stroll, don't sneak, I know," Michael answered. "And if one of them gets close and sees we're not one of 'em?"

"We'll deal with it," Zed said.

"You can't be killing the guards, man," Joto objected. "She's connected to them. The minute you kill

301

one, she'll be on to you."

"We know, Joto," Michael said. "Just be ready, we don't know how the boys are. They may be running. We may be carrying them." Michael held out his hand. "You bring the other thing?"

Joto blew out a long breath and unfolded the cloth around the pebble from the Crossroads. "You sure about this?"

Michael reached between the seats and plucked it from his palm. Zed caught his wrist.

"That's Samedi's magic," he warned.

"Which also means it's Ghede magic, right?" Michael asked. "I can handle it."

Michael dumped the pebble into his gris-gris bag and led Zed out of the side door of the van. Joto drove to the end of the block, made a u-turn, and stopped. Michael settled the ball cap low over his eyes and marched toward the back lot of Queensland. Zed moved up next to him, holding a paper bag at his side.

"You pack a lunch?" Michael asked.

"Nothing but dust and a cold breeze," Zed said.

They made their way through piles of earth and stone as big around as houses.

"There's enough dirt here to build a small island," Michael said.

"It had to come from somewhere," Zed added and pointed ahead.

The half light surrounded a darkened maw. It seemed to swallow what little light fell toward it. Fifty feet from it, Michael saw two shadows detach from the darkness.

"Wonders never cease. Look, Oscar, relief at last. And only five minutes late."

Michael pitched his voice as deep as he could manage. "Sorry. We have our own orders."

He moved ahead of Zed and tried to walk past them, but a hand in the center of his chest stopped him.

"Hold up there, *ese*," Oscar said. "Nobody goes in here. You know the rules."

Zed stepped forward. His left hand opened, revealing a small pile of fine dirt. He depressed the nozzle on a can of compressed air in his right. The dirt turned to a small focused dust storm. It blew across the two guards in a tight, thick stream. Michael ducked away, and when he looked back, the guards were gone.

"Okay, Zed," Michael said. "How'd you do that?"

"Told you, dust and a cold breeze. A can of air to create a stiff wind. A bit of dirt from a desert mountain out west. Imagine how hot they're gonna be when the sun comes up in Arizona tomorrow."

"Not hurt, but not here," Michael said. "Crafty."

He turned toward the dark entrance.

"Wait," Zed said. He nodded back toward the two shadows walking toward them. "Relief's late, remember?"

Michael nodded. "Send these two after the others, might be awhile before anyone else comes by this way."

"Seems likely."

They waited until the two silhouettes got closer. Michael waved when they waved. One of them grunted and handed him a clipboard. He couldn't make out what it said, but it didn't matter. Zed stepped out from behind Michael, dust and can in hand. The dust struck both men in the face, knocking them backward as they blinked out of sight.

The darkness in the cavern was so complete that phosphenes danced in front of Michael's face, but it didn't seem to bother Zed. Michael concentrated on following the sound of the old man's footsteps into the still air. He paused. Michael stopped behind him.

"Left turn. Another turn a few steps later. Stay close. There's light up ahead after that. Cover your eyes just 'fore we get there, so it won't blind you."

"How can you tell?" Michael asked.

"I been walking the swamp at night about as long as you've been walking upright."

He followed Zed's steps until they stopped again, covered his eyes, and faced the light. Slowly, he opened his fingers and dropped his hand. Almost immediately, he wished he hadn't. What it revealed was more than brightness.

The cavern below them was massive, nearly twice as deep as Queensland was tall, and the boys were at the bottom. The narrow, ragged walls were dimly lit by a fiery glow. The heat it produced made it hard to breathe. Michael set a tentative hand against the rock but jerked back instantly. Not just hot, *scalding*. A couple quick glances at the boys' shoulders hold Michael it was a lesson learned from experience, not warning.

He watched them shuffle back to the intersection of three different caverns. All the boys carried something; shovels, picks, ropes, though most of them had canvas sacks filled with dirt and rock. They struggled to dump them into a massive cart before shuffling back for another load.

"This is inhuman," Michael breathed.

"Let's get to it."

Zed scanned the lip of the chasm for guards and found none. "We're going to have to go down and bring them up to here."

Michael nodded and followed Zed. They marched down the winding ramp cut into the stone. The sounds of digging and scraping grew louder, and the air got thicker. The uneven floor wound down to the center of the cave.

"Where are the guards?" Michael whispered.

"We are the guards, son."

The boys shuffled past him without so much as an upward glance. Some faces he recognized, but most he didn't. He resisted the urge to reach for any of them.

"There's a few more than I remember," Michael said.

By about double, which only further complicated getting them all out of there.

Michael spotted Maurice and Rene standing over a hole in the center of the floor. They worked together to pull a sack of dirt over the edge before hefting it onto the back of a third boy.

He found several more holes positioned throughout the cavern, two boys on top and one more, presumably, at the bottom, carving out core sections of rock.

"They're already starting the next level," Michael said.

Zed motioned him for silence. A guard stood in the center of the room.

"About time you got down here!" the guard called. He started toward them, jerking a thumb over his shoulder. "One of them fell down the hole. Thinks he might'a broke somethin'."

When he reached them, Zed blew the dust at the guard and the guard fell back. Just as the first guard disappeared, his partner's head popped up from the top of the hole.

"It ain't broke. He can work it off just like the others. Lazy little bastard."

The second guard dusted his hands together as he stood. Zed started forward, but Michael was closer. He caught the guard by the collar, jerked him forward, and head-butted him in the nose. Blood flooded down his face, his eyes glazed over. He fell to the earth, unconscious.

"That feel good, Rambo?" Zed asked. He knelt down in front of the guard and felt for a pulse. "He's breathing. Maybe we got lucky. Bridgette probably don't keep track of anything less than death."

Michael rushed to the hole, squinting through the dust.

"Father Michael?"

"Gabriel?"

A beat of silence followed before a thin, tired voice answered him.

"I didn't fall. I jumped." His hands rose over his head, palms outstretched and holding a large, bald rat. "Roben fell. Had to get him."

"Gabriel, can you climb out?"

"I don't think so."

"Can you stand on the ladder?"

"Yeah," he said hesitantly. "I can stand."

"Hold on. I'm bringing you up."

Michael hauled him up as smoothly as possible. Gabriel rolled off the ladder onto his back. Michael knelt over him, feeling for broken bones or anything out of place. He worked his way back to Gabriel's face and stared at him.

"It's really you," Gabriel whispered.

"It's me."

When Gabriel threw his arms around his neck, Michael felt something tight and painful release from his gut. He blinked away tears and noticed the rat peeking out of Gabriel's ragged collar. It chittered at Michael before darting beneath Gabriel's shirt again and dropping to the floor. It lifted its snout into the air, and Michael saw the tattoo etched across his skin. The rat turned back and fired off another series of quick chirps.

"That really is Roben," he said.

Gabriel nodded. "And he says we need to go. There are more guards coming."

"Then let's get out of here. Zed?"

"Almost ready. We don't want them to panic on the way out."

He'd already managed to gather the rest of the boys in a loose line and was working his way down them, dabbing white birch oil onto their foreheads.

Michael turned back to Gabriel. "Straight up and

out, okay?"

Roben screeched again, and Gabriel shook his head. "We can't. They're up there."

"Is there another way out?" Zed asked. Michael realized he was talking directly to Roben. The rat started forward, stopped, and looked back.

Zed's attention flew to the lip of the cavern, his eyes searching the rim as tension settled his jaw into a hard frown.

"*I can feel her,*" he whispered.

Michael could, too, he realized, but not the way he had. This was like being stalked inside a dream, sensing a predator just out of your vision, watching you, waiting for you.

Zed looked to Roben. "Lead on, critter."

Michael carried Gabriel. Roben led. The other boys followed. Together, they left the dim light and hurried into the darkness at the far edge of the wall. Roben vanished inside it, followed by Zed.

Gabriel whispered into Michael's ear. "Duck, Father."

Roben's fast squeaks echoed down the dark corridor ahead of him, pulling in the sound of the shuffling feet that followed. A hundred yards, maybe more. Michael felt the outside air well before they reached it. He sucked in deep breaths just to assure himself of its presence. He tightened his grip on Gabriel, clutching him to his chest.

Bridgette's power chased them. He felt her breath on his neck, hot and damp.

The cave ended, but it took Michael a second to

find their position. They were five-hundred yards from Queensland at the foot of a runoff canal, but still a block away from Joto and the van.

Zed kept the boys together, collecting the stragglers as they trickled out of the cave.

Michael eased Gabriel to the ground, making sure he was steady before releasing him.

"Gabriel, go with Zed." Michael stood and looked at Zed. "Follow the culvert east until you smell seafood. That's the back of Harper's. Cut across the alley. That should take you right back to Joto."

Zed caught his elbow roughly. "Stick to the plan."

Michael gave him a swift nod. "Go. *Go!*"

He watched Zed and the boys until they were out of sight, then hurried back into the tunnel. The cool air turned hot again, but he stopped just before rushing into the main cavern. He let himself feel everything, the rocks, the dust, and the sensations floating on the waves of heat. There were at least ten guards in the center of the room now, several others on the way, but as far as he could tell, no Bridgette.

Michael stepped forward.

The guards spotted him instantly but didn't move to intercept him. They parted instead around Laurent, who was firing rapid, angry words into a cell phone. His sneer spread into a smile when he saw Michael, and he pulled the phone away from his ear.

"Oscar says hi," he told Michael. "Actually, he said he wanted to spit you, roast you, and eat your balls for dinner. Lucky you, he's going to have to get in line."

Forty-Six

Laurent escorted Michael up the path, not that his feet touched the ground more than a few times. The guards carried him, more or less, between them, but eventually even they grew tired. They dropped him to his knees and sent a hard shot to his kidneys to stand him back upright. Michael flinched and kept walking.

They stopped again at a heavy metal door. It slid sideways into the rock wall and fluorescent light washed over them. It was meant to be a locker room, but it looked more like a slaughterhouse. The white, floor-to-ceiling tile tapered where it reached a drain in the center of the floor.

Two guards shoved Michael inside, across the room, and face first into a wall. One of them blocked his escape while the other turned on a hose. Water ripped at his skin and clothing, running black then gray, and finally clear. The water stopped suddenly. The silence made Michael's ears ring. He spit a mouthful of water across the tile.

Laurent snapped and yet another guard stepped

forward with a bundle of black fabric in his arms. Silk pajamas. Of course.

"Strip," Laurent said.

Michael crossed his arms and glared at him. "Fuck you."

"Easy way, hard way, *homme*." Laurent flashed a cruel smile. "I'm hoping you pick the hard way."

Michael forced his arms to settle at his sides and began to work his clothes off for himself. The boots came off his feet with a thick sucking sound. The remaining mud slung outward toward the guards. It helped to create some distance when they jumped back from the spray. Michael pulled the soggy sweater over his head, using the stretched, bedraggled nature of the fabric to hide palming the nail and his gris-gris bag.

While the other guards found spots on the wall to stare out, Laurent held Michael's eyes the entire time. Michael ground his back teeth against his tongue. It was meant to be humiliating, but he wouldn't give Laurent the satisfaction of seeing him turn away. Michael jerked his pants down to his ankles and stepped free of them.

The guard to his left tossed the pajamas against his bare chest. The silk pants were an inch too short, but they had pockets. The nail slid inside without a sound. The top was a wrap around, with a wide, deep crimson belt.

"Give it to me," Laurent said.

"Give you what?"

"Gris-gris bag. Every want to be witch doctor has one."

Michael pulled it from the bundle of clothes and

tossed it at Laurent's feet. He bent to retrieve it.

The wall opposite the entrance to the caves was smooth and matte-white, marked with the elongated silhouette of a lily. Laurent passed a hand over the center of the flower and the wall rose up out of sight. The guards prodded Michael inside. Laurent followed. The door slid down and the elevator rose, carrying them up into Queensland.

The ride was short, and a few hallways and a couple of turns later, they passed through a set of double doors. The hallways had been sterile, unmarked, but nothing unusual. Unusual was just the beginning of the words that described what waited on the other side of the doorway.

Sumptuous, garish... *obscene* came to mind. It was hard to see where the orphanage had been, or if it even *was*, under the new decor. Candles hung in sconces on the high walls. The flickering light cast wavering shadows over the room. Every piece of furniture was rich and overstuffed, adorned in Victorian patterns and mounted on heavy oaks and mahoganies. The walls were covered in tapestries that portrayed one carnal and outrageous act after another.

The carpet was thick and soft against Michael's bare feet, until his foot came down on a damp spot. His recoil was purely reaction, it caused Laurent to slam into his back.

"Mind your step."

Michael glanced down. He'd been in enough boys' dorms that, even in the shadowy light, he recognized the wet stains for what they were. Then the smell hit him, musk, acidity, and sweat; the decaying stench of stale sex. He shuddered and wiped his foot against the carpet.

Laurent pushed him forward again.

Something silver flashed past the corner of Michael's eye. He searched the moving shadows, but couldn't find a source. Halfway across the room, Michael realized he was in the cafeteria, or what used to be. That meant the cavern entrance was just past the kitchen, and the next room should be…

Well, not Sister Ned's office anymore.

He could feel the magic coming off the walls and floors in shuddering bursts. Chandeliers floated impossibly high over his head. Palm trees and tropical flowers surrounded a series of small waterfalls. He spotted another flash in his periphery, but by the time he looked, it was already gone. Whatever it was, it was large and ghostly silent.

The room was lit from all sides. An empty, bone-white throne dominated the far wall. The back was framed by large, sculpted clitoria in a bawdy lavender. He expected to hear violins, or an orchestra. Anything except for the rush of his own breath.

By the time Michael realized Laurent was no longer behind him, he heard the giant doors slam shut, and in an answering echo, unseen doors all around the great room slammed as well. He caught a final skip of movement, just before the lights went out.

"We could have been quite the pair, *meyse*."

Bridgette's voice came from everywhere, insinuating itself into his head like the aroma of a fine wine.

"I could have given you such pleasure you would

have *begged* for the pain. You still might."

Her voice floated down around him at the same time it rose from the floor. The sensation crawled across his skin and met at his waist.

Lights flared around the room. Bridgette was draped across the throne, encircled with flickering white flame. Her bare feet dangled over one arm of the chair, one hand dropped lazily against the head of the largest dog he'd ever seen.

Its silver hair glistened. An impossibly long, reptilian tongue slid out from serrated teeth, and its mouth was large enough to swallow a man's head easily. How could something look so graceful and yet so terrifying?

Bridgette watched him idly.

Right.

Her face wasn't the red-haired beauty from the diner. This was the face of an insane monster. Her porcelain skin had stretched to the point of translucence, and beneath it, a skull flexed and grimaced at him. Her lips moved when she spoke, but they weren't lips at all. They were teeth. They moved again, speaking to him.

"I said, what do you think you have accomplished, Michael?"

Michael swallowed hard, but didn't answer.

Bridgette uncrossed one leg and slid forward in a movement that was weightless, precise, but totally inhuman. She slunk down to the foot of the dais and snapped at her dogs.

"*Chache l'leve.*"

The hounds rose as cleanly as she had, moving with

silent, deliberate steps, flanking him. Michael took a step forward without even meaning to, followed by another. He stopped within reaching distance of Bridgette.

The lithe lines of her body were barely covered by the length of her skin-toned dress. Her skin shifted and rolled, pressing outward against the fabric to form a hand, a breast, and a face before they drew back into her.

"*Kneel*," she said. "Or I'll take your knees."

She sank one hand in the air above his head. Michael fell beneath the crush of her power, vaguely aware of the breath on his neck and the fetid stink of the two beasts panting just beyond his periphery.

"Such a good little priest," she mocked.

The play in her voice fell to pity as she knelt in front of him. "All those years, praying for salvation. And what did it get you?"

She swept long, cold fingers under his chin and lifted his eyes to hers, implacable green, infinite, piercing, but still lovely. A tremor worked its way up his spine, rattling his teeth as he fought to hold her gaze. Her free hand slid into his silk pocket, gliding across his thigh until it found the nail. She held it up between them, balanced on the tip of her index finger.

"I can give it all back to you. Your soul, the priesthood, everything you want. Everything she took. All you have to do, is *kneel*."

Michael's hands pressed into the carpet. He tried to lift them, bend them, but they were pinned under her power. Every part of him was immobilized, trapped under what felt like the crush of a thousand suns against his skin.

Even his jaw tighten as he struggled to speak.

"I…will not…bow…to you."

The tension released and threw him to the carpet, gasping.

"Pride," Bridgette sneered.

Her skin brushed his face as she stepped over him. He was pulled, head over feet, and landed upright in her throne. The nail dropped to the floor with a sharp *ping*, and she stepped to the center of the room.

"Do you know what happens to men of pride?" she asked.

The tapestried wall began to shift. Hands and faces pressed to breast and groin, bent at angles that didn't seem possible let alone pleasurable. Embroidered bodies moved across each other, images trapped in thread becoming oscillating flesh.

His eyes were drawn to the man at the center of the orgy. He began to slide down the wall, bleeding toward the edge of the tapestry. Sewn feet became real feet, then legs, then a chest. He sank onto all fours. Michael recognized his face; the cop, who had held a gun to Danni's head.

"Bouchard." Bridgette curled one finger toward him. "*Ici.*"

Sweat clung to his rippling muscles as he crawled his way to her. He looked exhausted, near collapse, but the half-rigid flesh between his legs suggested otherwise. When he reached Bridgette's feet, she toed his shoulder and spread him prone against the floor. Her ruby lips pouted out to form a tiny 'o' and blew a molten wind across Bouchard's groin.

The back-end of the breeze struck Michael, but carried only half the effect on him as it seemed to have on Bouchard. Bridgette's palm smoothed the sweat from Bouchard's thigh before she encircled him with her hand. A few, hard strokes pulled his back away from the carpet as he fought to drive himself deeper into her palm.

"Three-point five billion of your gender on this blood-soaked planet, and every single one of you is after the same thing," she said.

Bridgette stood. Bouchard continued to pump his hips into the empty air. Michael's stomach clenched when Bouchard's hand resumed Bridgette's work.

She moved toward the throne again, her gaze trained on Michael with a weight he could feel long before she draped herself against him. She writhed in his lap, letting her hair spill over his shoulder. Michael fought the sensations brushing across his skin. Laurent had meant to humiliate him. She was trying to conquer him, control him, and she was going to use his own body to do it.

She arched her back, snaking one hand around the side of his head and forcing it back to where Bouchard lay in the center of the floor.

"Rise, *sevi*. Let us see you."

Bouchard didn't miss a beat as he rocked forward onto his knees then stood.

"That's the irony about pride, Michael. Men think so much of it, and yet they have so damn little."

Bridgette's voice slithered over his senses, humming down to his stomach then lower as she pressed into him, keeping him just on the brink. Michael was vaguely aware Bouchard was sobbing, begging for release, but Bridgette wouldn't allow that either. He closed his eyes and tried to find a calm place inside his mind.

Danni. He saw her seated at Zed's working table, still safe in the swamp, and beyond Bridgette's reach, which made what he had to do now that much harder.

He used the last of his strength and shoved away from the chair, sending Bridgette out with a startled cry. She bounced when she struck the floor, but was already rolling and coming up again. Michael dove for the nail and clamped his hand around it. He held it out in front of him and screamed.

"*Akeyi yo, Jiji!*"

Light exploded into the room, blinding and brilliant, contained in a Danni-sized orb. She stepped out of the light and it fell in on itself behind her, darkening even as the fire in her eyes blazed to life behind the mask on her face. It was a traditional Ghede skull, but where sharp bone and teeth ruled the features of Bridgette's, Danni's bore ribbons and streamers.

Not ribbons. Veins. Her skin was alabaster white, more sculpture than skin, covered in graceful arcs and streaming patterns traced in blood. Her raven hair flowed in waves as she stormed across the room.

Bridgette's dogs moved to intercept her, launching themselves with open-mouthed snarls. Michael heard a yip and a solid crunch before both beasts slumped to the floor. Danni trampled over them, set on her own warpath. Directly for Bridgette.

Black met red with a hard, bodily strike. The wall

behind Bridgette exploded and collapsed as she was driven backwards through the tapestries and the underlying brick. Michael ducked his face into his sleeve but felt the cooler, damper air of New Orleans rushing in to fill the void.

Ahead of him, Danni floated, arms wide at her sides, head rested back so her voice pounded against the sky.

"This is my house!"

Forty-Seven

The shifting weight of the building brought a slow avalanche of sounds as loose bricks thunked off each other. The wall was, more or less, gone. Michael shook plaster and debris from his head.

Danni hovered for a moment longer before kneeling beside Bouchard and laying her hand against his chest. Recognition passed over his face before going deathly still. The blade of her knife flashed where it was wedged in her back pocket.

"Now you serve me," she said.

It was her face, but it wasn't her voice. It was fuller, a collection of sounds that seemed to echo even at a whisper.

Michael felt her attention find him.

"The boys?" she asked.

"Safe. But I've got to find Laurent. He took my gris-gris bag." He stared down the front of his body. "And my clothes."

Danni stroked his jaw with the back of her fingers,

and he felt himself lift slightly off the ground. He looked down. The silk was gone, replaced by his jeans and a loose cotton work shirt, even his boots.

"Thanks." He kissed her quickly. "Is she—"

He followed Danni's eyes to the largest pile of rubble in the street. A heavy, wet fog leaked from inside the bricks, slipping out over the grass as it climbed back into Queensland.

A shriek rose behind them, joined by the sounds of rending and tearing. The dogs rose as one, twisted together and biting at their own flesh with sharp, jagged teeth. Their silken fur fell into bloody piles at their feet. Paws reached out and became claws as their bloody skulls widened and flattened. By the time Michael realized he was holding his breath, they'd gone from ghost dogs to hellhounds, and their blood-red eyes were trained on him. Amazingly, they didn't attack and instead, turned and leapt through a window.

"Where are they going?"

"To find their master," Danni said. "We need to move."

Outside, the world burned. Trees were on fire, set off by the electrical wires hanging loose in their branches, while water sprayed from a broken line somewhere. Michael hurried to keep up with Danni but paused to look back at the raw shape where Queensland used to be.

Zed met them at the curb.

"One of you made a mess," he said.

Bridgette's hounds bayed and dug at the pile of bricks. It began to vibrate and shift, and the dogs whined.

The tremble grew to a quake. Thick, red light burned from inside the pile and reflected off the smoke to cast the street in a hellish haze. One slender, white arm reached from it, followed by the rest of her as Bridgette shook off several tons of rubble.

"I thought I *killed* you, whore."

"Not your only mistake," Danni said.

Bridgette's laughter was sharp like a razor blade drug backwards against Michael's skin. She nodded to Zed. "Old man. Come out of the swamp to play finally?"

He shrugged. "Finally found a loa worth backing."

The smile on Bridgette's lips vanished. The two hounds circled up around her. Their bleeding bodies rose on hind legs, their muzzles drawing in and shoulders expanding. Fresh, soft skin formed around them as beast became man, half-naked but whole. Laurent ran his tongue across his bottom lip and winked.

"This is between you and me," Danni said to Bridgette.

"*No*. This *was* between you and me, until they took something of mine."

Light flashed and expanded between them, then vanished. Gabriel stood in its place.

"Jiji!"

He ran towards her, but Bridgette's hand slammed into a fist. Gabriel choked and staggered, frozen just out of Michael's reach.

"*Ah, ah,*" Bridgette said. "I own them now."

Danni opened her hands at her sides, flaring fresh heat and ash inside her palms.

"Let him go."

"Come get him, if you think you can," Bridgette said, cooly, *before I snap his neck.*"

Michael raised his arm against Danni's chest and Bridgette laughed again.

"Look at her, Michael. She's willing to risk his life just to satisfy her vendetta. How many would you be willing to sacrifice to defeat me, *Jiji*? One? *More*?"

The light flared again and all the boys appeared, and Joto was with them. He spun around in his chair, found Bridgette, and visibly sank with dread. Michael started towards him, but Bridgette raised another fist and flexed her power over the street.

"You have no claim to him!" Michael yelled.

She shrugged. "Call it marital privilege."

Flames formed in her palm and began to dance, pulling Joto to his feet. His legs jerked beneath him in a boneless soft shoe while his hands fought against the steps. The result was the stilted jerks of a life-size marionette. Michael met his friend's eyes and saw the anger and the helplessness. Still, Joto never made a sound.

"Enough!" Danni shouted.

Her voice carried a force that blew Bridgette's hair off her shoulders. Whether it was the distraction, or the power of Danni's objection, the flames in Bridgette's palm died, and Joto dropped to the ground with a thud.

"*C'est bon,*" Bridgette said. "Let's move on to the sacrifice. Shall I burn this one first? Or shall we make a pyre of them all at once?"

Smoke rose and fell behind Bridgette like a tidal

wave, but when it reached its crest, LaCroix, Cemetrie, and Samedi stepped through it.

"Dear brothers." Bridgette's green eyes thinned on Samedi. "*Husband.* You're just in time for a barbecue."

Wordlessly, the Barons' divided around her, moving in to flank the neutral ground, Cemetrie on the left, Samedi and LaCroix on the right. For the first time since Danni had met her, Bridgette looked genuinely surprised.

"Ghede?" she asked.

"Only two Ghede here, sister," LaCroix said.

Bridgette turned to Samedi and ran a fingernail across his jaw. "Will you not stand with me, lover?"

Samedi seized her wrist, his eyes lit with fresh fury. "As you stood with me at *Belle Marseille*?"

Bridgette jerked back and spit in his face. "I can smell her blood on your lips! *Kenbe pawòl, bata!*"

Samedi chuckled low and long as he wiped her spit from his cheek.

"You want my faith again, *wife*? Then prove yourself."

Cemetrie nodded. "What we have is a house divided, and what we need is proof of legitimate claim."

Danni rolled her eyes toward Cemetrie. "Not this again."

"What was it you came here to do, sister, if not strip her of her charter and claim head of household?"

Bridgette shrieked. "She cannot strip me of my birthright!"

"Perhaps," Cemetrie said. "Perhaps it's not a birthright at all. Either way, we can't have the two of you knocking down every building in the city to decide it."

He glanced at Michael and Zed, Laurent and Tomas, and went on. "The power of the loa resides in the strength of her priests. What luck. We seem to have even numbers."

"This wasn't exactly what I had in mind," Danni said.

Bridgette nodded at her. "For once, whore, we agree."

Cemetrie, LaCroix, and Samedi shrugged in unison. "You're outnumbered," they said.

"For now," Bridgette growled.

She stalked away from Samedi and raised her hand. The children, plus Joto, vanished and reappeared on the far side of the street. She centered herself behind Tomas and Laurent, and lifted a single, white finger toward Michael.

"I want his soul when you're done."

"Michael?" Danni asked.

"We've got this."

He kicked the rubble away from his feet and squared his stance. Zed gave Danni a solid nod before moving up beside him. He cracked his knuckles inside his fist and asked, "You want the fool on the left, or the fool on the right?"

Michael nodded at Laurent. "That one has something of mine."

Laurent smiled back. "I've had many *things* of yours, *homme*."

The Baron's lifted their arms above their heads, followed by Bridgette and finally, Danni. The power of the Ghede met on all sides of the circle and burned a white line around the four men.

      "Only rule in this circle, gentlemen," Cemetrie said, "is *to the death*."

Forty-Eight

"Not so sure how I feel about killing two men," Michael said low enough only Zed could hear him.

"Well, I shouldn't have to tell you how they feel 'bout killin' you." He flashed Michael a quick grin. "Don't let that happen. Only one of us goes down, they'll call it a draw."

"I wish I had your confidence."

Zed shrugged. "Comes with age."

Across the circle, Laurent lifted Michael's gris-gris bag up by the string.

"You want this so badly, I can see it in your eyes. Come and die trying."

Michael rushed forward, aware that whatever battle Zed was fighting had begun two beats earlier. A switchblade appeared in Laurent's hand. Michael ducked as it slashed out over his shoulder, then used Laurent's momentum to toss him through the swing.

Michael's fingers began to work in the air, shaping figures down beside him. Laurent wagged the knife side to side.

"Ah, ah. No bag, no magic, *homme*."

"You think so? You should have spent some time in a swamp."

The string around Laurent's hand began to glow before catching fire. It scorched its way across his hand and Laurent cried out, dropping the bag.

Michael swung. His fist landed firmly against Laurent's throat. He fell back, gagging, and Michael picked up the gris-gris bag.

To his left, Zed waved a hand at Tomas's feet.

"Ever had that sinking feeling?" he asked.

The ground turned to water, and Tomas sank up to his knees. The earth solidified quickly into hard pack around him. Tomas jerked and twisted but stayed in place. Zed's fist landed with a hard smack to his nose and knocked him flat on his back.

"Stay down and stay alive," Zed warned and turned to Michael. "You got to keep some distance, boy! They have to touch you to use their power. He gets his hands on your skin, every night terror you ever had as a kid will be right here in this circle with us!"

Laurent rushed forward again, taking Michael down around the waist. They rolled to the edge of the circle. Fire shot up from the boundary and burned Michael's boot. His panicked knee-jerk to escape caught Laurent in the stomach.

"You got terrors of your own to deal with," Michael yelled back at Zed.

Tomas' fingers clawed at his skin, ripping it down

his body. The bloody muscle and sinew beneath swelled, twisting and changing into the hell-hound again. His lower legs pulled free of the ground and left a shell of skin imprisoned in the dirt. He rose up on his new hind legs and roared.

Laurent latched onto Michael's arm, tearing his attention away from Zed.

"You heard the old man, just one touch. You can't run forever."

Michael smiled grimly. "I'm not even walking."

He twisted them down to the ground. They hit with Laurent on bottom, and Michael locked his knees on either side of him. He drew back his fist and felt fresh power ratcheting down his arm. He tasted iron and realized it was *inside* him, brushed down his shoulder and into his fist by Danni's power. She was crouched at the edge of the circle, but he could feel her focus shaping the weight inside his bones.

The first blow landed against Laurent's jaw, but the next missed and slammed a divot into the dirt. Laurent bucked beneath him, twisting his head sideways to sink razor-sharp teeth into the meat of Michael's arm. He didn't feel it, but Danni did. She fell, clutching her chest as her power receded from his fist. Bridgette's low laughter rumbled across the ground.

"If you touch him, I can touch you," she warned Danni.

Michael tried to shove himself away from Laurent, which resulted in a grappling struggle until a hand caught Michael's throat. His eyes rolled back in his head. The world stuttered out in quick electric flashes. Laurent rushed across his mind, his memories, hunting for his pain and seized the first thing he found.

Joey's face took shape, aged-up so his jaw was wider, his hair slightly darker, but his eyes matched Michael's. It was the only thing that had ever marked them as brothers. Their mother hadn't had them at all, which meant they were the last, living hallmark of their father, whomever he had been.

Michael reached for him. Joey's image shuddered, and when Michael looked at his hands again, they were covered with blood. A hotter, thicker heat dripped down Michael's face. Laurent's power, or at least, what felt like Laurent's power. The man was absent, but Michael could still smell his breath, a mixture of overripe fruit and decay, somewhere outside his mind.

This time, Joey reached for Michael. There seemed no sense in avoiding him. It was his brother! Long dead, but still his brother. Michael crushed him against his chest, felt Joey's arms come around him and his voice whisper against his ear.

"I'm in Hell."

Michael jerked back to see his face. "What?"

"I'm in Hell," Joey said again. He laughed, choked, spit blood, and laughed harder. "You put me in Hell!"

Before he could answer, Michael's body was forced around, away from Joey. He tried to turn back, but Danni held him firmly in place.

"Focus on me," she told him. "Focus on my voice, not his."

Behind him, Joey's gagging cackle turned into a high whine.

"Yoooou put meeeee in *Hell*!"

"It's not real," Danni said. She shook his shoulders. "It's *not* real."

But it felt real! This was his fear come to life. The real reason he had never told his mother about Joey. The shame, the regret, he could deal with, but knowing exactly what the lies had done to Joey's soul...

His high-pitched shrieks re-doubled on a single word.

"Hell! Hell! Hell!" he sang. "Michael sent me to Hell!"

Danni's hands tightened around his shoulders. She shook him again. The whiplash snapped his head forward and back.

"Me! Look at me!"

He tried, but tears clouded his vision, slipping her in and out of focus. Danni's hands opened as she made a painful sound. She gripped the sides of her head and bent over at her waist.

Joey vanished behind him, his voice zeroing out in the middle of his maniacal song before being replaced with a deeper, softer melody. The opening saxophone riff of a familiar song made Michael's stomach tighten with dread. The smell shifted from sweet to smoky, cigarettes and spilled beer. The cinderblock walls were painted a sick yellow, the same color of the old popcorn in the bowl in front of him. The sharp lines gouged into the Formica tabletop read: Jack-Ray's sucks. And it still did. Michael had carved the message almost thirty years ago with the edge of his mother's keys.

Her standing joke doubled as the reason she was allowed to bring her six-year-old son into a bar at all. *He's my designated driver*, but she hadn't owned a car or even had a license as long as he could remember. What he did recall were steady meals of stale popcorn and cherry cokes, the latter of which were given to him, mostly out of pity. He sipped them through thin, red cocktail straws, and made a game of stabbing for the cherries as they sunk to the bottom of his glass.

It was everything he saw now, scored by the low buzz of Basin Street Blues. Cooke, not Prima, piped from a Seeburg jukebox with one blown speaker, while his mother clung to the casing for her umpteenth 'last song before we go.'

His memory recorded her as twenty-two, but she could have passed for thirty. She looked emaciated in her favorite black mini skirt and red, sequined top that slipped off her shoulder and hid the snagged threads and missing row of sequins. It was dry-clean only, Michael understood now, but only enough that he was careful to leave it at the foot of her bed and out of the wash.

She swayed two-beats behind the music, which was good. It meant more of her drink went on the floor than in her mouth. She pushed herself off the wall at the bridge, one heavy footfall after another until she was leaning over the table of men who had been watching her all night. Two fishermen in off a trawler and a third, dressed in blue jeans, folded leather chaps, and steel-toed boots. Michael liked him the least.

Then again, he had never shared much in common with his mother, least of all her taste in men.

He watched her snake a fresh cigarette from the leather-man's pack, light it, and then drop into his lap. The man swept the hair back from her neck, said something in her ear, and Michael's mother's eyes traveled around to meet his.

He glanced down at the ice melting in the bottom of his glass and didn't look up until her reflection was looking back at him, standing over him.

"Hey, sweetie. Mommy's gonna go outside for a minute. You be a good boy and stay here."

Michael nodded, but didn't watch her and the man leave out the back door. Horns joined the labored swing of the music.

"Down in New Orleans, in that land of dreams. You don't know how nice it seems..."

Time passed in odd bursts in those days. A few minutes seemed like hours when he was a child, weeks like lifetimes. Months were denoted by holidays: Christmas, Easter, and parade season. Times when the sisters stuffed his pockets with candies and gifts. Those days passed quickest of all. Nights at Jack-Ray's, the slowest.

The door opened again. The leather-man dropped into his seat, but it took his mother's eyes a second longer to find Michael. When they did, she seemed to recognize him less than she ever had. Still, her momentum and staggering steps carried her forward until she was leaning over his table once more.

"Well, hey there."

Michael looked up from his glass again, but this time, he was eye-level with her, no longer a boy. The look in her eye was familiar, vile, and filled him with a strange horror. She'd never looked at him, not *that way*.

She dropped into his lap, feather-light on the edge of his knee. The sequins scratched the side of his jaw.

"I've never seen you around here before," she said.

The leather-man looked at him from across the room.

"She's good," he said in a deep, smoky voice.

"Got anything in that bag for me," she asked.

Michael glanced at the gris-gris bag on his hip and back to her face. Blue eyes widened and then relaxed. No. *Brown*. His mother's eyes had been brown, the same color as the rich, dark chocolate the nuns gave him at Easter. *Danni's* eyes were blue, and those were the ones he was looking at now. The eyes he loved so much in the face of the woman he only ever wanted to love him.

Two kinds of debt to two very different people.

Zed's words came back to him at the same time he realized why. Why he couldn't hold on to both of them. And why he had chosen the one he did.

Danni.

The battle for Queensland. The boys. He was still there, though how much time he had wasted, trapped by his own fear, he couldn't say. Nor did it matter. Just like waking up inside a dream, realizing it was a dream, the music, the bar, and the weight of his mother's body in his lap began to fade. The low-ceilinged air of Jack-Ray's evaporated. His mother screamed with rage, but it wasn't her voice, her face or Danni's anymore. It was Laurent's.

Michael swept his focus into his gris-gris bag. The heat found him first, followed by the burning air and the roaring scream of a thousand souls. The pebble from the Crossroads. He reached for it and channeled the fire into Laurent's brain.

Dirt filled Michael's nose, inhaled as he was dropped to the ground again. Laurent's arm came down hard on the back of his neck, grinding his eyes into the sand. It didn't matter. Michael pulled a tighter focus on the pebble until it was the only thing in his vision. It pulsed and glowed in the space behind his eyes, red and then white hot.

Michael had always believed in Hell, and Samedi was the closest thing he'd ever come to a devil. There was more than enough pain in The Crossroads, more than enough fear, but Michael only saw it briefly as it filtered past him. Lifetimes of torment. Death. Despair. The blistering heat and fear hammered inside Laurent, pounding everything else into nothing.

Laurent collapsed to the ground beside him, snarling through fresh tracks of blood leaking from his eyes, nose, and ears. His fingers clawed at his throat as he tried to shift back into the hell-hound. But it was too late. His skin was suddenly dry, brittle, and broke off in hunks of ash.

Bridgette sank to the edge of the circle and screamed. "*NO!*"

At last, Laurent's hands fell, limp and lifeless at his

sides.

Michael rolled to his stomach, then onto his knees, struggling to find his bearings. He saw Danni first. She, too, was struggling to stand while motioning wildly across the circle.

"Zed!" she screamed. "Help Zed!"

Because she couldn't, he realized. Whatever force it had taken her to find him inside his mind, Bridgette had returned in kind, and Danni was paying for it.

Michael spun in the dirt. Zed was playing bullfighter to the hell-hound while simultaneously trying to heal a deep gash across his thigh. He tripped along the edge of the circle, baiting Tomas forward and then deflecting his advances with hard bursts of dust and air.

"You got something left for a little help!" he yelled at Michael.

Tomas shot forward again only to meet a hard blast of dirt, but he was gaining feet with every attempt.

"What do you want, a net?"

"A little fire would do!"

Michael tried to focus on the fire agate in his bag, but he couldn't feel it. He was too tired. He dug around inside the gris-gris bag until the ragged edge and concave shape hung on his fingertip. He pulled the agate out and held it up.

"Ready!"

"Coming to you!"

Zed ran toward him. The hell-hound followed only a few steps behind. As he passed Michael, Zed turned and fired the can of air across Michael's hand. The agate turned it into a flamethrower, arcing out several feet of bright orange flames. It stopped Tomas in his tracks, but he only lolled his head inside the fire, lost in some stuporous pleasure.

"I think he likes fire, Zed."

"Yeah, that's just part one. Get ready to give us a shield."

Zed reached into his pocket and pulled out a scrap of blue cloth. A shape formed inside it and he shook it out into his palm. The small white cube smoked in his hand.

"Dry ice?" Michael asked.

Zed nodded. "From the cooler at Del's. Here we go."

He took a deep breath, held it, and stuffed the ice in his mouth. His exhaling breath came out as a cloud of popping crystal. Superheated flesh met subzero temperatures, and Tomas exploded.

Michael barely got the shield in place to divert the largest flying pieces around them. Flesh and fire slammed into the boundaries of the circle, but even the flames couldn't keep all of the carnage inside. Bits of bloody, smoldering hell-hound spattered across the Barons.

The circle flared and broke, but the aftermath lay deathly still against the scuffled dirt. Bridgette surveyed Laurent with clear disgust and flicked a piece of Tomas off her bare shoulder.

Michael caught Zed beneath the arm and limped him back to Danni. She pulled him down beside her, beginning to heal what wounds she could see. She ran quick hands over his decimated thigh as well as a few shallower cuts on his face.

"Where else?" Danni asked.

Zed said nothing but opened his mouth. The skin across his tongue was blistered, white and red. Danni pulled his face into her hands. His eyes widened then relaxed when her lips touched his. When she pulled away, Zed was blushing. Michael couldn't help but smile.

"Something, isn't it?" he asked.

Zed nodded. "*Akeyi yo*."

Cemetrie stepped to the center of the circle. "Well, now. Seems we have a winner."

"Like hell we do," Bridgette growled.

She launched herself into the air. Bare flesh melted to expose the underlying muscle and sinew in wet, red lines. Her bones glistened, joints flexing and working as she stretched against the open air. Then, her cool, slick muscle began to blister as fire unfolded from the center of her chest. It flowed out in blue waves, consuming, charring, and peeling away the tissue until every appendage was just bone. She cocked her head to one side, eyes filled with the same blue and orange flame. Her lipless mouth opened in another scream.

Danni stood and raised her arms at her sides, mimicking Bridgette's gesture, except where Bridgette's hands were full of flames, hers were clouds of cold ash.

The power vibrated the air between them and made Michael's vision swim. Bridgette shot forward and struck Danni hard, driving them both into the dirt. The earth rumbled and opened, sagging and then swallowing them both in a cloud of cinder and ash.

Michael crawled to the edge of the hole. A stale, wet heat wafted up into his face as he searched the darkness for any sign of movement. All three Barons crowded at the opposite side of the chasm.

"Where did they go?" Michael demanded.

"*Rivyè Sangen,*" they said in unison, but it only made it sound more doleful.

"Bridgette's hell away from home," Samedi said. He toed loose gravel over the edge and watched it disappear into the void. "Farewell, *cher*. I will miss you."

"Wait! What?" Michael staggered to his feet. By then, Samedi had already turned and was walking back toward the street. "Samedi! Don't fucking walk away from me! What happened to Danni?"

Samedi whirled around, but his expression startled Michael back a step. The anger he understood, it was always there. But the tears?

"She is dead, Michael," he hissed. "*Dead.*"

"But we…" Michael gestured to the carnage behind him, around him. They had won, hadn't they?

"Bridgette never was one to play by the rules," LaCroix said with a sigh.

Michael screamed, this time at Cemetrie. "*Do something!*"

"I cannot," he said. "None of us can."

Zed placed a gentle hand on Michael's shoulder.

Michael turned and grasped his at his sleeves. "*How?* How can she be dead?"

"Flesh can't pass between worlds, Michael," Zed explained, his voice patient but firm. "When Danni hid in

Bel-Koté, she left her body here. Now, it's somewhere down there."

Beneath a thousand tons of earth and rock. Michael dropped to his knees, balled the loose dirt in his fists, and let out a frustrated scream. When his air ran out, he sank back, and found Samedi seated beside him, his feet hanging over the mouth of the hole. Michael searched the void and then the Baron's face for an answer.

"What happens now?" he asked dimly.

"One of two things is going to come out of that hole," Samedi said. "My wife or your beloved, but neither of them will be the same. What's more likely is, if it is Bridgette, all of us will burn."

Wait for death or wait for Danni. Michael shrugged. What else could he do? He looked at Samedi. What could either of them do?

He turned the gris-gris bag out into the dirt beside him, shuffling through the pieces until he found the pebble from the Crossroads, and offered it to Samedi.

"Just in case I don't get the chance again," he said.

Samedi withdrew it from his palm. "I often underestimate you, Michael."

If it was a compliment, it was probably the best he was ever going to get.

Forty-Nine

Bridgette roared.

Their powers collided as they fell, their two wills working against each other until the terminal velocity took over and sent them into a tangled tailspin.

Embers fell into Danni's eyes, belched from rows of Bridgette's serrated teeth. Danni fought for control, arching and twisting for a position that didn't leave her exposed to Bridgette's crushing blows, but for each one she was able to avoid, three more landed in her gut. But they were more than just punches. It felt like Bridgette's hands were burning *through* her, cauterizing one wound before opening another in its place.

Fast-falling air whipped Bridgette's hair into thin, blistering straps. They wrapped around Danni's wrists and pinned them to her chest. It didn't matter. There was no strength in her arms, anyway. The only thing that seemed to matter now was not coming up on the bottom as they approached the hard, raw earth at the belly of Bridgette's newly-carved hell.

The closer it got, the more of it Danni could see. Towers of bodies stood lashed together in varying height, immobilized in positions as humiliating as they were obscene. Dark, red waters churned around them. An infinite sea of blood. Danni kicked hard against Bridgette's chest and shot for it.

The impact wasn't hard, but it wasn't water either. She sank into a fetid pool of thick, coagulating liquid. It filled her mouth, and she tasted sweat and skin, blood and semen. The last, living remnants of all the men and women who had died under Bridgette's thrall, pooled into a hell she, too, was about to become part of. She sank deeper and deeper until the surface was only an arbitrarily chosen direction. Still, Danni kicked against the aqueous heat.

Bridgette's hands found her throat from somewhere above and forced her deeper. A brief wave of panic passed through Danni's gut, crushed on the inevitability of Bridgette's power. She couldn't fight her here. Not on her ground. Bridgette was simply too strong.

If I should die, before I wake, I give to you my soul to take.

She heard their voices around her. Above her. Gabriel, Rene, Maurice. Even Michael.

"My soul to take…"

Her vision flashed over Michael's face as he repeated the last line in solitude and tightened his fist around the nail.

"My soul to take."

Danni reached to Bel-koté. They, too, were calling her, pulling her back to safer places and away from the grief and desolation. But Bridgette had no intention of letting her escape, body or soul. Danni felt herself lifted, then yanked, in the opposite direction. She landed facedown on a hard, black precipice, out of the river of blood, but staring into the Hell yawned out in front of her.

Naked hands clawed from holes cut into the ground, while overhead the towers of bound flesh seemed to move as one, angling down for a better view. Hot, hissing geysers blasted them back. Danni rolled away from them, but rolled into something much worse.

Bridgette rose from the river, shaking like a dog coming out of water. The flames around her extinguished, replaced with rippling white skin. Naked, but still horrifying.

Bridgette screamed again. "*How* are you not dead yet!"

She snatched a handful of Danni's hair and dragged her across the ground. Her head found every rock and short spire of bone littered across the island.

Bridgette stopped abruptly but gave Danni no time to find her feet. Instead, she tossed Danni a full one-eighty over her head and slammed her down on the other side. Bridgette repeated the motion, slapping her against the ground so many times, the sensation stopped being real. Bones broke, but Danni didn't feel them. Her skin stopped looking like skin, but she couldn't feel that either.

Danni was floating above herself. She opened her mouth, or what felt like her mouth, but no sound came out. She studied the ground around Bridgette, found a familiar shape, and reached for it. The knife flew to her hand at the same time her fist formed around it. Bridgette stopped thrashing her body across the rocks, looked up, and smiled.

"Welcome to *Rivyè Sangen*, soul."

It sounded right, looked right, but nothing about Danni felt as small as a soul. Bridgette screamed, but this time it was a sound of mad glee. Victory. Triumph. Danni followed its source, letting the knife lead the way as she drove through the center of Bridgette's smooth, angular forehead. It passed through her skin easily and into the softer parts of her belly until the tip struck something hard. Whatever it was held immense power. Danni let loose of the knife and chased it. Her fingers clamped around a cornerstone.

She smelled the syrupy boil of sugar, tasted the heat on the back of her tongue. The sun that should have warmed her face seared it. The lash of a seasoned whip as it tore across her skin, and a clash of voices roared against the injustice of it all. How long had she held them this way? Gorging on their agony. The memories and terrors of hundreds were concentrated into a rock the size of her palm, and the souls inside it were long overdue for reckoning.

It was the real source of Bridgette's power: the sick, self-sustaining miasma, spider-webbed like a malignant tumor. Only this cancer reached into the earth, into the communities, eating its way through the wards and the people of New Orleans.

Danni drove her hand deeper into Bridgette's belly, raking around the wet cavity in search of another stone. Bridgette twisted around her, but there was no strength in

344

her resistance anymore. The souls were already disentangling themselves from their master, pleased to be free, but no less wrathful in the face of their lifetimes of torment.

She found another stone and knew immediately where it belonged. Though, what it was doing in Bridgette created a few more questions than it answered.

St. Louis Cemetery One. She saw the memory of Bridgette moving through the white maze of headstones, rustling up the dead. It was a petty thing to do, even Bridgette knew it. But she also knew the secret Cemetrie had shown her, long before Danni was a Ghede.

Not all of St. Louis One was still in the cemetery. Time and money had seen family plots lifted and redistributed across the city. Bones carried to new plots as if they were simply signing new leases on their graves. Lafayette to Madisonville to Treme. Humans had unknowingly done what the Ghede could not and connected common ground.

Katrina had done the rest and carried bodies away from their resting places and into others. Now, the entire city was a graveyard, and St. Louis One's cornerstone held them all. It only seemed natural that Bridgette steal it from Cemetrie.

The next cornerstone needed no provocation and found Danni's palm itself. Ville Noire hadn't always been Bridgette's. Visions of previous owners flashed over Danni's mind. Men, white and rich and nursing on the underbelly of Storyville like it was a crawfish boil.

Fresh torment cabled up her arm and into her throat,

spilling out in a sound that felt as real and wrenching as the strange hands pressed against her flesh and the chains around her wrists.

But this wasn't the sharp bite of a whip or the soreness of hard labor. This was a prickling, lingering wound. Long lived before it died, burning its way into the hereafter. It was indignity and humiliation, amplified by the thousands.

Finally, Bridgette stopped fighting. Her voice was broken and raw, as if she had experienced every moment with Danni, and it left her as hollow and shapeless as Danni felt.

"You understand now," Bridgette wheezed.

Danni did…and she didn't. But she was out of time. The blackened earth began to rumble and unfold. Towers of bodies toppled, setting off a domino effect and knocking them into the river of blood. She rode Bridgette up and out on the shockwave that followed.

A glint of steel caught her eye and she reached for it, calling herself up toward the nail. Toward Michael.

Danni landed in the wet mud on her hands and knees. A startled gasp echoed across Queensland. She crawled forward, stared at her reflection in a puddle, and found two menacing, green eyes staring back.

Fifty

A tremor ran down Michael's spine. He tried to stand, slipped back, and gave up. Seeing Bridgette erupt from the hole stole the last bit of hope from his heart. Danni was dead, and he couldn't force himself to care what happened now.

Samedi stood but made no move to approach her. Instead, he called, "Brothers."

LaCroix and Cemetrie kept their eyes on Bridgette as they moved in beside him. Only then did Samedi approach her again.

"Dearest wife, you're in a *great* deal of trouble."

Bridgette's responding laughter was wet in her throat.

"I'm not—"

She started and stopped, several times, pressing her hand against her throat as if she were gagging on the sound of her own voice. She staggered and fell, laughed, and tried again. Michael felt a stab of victory, albeit slight. At least Danni hadn't gone down without a fight.

"Strike now, brother! Before she finds her wits!" Cemetrie screamed.

Still, Samedi hesitated. Bridgette struggled to take shape. Parts of her were either faded to a shadow image of what they had been or missing completely. An elbow, a knee. Even her brilliant red hair was blackened at its roots.

"If he won't, I will," LaCroix said.

"*Wait!*" Samedi stepped forward, his hand held out as if he was testing the air around Bridgette. "She's not—"

The words never made it past his lips.

"Will *someone* finish that damned sentence?" Zed demanded.

Bridgette turned toward him and smiled.

Michael's heart jumped forward. There was no malice in her face, only the soft, wry amusement he'd always known.

"*Danni.*"

A rumble shook the ground below Queensland, followed by a distant *thump* like a mortar launched from somewhere deep inside the earth. Light burst like a supernova, unfolding with Bridgette's image at the focal point. Michael felt it pass through him, the Barons, Zed, and the children.

When Michael looked back, a new silhouette stood burned against the backdrop of settling mist. Danni shimmered out of it and caressed her newly-formed skin from shoulder to fingertip.

Zed carried Michael to his feet but kept a steadying hand on his shoulder.

"Believe the lady's looking for you, son," he said

before prodding Michael the last few steps into her arms.

She felt real, smelled real, even *tasted* real when he pressed his lips against hers. It was only his mind struggling to catch up with the rest of him that made him ask, "How did you…"

Danni unfolded her hand between them. Four smooth stones sat in the center of her palm. They weren't exactly what he'd envision, a little bigger than an egg and similar in shape, but their power leeched the warmth away from the air.

"I believe we had an arrangement, *cher*," Samedi said.

Danni nodded, and one of the stones flew toward his face with the speed of an overhand shot. Samedi caught it and immediately fed it past his lips. His jaw worked side to side as it slid down his throat with an audible gulp.

"Ah, Belle Marseille," he whispered. "Tastes like home."

Michael stared at the remaining corner stones.

"You're not going to do that, too, are you?" he asked her.

"Not quite."

She waved her free hand over the remaining stones. Two floated up into the air. The third drifted toward Cemetrie but stopped just seconds from his reach.

"The cornerstone to St. Louis Cemetery One," Danni told Michael and then raised her voice so everyone, especially Cemetrie, would hear. "The *real* reason Brother Cemetrie is having so much trouble keeping people in their graves. Isn't it?"

LaCroix's mouth dropped open. He slapped the back of Cemetrie's head, knocking his hat into the mud.

"You damned old fool!"

Cemetrie stooped to retrieve his hat, but didn't place it back on his head. Instead, he held it out, just beneath the cornerstone, and waited for it to fall. When it didn't, he glared at Danni.

"You made your point."

"Not quite," she said. "And before I give this back to you, I need your word. All of you."

She walked off a slow circle around the three Barons.

"Take your dead. Bury them. Keep them there. Nothing less. And *nothing* more."

"And what of my brothers' encroachments upon my realm?" Cemetrie demanded. "Am I to simply allow it?"

"Oh, I think they'll be too busy cleaning up her *other* messes. Won't you?" she asked Samedi and LaCroix.

"You mean to task us with Bridgette's amends?" LaCroix scoffed. "Without payment?"

Danni called Ville Noire's stone up between them, but LaCroix only shook his head.

"I have no patience for strippers and pimps," he said. "However, Bridgette has a lovely house in the Garden District."

"Take it."

Danni looked back at Cemetrie. "Well?"

He nodded, however grudgingly, and Danni let the stone fall into his hat. "As you wish, *maman*," he grumbled.

Samedi was laughing when he stepped forward

again, wiping a hand across his face to cover a smile that refused to die.

"*What?*" she asked.

He tucked his hands behind his back and rocked forward on his toes. "Nothin', nothin'." Finally, he shrugged. "Our deal is satisfied. I'm not, but—"

"Another day?" she asked.

He nodded once, tipping the brim of his hat. "Aye, *cher*. Another day."

A wave of smoke rose around them. When it dissipated, the Ghede, past and present, were gone. Except one.

Danni moved back to Michael and took his hand. She reached for Zed with the other. He came without hesitation, falling into a three-way embrace before being parted by a staggering round of cheers. Michael and Zed stepped back to let the boys pull her down into them.

The bricks around Michael's feet began to move, swirling up into the air as the broken pieces became whole. They shot past him, rotated, and reformed into walls. The fire in the trees snuffed to trails of smoke, which slowly became new growth. The power lines snaked back into place, along with the windows, the doors, the roof. Every chip of brick, every notch in the underlying foundation, stitched itself back into place until Queensland stood whole again. Interior lights flickered to life, filling the windows with familiar warmth.

Finally, Danni stood and swept the boys toward the doors. "Past your bedtimes, isn't it?"

Only half of them moved on to reclaim their home.

Gabriel and the others held back. He called her down beside him.

"Jiji, they don't have anywhere to go."

Michael held his breath as Danni's eyes coasted over the lot of them. They were ragged and sick, covered in the grizzled aftermath of Bridgette's mines.

Danni turned Gabriel out to face them, but kept her hands on his shoulders and her voice in his ear.

"These are your brothers, now. Teach them the way of things around here. Questions go to Michael. Problems always come to me."

"Yes, Jiji."

Gabriel gave her a final hug and called the others to follow him up the stairs, barking off orders as he went.

"First things first, we wash those hands."

Danni chuckled. "Someone should probably call Sister Ned, or that place is going to be a *wreck* in the morning."

Michael nodded. "I'll do it, but first…"

He caught her hand and pulled her to him to kiss her.

"Hey, uh, love-birds? A little help for a man with no legs!"

Michael pulled back. Joto leaned on his elbows against the grass and tossed his chin to where his wheelchair lay some yards away. Danni snapped and a new chair materialized a second ahead of Joto.

He pushed the wheels forward and back. It was sleeker, quicker, but Joto was still frowning.

"What's wrong with my old one?"

Danni shrugged. "It always bugged me."

"You could just… you know."

He stared down at his legs, but Danni shook her head.

"That deal is with Samedi. Not me."

Joto opened his mouth, as if to debate the point, but stopped and asked, "Can I still sell the St. Jiji dolls?"

Danni nodded, but a hard line drew itself across her face. Her eyes travelled out to the edge of the horizon. Zed did the same, and eventually Michael joined them.

His focus opened to the voices of the city. Ten became a hundred. Then thousands. From Lakeside to the Garden District, Treme to the deep, lightless bayous. The city was singing her name.

Finally, Michael turned back to Joto. "You might want to order a few more."

Fifty-One

"So, how was church?"

Michael and Gabriel sat, shoulder-to-shoulder, on playground swings behind Queensland. The piles of dirt were gone, replaced by a long, rolling lawn covered in more slides and jungle gyms than Michael could ever recall seeing in one place.

Gabriel toed a small rubber ball across the grass at his feet, and Roben bounded after it. Michael wondered just how much of the man was left inside the little rodent.

"It was okay," Gabriel said.

"But?" Michael pressed, hearing the hesitation in his voice.

"The new priest isn't from here. He kept talking about the one true God and stuff. Nobody said anything to him, though. I guess he'll figure it out."

Michael suppressed a smile and handed him a thin cardboard box.

"I brought you something, but I didn't wrap it because it isn't really a gift. Just something I wanted to give back to you."

Gabriel pulled off the top and lifted out a slim leather bound notebook. He unfolded it across his lap, and his grin became a full-blown smile.

"The Legend of St. Jiji!"

"I think it's all there," Michael said. "I hope so. It helped me a lot. And I figured maybe it will help some of the new guys, too."

Gabriel's hands smoothed the soft leather from cover to spine and back again.

"This is a lot nicer than the one I had."

"The cover isn't the important part. It's what you put in it that makes it special." Michael bumped Gabriel's shoulder. "I hope you don't mind. I added a secret of my own."

Gabriel considered him for a long moment, making his own assessment about Michael's contribution, even before he had seen it. When he did speak again, his voice was solemn but polite.

"You can't put something in there that isn't true."

Michael nodded once. "I promise."

Gabriel unfolded the book to the last page and scanned the last page with quiet suspicion. His eyes shot wide.

"Is this a ring? Are you gonna—"

Michael pressed a finger to his lips. "*Shh!*"

Gabriel clamped a hand over his mouth, lifted it, and whispered.

"Does Jiji know?"

"I think she suspects, but do me a favor and keep

that thing hidden until its official."

Gabriel stood in front of Michael, his expression suddenly serious.

"Can I tell the others?"

"Let's wait on that a bit, okay?"

"What about Sister Ned?"

Michael laughed in spite of himself. "Hell, no."

Gabriel's hand shot out. "Quarter!"

Fifty-Two

Magnolia petals drifted down across Bel-koté. Their sweet perfume filled Michael's nose. He rolled over them, back to Danni, and traced her thigh with a single white petal. He moved up to her hip and across the lines of her back.

"How long can we stay here, like this?" he asked.

Danni lifted her head and looked back at him.

"Reasonably? Until Sister Ned calls. Or one of the boys gets in trouble. Or Joto gets a new *whatever* he has to share... So, maybe another fifteen minutes?"

Michael smiled. "I'll take it."

She rolled onto her back and stretched against him. "You could come back to the city, and we could do this every morning, and afternoon. And potentially evening."

And not just when Zed left the cabin to fish. Now that he had the nail, he didn't have to die to be with her in Bel-Koté. The privacy to lay down and dream, however... His focus drew back to the earthy scent of the swamp and the sun there. They still had another hour.

Michael stared up through the canopy of magnolia branches. The clouds drifted against a blue, satin sky. It was peaceful just to watch.

"What's wrong with here?" he asked.

Danni laughed and ran a hand through the top of his hair. "Not a damn thing."

"Soon, but, Zed has a few more things to teach me."

Danni sighed. "Just as well. *Ville Noire* is a mess. If you come home now, you'll just be relegated to the renovation."

He propped his head against his fist.

"You still think you can pull together a working night club?"

"Get rid of the beds, the regular clientele, and that god awful carpet, but yeah." She shrugged. "I successfully united voodoo with the church. Doesn't seem so hard."

"*United* might be a bit strong." Michael laughed. "Mother Superior does seem happier now, though."

"Did you two make up?"

Michael thought about it and nodded. "Forgiven, but not forgotten. What about you?"

"I need her," she said simply. "I need *all* of them. But killing Bridgette helped me understand why. I don't want to force the boys, or anyone, to believe in me. If I want their love, I have to earn it."

She reached up and tugged at the nail around his throat.

"You have it," he assured her. Michael rolled them across the bed of petals. "*At least* for another fifteen minutes."

Fifty-Three

Minutes before dawn, the quiet lull between the big brass of the night and the jazz reveille of morning passed over New Orleans. Down Camp, west toward Canal where the sidewalks ended and the lanes opened up four-wide.

Jiji ran.

Puddles rippled in time with her footfalls before flashing to mist. Steam rose in her wake, peeling off the pavement to glaze every window overlooking the French Quarter. Her pace stayed just below the sound barrier, slow enough to hear the chorus of late morning dreams and early morning prayers.

Some she left to chance, while others she answered. Not in gestures of gross magnitude or perilous deals, but in kind words and soft hands.

Get book three:

VIRTUE AND VICE

Coming 2015

Other Books by C.H. Valentino and Eldon Hughes:

Poison and Wine

For more information, visit:

www.chvalentino.com
or
www.ifoundaknife.com

Intentionally Blank

Glossary

Baron: a rank afforded to a loa inside their house. In the House of Ghede there are three: Samedi, Cemetrie, and LaCroix.

Bel-Koté: (pronounced "bell-coat-te")literally translated, means "a beautiful place." Bel-Koté is Danni's center of power, where she keeps the souls she has either taken in death or protects in life until they die.

The Crossroads: Samedi's center of power. The Crossroads is a dark, hellish place with an endless ocean of souls who scream and lament for their freedom.

Débouyé-a: (pronounced "deb-oo-ye-a) a powerful curse that can destroy a loa.

Endymoin: a New Orleans super krewe.

flé: Haitian Creole for "flower"

Ghede: (pronounced "Ged-day") a family of loa who control death

Golden Eagles: an Indian tribe of New Orleans

gris-gris bag: a voodoo talisman that contains objects representing the houngan's power.

houngan: a man who practices voodoo

Jiji: Danni's loa name; Haitian Creole for "the judge."

jou-jou: a voodoo spell, most of the time, of lesser power and meant to entertain.

Jou Mon Mouri: Haitian Creole meaning "party of the dead."

koulev: (pronounced "coo-lev") a large creature that is half-human, half-snake.

krewe: (pronounced "crew") a social club or organization that puts on parades during the Mardi Gras season. Super krewes are the larger, more well-known krewes that often include celebrities.

lam te mouri: a "death blade" used to sever souls from living bodies. It is a double-edged blade with a bone handle. Danni's lam te mouri originally belonged to Samedi and can deal a great amount of damage to any loa.

loa: (pronounced "low-a") a voodoo god

mambo: a woman who practices voodoo

Maman: 1. Haitian Creole for "mother" or 2. A rank afforded to a female loa inside their house. Calling any female loa "maman" is considered a sign of respect, regardless of her actual rank.

Muses: an all female krewe

portmanteau: (pronounced "port-men-toe") a voodoo box made out of skin and bone.

Rivyè Sangen: Bridgette's center of power. A hellish, violent place.

second-line: a type of parade where participants walk and/or dance behind the head of the parade. In New Orleans, it is customary to walk the 'second line' to a grave site.

Wild Tchoupitoulas: (only true Who'dats can pronounce this one) another Indian tribe in New Orleans.

veve: a voodoo symbol associated with a specific loa.

vire-pys: the gold coin used to control a koulev. It has two sides, stamped with the face of a man on one side, and the face of a snake on the other. When the two halves are connected, the master can communicate and control the creature.

Zulu: a parade krewe known for their blackface and painted coconut parade throws.

About the Authors

C.H. Valentino lives in the metro-east St. Louis area with her husband, two dogs, two cats, and a snake. By day, she is a veteran 911 operator and police dispatcher. She is an unrepentant smoker and whole-heartedly believes Earl Gray makes the best tea.

Eldon Hughes is a writer and a storyteller who lives in southern Illinois with his wife and their menagerie of four-legged freeloaders. He has been known to run with scissors and not get a scratch. Once.